The Wolf and the Lamb

Books by Frederick Ramsay

The Ike Schwartz Mysteries
Artscape
Secrets
Buffalo Mountain
Stranger Room
Choker
The Eye of the Virgin
Rogue
Scone Island
Drowning Barbie

The Jerusalem Mysteries
Judas
The Eighth Veil
Holy Smoke
The Wolf and the Lamb

The Botswana Mysteries
Predators
Reapers

Other Novels
Impulse

The Wolf and the Lamb

A Jerusalem Mystery

Frederick Ramsay

Poisoned Pen Press

Copyright © 2014 by Frederick Ramsay

First Edition 2014

10 9 8 7 6 5 4 3 2 1

Library of Congress Catalog Card Number: 2014938598

ISBN: 9781464203268   Hardcover
       9781464203282   Trade Paperback

Poisoned Pen Press
6962 E. First Ave., Ste. 103
Scottsdale, AZ 85251
www.poisonedpenpress.com
info@poisonedpenpress.com

Printed in the United States of America

To The Rt. Rev. Robert Wilkes Ihloff,
Bishop of the Diocese of Maryland (Retired) and
erstwhile Rabban

Acknowledgments

First, the usual and necessary thank you to the folks at the Poisoned Pen Press who make all this happen for me and for you. In an age of e-books and instant authorship, it is easy to forget that publishing is more than just a business. It combines art and craft in ways that are not often understood or appreciated. Readers sometimes forget that for a publisher to put a book into their hands involves more than checking for spelling, comma placement, and digitalizing. Book publishers must also judge whether you will like a particular piece and will buy it, whether the story needs to be told and, indeed, if either of those things even matter for a particular book. Sometimes a book will be released just because it is something that needs doing. Anyway, this is number sixteen for the Press and for me, and I want to make sure you know and they know how happy that makes me (and I hope you, too).

Second, I want to thank all those people who, over nearly eight decades, stuffed my head with the facts, speculation, history, and outright lies, all of which is the primary source of what passes for what I call research. I could not write about Jerusalem in the First Century without them.

Finally, to all of the folks—especially my patient wife, Susan—who have supported me in this giddy late-in-life career as a storyteller, many thanks.

Frederick Ramsay
2014

A Few Explanatory Notes

For those readers who have already experienced Gamaliel and his investigative skills in *The Eighth Veil* and *Holy Smoke,* the notes carried here and in the Appendix at the end of the book may be repetitious. For new readers, I hope they help clarify some of the complexities of life in Jerusalem during the early part of the first century. I urge readers to slip a paper clip back there somewhere for quick reference.

Another note is in order for those who are reading this series in sequence; I have had to alter the map of the city. Gamaliel's house has been shifted slightly to the west to make room for the hippodrome. (Yes, there was one in Jerusalem at the time. It was not as large as that depicted in *Ben Hur*, but it did exist.) The Antonia Fortress and its controversial placement is discussed in more detail in the Appendix.

Days of the Week

Yom Rishon = first day = Sunday (starting at preceding sunset)
Yom Sheni = second day = Monday
Yom Shlishi = third day = Tuesday
Yom Revi'i = fourth day = Wednesday
Yom Chamishi = fifth day = Thursday
Yom Shishi = sixth day = Friday
Yom Shabbat = Sabbath, seventh day (Rest day) = Saturday

Chronology

Given the number of events that had to take place, this author believes it unlikely the narrative as presented in the Synoptic Gospels could have occurred as written. If, however the Last Supper was celebrated on a Tuesday (Yom Shlishi) with his Essene friends (their Passover), then, there is time enough for an arrest late at night with a flogging, a hearing before the Sanhedrin, two trips to the Prefect, one to the King, another flogging, and a march through the streets of Jerusalem to Golgotha and a crucifixion by nine in the morning.

With these thoughts in mind, you will find a fuller explanation and resultant chronology in the Appendix.

Schematic Map of Jerusalem, 30 CE

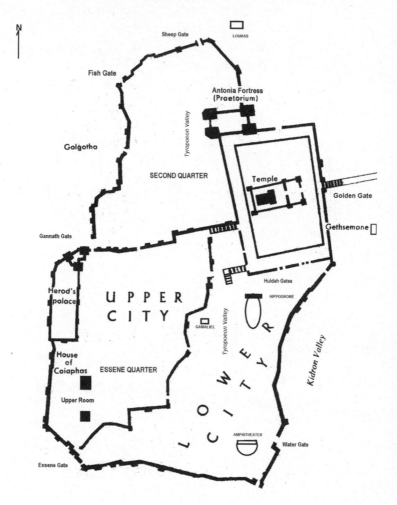

The wolf also shall dwell with the lamb,
and the leopard shall lie down with the kid;
and the calf and the young lion and the fatling together;
and a little child shall lead them.

Isaiah 11:6, King James Version

A Tale by Aesop

The Wolf and the Lamb

The Wolf, meeting with a Lamb that had strayed away from the flock, resolved not to resort to violence, but to find some legitimate justification for the Wolf's right to eat him. He addressed him:

"Young sir, last year you insulted me."

"Indeed," bleated the Lamb, "but I was not born yet."

Then the Wolf said, "You feed in my pasture."

"No," replied the Lamb, "I have not yet tasted grass."

Again said the Wolf, "Well, you drink from my well."

"No," pleaded the Lamb, "I never drank water yet, for my mother's milk is both food and drink to me so far."

Upon which the Wolf seized him and ate him anyway, saying, "Well! I won't go without my supper, even though you refute every one of my imputations."

Moral: The tyrant will always find a pretext for his tyranny.

YOM REVI'I

Chapter I

He couldn't remember venturing this deep into the labyrinthine corridors and arbitrary passages of the Antonia Fortress. He'd never needed to. He took one tentative step forward and paused, put out his hand and felt the stone wall—damp. He inhaled acrid smoke, burning pitch from the torches. Why had Priscus asked him to meet in this dank and dreary hallway? Located as it was deep in the bowels of the building—the *cloaca*, he would have said—Priscus must have had a great need for secrecy—routine in Roman politics. Half the torches were dark and those that still glowed sent tendrils of smoke to the ceiling. Had they been extinguished recently? If so, by whom and why? Lighted or dark, they lined either side of the corridor and projected from sconces at angles as if to salute any passerby. He hesitated and peered into the darkness. Like one of his hunting dogs when it caught the scent of a stag in flight, he went into full alert, unmoving and listening. If he had shared the dog's cropped ears, they would have been twitching this way and that. The only sound he heard was the beating of his own heart.

He strained to see into the hallway's depths. It was impossible to determine where it led or how long it might be. It could as easily disappear into an abyss as come to an abrupt halt a few cubits farther along. Then, it might end at an intersecting wall or continue for a half mile and out into the night air beyond the city walls to the north. He knew the last wasn't the case, but this inky hallway with half its torches unlit created that illusion. Perhaps the fort's builder, the first Herod, in assembling this monument to the late and, for most, unlamented Mark Antony, thought a siege inevitable or that Antony would retreat from Egypt to Judea with his Ptolemaic Queen to make his stand against Octavian. Or perhaps it was simply another manifestation of that King's diseased and suspicious mind. Throughout the year the space housed a resident contingent of legionnaires with a Centurion in command. It could have served as well if half or a quarter its current size.

Priscus' message made it clear he wanted to meet at this place, that he had something important to tell him, and that it required privacy. The message had been vague and the legionnaire who bore it nearly inarticulate, but he'd no reason to suspect anything out of the ordinary so he'd come as asked. Priscus, after all, was a loyal member of his entourage and a serving officer. On the other hand, he knew that all Roman politics operated on intrigue and duplicity. He shuddered. He didn't know why. It wasn't as if he were afraid.

He took another tentative step forward and reached up to free one of the lighted torches from its bracket. He held it aloft squinting into the darkness, straining to make out what lay further on. He touched its flame to the still-smoking pitch-soaked fabric at the end of a nearby staff. It burst into flame and a bit of his anxiety waned as the light penetrated deeper into the gloom. He lit another and moved on. As he leaned forward to light a third, he stumbled against a form lying at his feet. Startled, he jerked his foot back. He looked again and recoiled at the sight of a corpse. He took a deep breath, knelt, and rolled the body over.

A dagger had been thrust in the man's chest. Its gilded and stone-studded hilt protruded from his bloody short toga. The knife's angle was all wrong. He lifted the torch to cast light on the dead man's face. Aurelius Decimus' lifeless eyes stared at the ceiling, the expression of shock at his unexpected demise still frozen on his face. None of this made any sense. He dismissed the notion that Aurelius Decimus had committed suicide. No one with that man's enormous ambition would consider such an action. Furthermore, to fall on one's dagger or sword took a measure of courage that he knew this man did not possess. Not suicide. That meant that someone had stabbed him, murdered him. It seemed so unlikely. A man murdered in the depths of the Antonia Fortress, the very symbol of Roman preeminence and a safe haven for its citizens. Yet, here the ambitious Aurelius lay in an expanding pool of blood.

He regained his feet and glanced around, uncertain what to do next. And what had happened to Priscus? Footsteps scraped against the stones behind him—several pairs, in fact. He stood and faced about.

"Priscus? Is that you? Come here."

"Pontius Pilate, Emperor's Prefect of Judea and Overseer of the Palestine, *tu deprenditur discurrent caede.*"

"I am to be arrested for murder? I only this moment arrived and found this man lying here. I did not murder anyone, Cassia."

"Yet our friend Aurelius Decimus lies dead at your feet, Prefect. The dagger in his chest is yours, I believe."

Was it? It was.

"And I can see no reasonable explanation for your presence in this remote part of the Fortress other than an assignation with him in order to remove the one man who could have sent you back to Rome in disgrace."

"My dagger? Sent back? Cassia, what am I being accused of?"

"Assassination, Prefect, as you well know. *Sicarius.*"

YOM CHAMISHI

Chapter II

"The Romans call them the Sicarii," the High Priest said. "Surely you have heard of them?"

Everyone knew about the Sicarii, this new and dangerous political sect, the Dagger Men. They had begun to make themselves felt in the country by killing men whom they labeled as enemies of the State. Thus far, only one or two minor tax gatherers and a handful of men whom they'd determined to be הלועפ יפתשמ, collaborators, had fallen to their knives. These killings worried the people, of course. They were inexcusable. What worried them more was the dangerous precedent they set. In a country occupied by an omnipotent Rome, what person could not be branded הלועפ ףתשמ? If you sold their legions salt fish, as the Galilean fishermen did by the barrel, and grew rich in the process, wouldn't that make you a collaborator? Or wine merchants, or bakers? What about Gamaliel's student, Saul, who came from a family of tent-makers? Legionnaires in need of a shelter light enough to be carried with their packs made up an important portion of the family's business in and around Tarsus. How would that rigid Pharisee describe those transactions? Where does one, or more importantly, where would the Sicarii, draw the line when branding someone a collaborator?

"The worst part, Rabban," the High Priest continued, "is I have been told they consider me to be one of Rome's allies. Me! It is an outrage. Do I have control over what Rome does?

I don't. Do I retain my position at the Emperor's sufferance? I do. How else shall we keep the faith? Do these fools think that the Nation could survive even a month without a functioning Temple? Would the Lord allow it? No, I tell you, He would not. If we abandon Him, He will judge us harshly and these misguided men, these cowards who creep about in the night terrorizing innocent people, they will end by begging the Romans to return and save them."

The High Priest wore worry like his priestly vestments. Gamaliel had listened to his worried discourses on many topics—from the price of incense to the status of itinerant rabbis—one, in particular—for years. This sudden concern about the Sicarii opened a new chapter. He wondered what had inspired it.

"You need not fear the Sicarii, High Priest. They only concern themselves with two things. They hope to terrorize Roman officials and thereby assume that they, in turn, will ease up on their oppressive practices and leave us in peace. That is no more than wishful thinking. Zealots thrive on wishful thinking. Yet, they are mostly brigands themselves and apply this patina of political activism to cover their acts of robbery and worse. Consider Barabbas. Shall we call him a patriot or a criminal?"

"Barabbas? What about him? How can you possibly know about him or any of this? You spend your days disputing the Law with your students and scholars. Scrolls and musty sheets of papyrus are your companions. What can you tell me of the world around us?"

"You do not do me justice, High Priest. You believe the pursuit of truth excludes one from the cares of the day? You may be correct, but I do not think so. I get out into the streets daily and I have contacts here and there. What I do not know, but should know, they will tell me. For example, did you know that this very Barabbas is currently raging away in a cell deep in the Antonia Fortress? Ah, I see you did not. So, which of us needs to be out and about more? Now, unless you have something else to discuss with the Rabban of the Sanhedrin, I will be on my way. I have things to do that are far more pressing."

That statement was not exactly true. Except to finish parsing an Isaiah scroll sent up from Qumran, Gamaliel had nothing pressing, but he could only endure the High Priest's company for short periods. Gamaliel nodded and started to move away.

"Wait, yes. I do have another matter. Passover is upon us next week."

"It is fair to say everyone knows that, Caiaphas."

"Yes, of course. I am concerned about riots, Rabban, demonstrations, misadventures, and so on. What if these Sicarii decide to use Passover as an excuse to cause trouble? I tell you that of all our holy days…this one brings more people to the city than any of the others combined and is, moreover, the logical one to inspire a revolt."

"And?"

"And, and what? Oh, yes, where was I? Yes, and it is ripe for the work of these dangerous people. They will say, 'Moses led us to freedom. This is a new Passover and we must continue the journey,' or some such nonsense."

Gamaliel started to respond but the High Priest rattled on. "That rabbi from the Galilee, for example, he is at it again, stirring up the people, instigating just those sorts of thoughts. Do you see? If this Yeshua comes to Jerusalem with his followers… no, not if, but when…he is always here for Passover. When he comes he very well could do something to provoke people. Riots could follow which would then require the intervention of the Prefect's soldiers and that would inevitably turn deadly. I received an edict from the Prefect who says he will accept no disturbance of any sort this year. Anyone who engages in such things and—listen to this—anyone who even appears to countenance such behavior, will be severely punished."

"Your country rabbi hardly constitutes a threat to the mighty Roman Empire, Caiaphas, nor does he pose one to you. You worry too much about all the wrong things."

"He has many followers. Some say hundreds, thousands."

"Thousands? Did anyone actually count them? And who are they, High Priest? I will tell you. They are farmers and fishermen, the forgotten, the landless, women, and shepherds. Shepherds, High Priest, imagine. I doubt you could find anything more dangerous on them than a gutting knife or pruning shears. They may be determined in their newly discovered faith, but hardly pose a threat to anyone."

"Their newly discovered faith of which you speak is not new and it is not from the Lord, as you surely know. And that is not the problem. What we fear is that in their zeal to proselytize, they will stir up trouble. Not everyone is as tolerant of unorthodoxy as you."

"You seriously believe that I tolerate a lack of orthodoxy? Surely you misspeak, Caiaphas. I am many things, but unorthodox, much less radical, is not one of them."

"And I tell you, Gamaliel, while you insist on being blind to the inherent danger these people pose, I foresee problems that could very well end in the undoing of us all. Do you not understand that Rome will leap at any excuse to destroy the fragile balance we have established here? Even a trivial uprising could topple it. One dissident rabbi and a handful of misguided Sicarii, and everything could collapse around us. And then where will you and I be?'

"It is a sobering thought if true, but I do not believe it. The Lord has promised us the land and the future. He will not desert us now or ever. Passover is about the flight from bondage to freedom, to the land promised to us. We are here. The promise has been kept, and even when we stray and are carried off to Babylon, he leads us back. So, to answer your question, where will I be? Rome or no Rome, I will be in my study with, as you put it, my musty companions. May I suggest that if you wish to ponder a problem of real import, you might turn your mind to discovering why our Prefect arrived early for Passover this year and why a party of Roman officials, who may or may not be part of the Prefect's entourage, have descended on the city as well, and both a full week early. What is in the wind?"

"And why is that a problem?"

"Romans are many things and most of them quite unpleasant, but the characteristics on which we have come to rely are their maddening consistency and predictability. The arrival of this group at this time lacks both. It is a problem to be solved and therefore it is imperative that you discover what they are up to. Now I must leave."

"And the rabbi and his ragtag band? What am I to do about them?"

"Forget them. One eccentric rabbi more or less should not be your concern. Rather, find out what Pilate and his bullies are about."

Chapter III

Gamaliel moved off toward his home. He had been listening to the High Priest's rants about Rabbi Yeshua ben Josef since the Galilean had first come to his notice as a person with something of a following. At least he boasted more than a floating minyan such as characterized most of his contemporaries. After the idiotic beheading of John the Baptizer by King Herod and Yeshua's alleged blood relationship to the Desert Prophet, Yeshua's presence seemed to have gained more *gravitas,* a fact which doubtless explained the High Priest's concerns.

The real problem for the Nation was Rome's heavy foot pressed on the neck of the Nation, so that each day began and ended in uncertainty and, for many, fear. In times like these, it was not unusual for messiahs of all shapes and sizes to crawl out from under every rock or lurk behind every tree. Unless and until the Nation wrested free from its oppressive overlord, that phenomenon would continue and grow. Its history demonstrated that when oppressed, the Nation would soon be rife with prospective saviors. Occasionally they would actually rise up and liberate the people for a time, the Maccabees, Gideon, Saul, and David...but they were the exceptions—exceptions that forged the Nation, to be sure—but exceptions, nevertheless. And now along comes this rabbi from Nazareth. He had amassed an impressive following and the hopes of some—who knows how many—rested on his claim to be *Mashiach.* So, messiahs, redeemers, would-be saviors, Moseses and this Yeshua. It had always been so. It would always be so, but Gamaliel, for one, did not see another Moses on the horizon, the High Priest's obsession on Yeshua ben Josef notwithstanding.

In any case, and for reasons Gamaliel would never understand, Caiaphas had determined that of all these self-proclaimed rabbis, prophets, and holy men, Yeshua posed a threat to the Nation. In one minor respect, Gamaliel thought, the High Priest just might have it right. If any one of the many itinerant preachers and prophets would have a lasting impact, he guessed this Yeshua could be the one. He had a message that differed from the others, even from that of his presumptive cousin. But did that justify the High Priest's obsession with him? Gamaliel thought not. There were so many other, more pressing issues confronting them at present that needed their attention.

Why, given this rather obvious situation, had the High Priest singled out this particular man? He'd once asked that of Caiaphas. "Why are you so concerned with this particular rabbi and not any of the half a hundred like him?"

"I hardly think 'half a hundred' describes their number and I am concerned about them, Rabban, but this Yeshua seems to touch people in ways that differ significantly from the others. Oddly, he seems to know the Law and the Prophets and yet presents them in ways that are well beyond the self-serving ramblings of his contemporaries. He is, shall I say, seductive. It is almost as if…"

The High Priest had not finished the sentence. Gamaliel had waited and then turned away. He did not care to hear the ending. He could guess what it would be. He'd heard it all before—many times. His own examination of the man had convinced him that with some training and a measure of discipline, this Galilean might make a passable scholar. Otherwise, he thought his teaching radical and borderline heretical. Interesting, in an offbeat near-Persian sense, but with all that, he could not see Yeshua as a threat to anyone, much less to the Nation. He deemed the idea absurd.

He left the High Priest with his rabbinic fixation and made his way homeward. The streets of Jerusalem were becoming congested with early arrivals for the Passover. The influx of men and women from all over the Empire occurred every High Holy day, but Passover always produced the largest crowds. Judging by the numbers already camped on the hills surrounding the city, this particular Passover seemed not only to be attracting many more celebrants than usual, but they were arriving earlier as well. He could not think of any reason why that should be, nor could he have quantified it. But he had the clear impression that the press of humanity was greater than the previous years and had a different feel to it. The air seemed to possess a tension which he could not explain. It reminded him of the malaise he often felt before a violent storm, before the lightning cracked open the sky and caused his heart to skip a beat.

He'd pointed out to the High Priest that the Prefect had traveled down from Caesarea early. Were they missing something? In his near single-minded attention to his studies and students and Caiaphas' equally absorbing obsession with vagabond rabbis, had they blocked out the possibility that something momentous, which they should have known or heard about, was about to occur? The High Priest had offered no enlightenment nor had Gamaliel any thoughts on the matter, although it crossed his mind that the Isaiah scroll resting on his desk might be a place to start. He would look into it right after the Passover or perhaps he would task his students to glean that particular field.

So occupied had his mind been with musings about pending catastrophes and messianic claims, he nearly missed spotting the young man loitering by his doorway. Gamaliel had an instinct for people. He paused to inspect this nondescript individual, who was shifting from one foot to the other, slouched in the shadows provided by the door's stone archway, seemingly impatient on the one hand and anxious on the other. Outward appearances, Gamaliel knew, could be deceiving. This young man, for example, in spite of his shabby clothing, would be someone's servant. A servant sent to him to solicit a ruling, a visit, or a loan of a manuscript? He couldn't be sure. The boy stared at him expectantly. His eyes lit up and he opened and shut his mouth. It seemed that if he didn't soon speak, the words would come vomiting out of his mouth. Gamaliel took a few steps forward and waited for the greeting and the reason the boy waited for him.

"Excellency, do I address the Rabban of the Sanhedrin?"

"You do, and I am not anyone's 'Excellency,' boy."

"Sorry. Umm, that is greetings, sir, and…"

"Yes, yes, speak up. What is it you wish from me?"

"Not me, sir, my Master bids you to attend on him."

So, definitely a member of someone's household and judging by his dress, not a Hebrew household. The shabbiness of the boy's cloak could also mean not a wealthy one or it could mean the person requiring the meeting wished not to draw attention to his messenger, and by indirection, to himself.

"He does. And who, may I ask, is this master of yours?"

The young man, boy glanced furtively over his shoulder, leaned in toward Gamaliel, and cocked his head to one side. In a voice the Rabban could barely hear he said, "The Prefect, sir."

"What? Are you saying Pontius Pilate wishes to see me?"

"Shhhh. Yes, sir, he does, now."

"I am confused. In the past, when the mighty Pilate required my presence, he did not send me an invitation in the person of a boy in a disreputable cloak. He commanded my presence and would send a contingent of his smartest legionnaires to escort me in the unlikely event I refused the invitation. My journey to the Fortress flanked by the best the local contingent of the army had to offer would always be both impressive and humiliating—impressive for the Prefect, humiliating for me. So, where are his soldiers? What has happened to the noble Roman that I no longer rate this treatment? Is he ill? I know a very fine Physician, if that is the case."

"They are not available."

"Who are not available? Pilate has arrived in the city with a full complement of soldiers and you tell me none of them are available to march me across the city to the Antonia Fortress like a felon? Truly welcome news, but I find it hard to believe."

"But it is so, Excellency."

"You are not listening. I am not your…Oh, never mind. Let me see if I have this right. Pilate sent you here, apparently in the worst clothes you could find, to summon me to his Eminence. Yet, with all his power and position, he cannot send his soldiers for some reason and so he sends me a boy. Am I to understand, that the reason for the latter is the explanation for the former?"

"Sir?"

"And the summons to meet with him has to do with both of the above."

"I don't understand."

"I ask…No, of course you don't. I am not sure I do either. Very well, let me go into my dwelling and freshen up. I need to tell my servant where I am going. Caution requires that one do so before entering the presence of the Prefect on the oft chance one never returns. Then at least your family and friends can guess what has happened to you. I see that you are confused, I know. People who deal with me often are. So, don't try to understand, my son. Wait here for a moment. I will return shortly."

"But he said to bring you straightaway. We must go, your Excellency."

"For the last time, I am not 'your Excellency' and also, I am saying to you that whether the great Pontius Pilate wishes it or not, I am not prepared to attend him just now. If the Prefect's need of me is both genuine and urgent, I would be standing in his august presence at this very moment. I would have been escorted to him by the legionnaires I just mentioned. Since he has not sent them, I must assume there is no such urgency. Wait here."

The messenger started to argue, then realized the futility of doing so. He sighed and leaned against the stone portico and contemplated the beating he would probably receive for not having produced the Rabban in quick time, as he'd been ordered.

Chapter IV

During the Hebrews' High Holy days, the number of Roman troops billeted in Jerusalem increased to a full cohort and a half, with the arrival of the Prefect of the Palestine, Pontius Pilate, and his household. Pilate and his entourage would make the trip southward along the coast of the Middle Sea from Caesarea Maritima to Joppa, and then climb the hills to Jerusalem. There, they would be joined by the resident legionnaires and staff assigned to the Antonia Fortress.

Passover especially attracted faithful Jews. Pilgrims were known to travel from places as far away as Hispania or Britannia, eager to be in King David's city for this celebration of the Flight from Egypt and its Pharaoh into the Promised Land. Worshippers, celebrants, and curiosity-seekers crowded into an area that could comfortably accommodate a tenth their number. Add to that the presence of the Emperor in the person of the Prefect and every radical, latent revolutionary, plus scores of fakers and frauds, and the mixing and mingling in their number made for an unusually tense time. Thus, the Empire bolstered its military presence. It was a cycle repeated every year—and one that would one day lead to confrontation and bloodshed and the destruction of a Nation.

Now, a full week before the beginning of the holiday, the city's population had already grown twentyfold. An official delegation sent by the Emperor had arrived unannounced. The Prefect had not been read into the reason for it being thrust on him, and that worried him. With Emperor Tiberius sequestered on the Isle of Capri, wallowing in depravity and madness, any sort of visitation commissioned by him that included people of rank and influence did not bode well for the residents of Roman Palestine in general, nor Pilate, in particular. Still, he had had to follow up on the Centurion's request. And now? The untimely death of his rival displaced all other concerns he may have had. The presence of these officials and their mission was overshadowed by a need to survive a charge of murder. Pilate found himself reduced to waiting for the Rabban of the Sanhedrin to come to his rescue. The eagle must seek help from the hare; the wolf must seek guidance from the sheep.

The irony would not be lost on either of them.

Try as he might, Gamaliel could not extract anything more from the boy except that the Prefect wishes to see the Rabban, and it is a matter of some urgency. The last time Gamaliel could remember having been summoned into the Prefect's presence, it had not been an easy meeting. He hoped this one would not be a repeat of that. As they approached the Antonia Fortress, his guide veered sharply to the side and circled the building. Gamaliel began to wonder if he hadn't been lured into a trap. The broad stairway leading up from the Temple Mount into the platform that fronted the Fortress was the only entrance he knew. Where was this boy taking him? Surely Pilate…

"Here now, boy," he said. "Where are you taking me? This is not the way to the Prefect."

"I am only following my orders, sir. Please, this way."

The boy hurried on. Gamaliel had no choice but to follow. He could have reversed and gone home, but he doubted that ploy would work. If the Prefect really did wish to see him, he'd be dragged back again and not nicely. Besides, his curiosity had been piqued. He knew that his curiosity often ended by putting him in situations that were less than beneficial, yet he yielded to it. Pilate could be arbitrary and cruel, but at the same time, any call into his presence would be intriguing. His best course was to follow the boy and see what the mighty Roman had in store.

Bypassing the Prefect's elaborate apartment, where in the past Gamaliel had been alternately scolded and cajoled, the boy led him through a small portal and into a rat's warren of corridors. After six or so turns, Gamaliel lost all sense of direction. He could not have found his way out to save his life. Now, he had no choice but to quick-step along with the boy. After what seemed a lifetime, the boy flung open a heavy cedar door and ushered him into a smallish room. There were no windows and the only egress seemed to be the door through which he'd just entered. The space was redolent with the nearly overpowering scent of burning pitch emitted by the flames of seven torches set about the walls in angled sconces. In the room's center Pilate sat in a rough chair behind an even cruder table. If Gamaliel had to guess, this room would normally serve as a gathering place for the soldiers stationed at the Fortress or perhaps a holding room for prisoners. That possibility nearly brought him to an abrupt stop.

"Greetings, Excellency," he said. "You summoned me and I came." He waved his arm in a circle, "I am sure there must be an explanation for this...ah...setting. I am here and at your disposal."

While he spoke, Gamaliel scrutinized the Roman. In all his dealings with the Prefect in the past, the man had been trim, well turned out, and supremely confident. But this Prefect slouched in his chair, wine cup atilt. He had not shaved his beard, the peculiar custom practiced by Gentiles. His clothing seemed rumpled. He had left off his signature decorative body armor and wore only a short toga and a crude leather belt which would have seemed more appropriate for a soldier than the Emperor's official overseer of the Promised Land.

Pilate waved him into a chair. "As you have noted, this setting is not my usual place to conduct business. To be perfectly honest with you, I am *in laribus*."

"Pardon?"

"I am under house arrest. That is if it is possible for one to place the current and only anointed Prefect in that condition."

"Excellency, you need to be more specific. By whom and for what crime have you been arrested?"

"Sit. It is a long story. Knowing how gossip floats about Jerusalem, you will have heard by now that the Emperor recently dispatched several emissaries to the city. I was to provide the usual hospitality afforded people of their rank and position. They, in turn, were to deliver dispatches, witness the city at its busiest, and report back on my efficiency. At any rate, I assumed that was the reason they were here. With the Emperor and his Commissions you can never be sure, but, as I had no other information, it is what I must accept as their purpose."

"That is all well and good but, with respect, you have not answered my question. Why are you here in this shabby room and arrested for what?"

"Patience, Rabban. You of all people should know that proper exposition requires time and a certain attention to detail and to context."

"I do know that. I did not realize you did as well. In all our dealings in the past I have never seen any evidence of this virtue on your part."

"Best keep a careful tongue in your head, Rabban. I may be constrained at the moment, but I am still the Prefect, and you are still a subject under the Emperor's rule."

"My apologies. Pray continue. I shall be silent and listen."

"Good. So, these men and their entourages arrived a few days ago. Among them I discovered an old rival. Do you know how it is to be walking along the street and there is someone behind you who wishes to pass but cannot? He presses hard and close and his boots continuously tread on your heels."

"I can't say that I have, but I take your point. So, one of these visitors has lusted after your position and place?"

"Exactly. For years, Aurelius Decimus has been the one dogging my heels. Within months of my appointment to any new position, he would begin a campaign to take it from me. It never worked, but it was never a pleasant experience. He spread one calumny after another about my character. I believe it is why I have been posted here and not to Africa or Sicily. I thought when Tiberius sent me to this godforsaken place, I was done with Aurelius. But no, he arrived with the detachment from Rome determined, I assume, to find fault with my performance and attempt to wrest the post from me by reporting my failures to the Emperor."

"This Aurelius had you arrested?"

Pilate raised his hand, palm out. "Listen, Rabban. I will tell all, but in my own time. No, he did not. He could not. He is dead, murdered, and I am accused of doing the murdering. That is why I languish in this dreary cell."

"And that is why I did not receive my usual detachment of legionnaires to escort me here."

"Your usual detachment of…? Oh, I see. Yes."

"And there is more. Of course there is. Sorry, go on."

"The man who put me in this position is named Cassia, Cassia Drusus. He has been commissioned by the Emperor to inspect the various outposts in the Empire, to root out disloyalty, inefficiency, and corruption, or so he says."

"You have some doubts as to his mission?"

"You will interrupt won't you, Rabban? I suppose it comes from a lifetime of disputation. We are not in that modality now, so please listen."

"But I only ask because it may bear on the rest—"

"Please…now, with these sorts of official visits, that is, visits ordered by the Emperor, one never really knows. He might be speaking the truth and, then again, he might not. Politics, Rabban, surely you have politics in your Sanhedrin."

"Only to the extent your Emperor imposes them on us, but that is a topic for another day. On what basis did Cassia Drusus determine you had murdered your rival? Obviously, if this Aurelius person was found dead, you must be a prime suspect if what you have told me is correct, but to arrest you?"

"Please do not barge in again. Cassia arrested me because he found me bent over the still-warm body of a very dead Aurelius, with his blood on my hands, and my dagger in his heart."

"Your dagger? That is unfortunate, but also interesting, importantly so I should say. Your dagger, truly?"

"Mine."

"I see. Well, to be fair to this Cassia person, it seems a reasonable conclusion. I must ask…sorry, I cannot play at this logical exposition you insist on following. I take it you did not, in fact, dispatch the man."

"Are you mad? Certainly not."

"But you were discovered with the body, red-handed, you could say. How did this incriminating scene come about and why were you at the scene in the first place?"

"If you want to hear the story, you must stop interrupting and listen. I received a message from one of my Centurions stating that he had urgent information for me that he needed to deliver in private. I thought he might have a line on my visitors' real purpose for being in the city. The message named the time and the place. When I arrived, there was no Centurion, only a dead Aurelius."

"And Cassia Drusus?"

"He arrived moments later."

"In time to find you in that compromising position. Yes, I see. Prefect, forgive me, but before you continue, I must ask you a question. Your story is indeed interesting, but why are you telling it to me and, as a corollary, why am I here?"

"I would have thought that would be obvious, Rabban. I did not stab Aurelius. Our law, as yours, requires proof of guilt. I assure you that Cassia and the rest of the Emperor's men have no interest in establishing my innocence. They may go through the motions of holding an inquiry, but it will only be for show, to meet the letter of the law. No, they intend to ship me back to Rome after the Passover to be tried by the Senate. In Rome, Rabban, they will send me to Rome. How can I possibly defend myself from the charges at such a remove?"

"I would say not easily, if at all."

"There, you see? If I cannot clear myself here and now, I am doomed. That is why I called you."

"Wait." Gamaliel started to rise but his legs failed him. "You dragged me to this wretched hole in the expectation that I would sort out Aurelius' murder on your behalf? It is impossible."

"Nevertheless, you will. We have very little time before they leave with or without me. You will see to it that I do not accompany them."

Chapter V

The two men contemplated one another across the table's scarred planking. How far had the Prefect fallen? The most powerful man in the Palestine, stripped of his powers, pleading for help from Gamaliel, the chief rabbi of the race of men and of the religion he despised. Gamaliel leaned back and gazed for several moments at this man he both feared and pitied. Except for the hissing from the burning torches, the room was quiet, and although he could not see them, he was almost certain he heard rats scampering about in the dark. The torches guttered and smoked. If fresh air did not find its way into the room and soon, Gamaliel believed, they would both expire from asphyxiation. Finally, Pilate spoke.

"You see how it is, Rabban. *Interveni pro me auxilium tuum.* I must beg for your help." He was pleading, but precious little humility found its way into his tone of voice. Gamaliel guessed it would be all that he would get. If he were to establish his position, it would have to be now.

"Indeed, I can see that. Tell me, Prefect…shall I continue to call you that? Tell me why I should be bothered with establishing your innocence or guilt? You know as well as I do that most, if not all, of my people would rejoice at your downfall. If you are not the most disliked man in all of the Palestine, you come in a close second. Furthermore—"

"Furthermore if you defend me and do so successfully, as I have no doubt you will, you will join me in the ranks of those hated by your own people. Yes, I know that."

"Yet, you bring me here to make the request. Why?"

"You have a weakness which, ironically, is also your greatest strength."

"What? A weakness that is also…please, do not burden me with Latin sophistry. I prefer not to deal in paradoxes, clever aphorisms, or word games. Why should I care about your sorry predicament?"

"Rabban, your weakness, and simultaneously your strength, is that you are a righteous man. You are *iustus,* a just man. It does not matter if you would prefer to ignore wrongdoing, even among your enemies; you are incapable of doing so. I am counting on that."

"You presume, sir. I may be, as you imply, blindly righteous, but at the same time, I am not a fool. I have a position to maintain and, believe it or not, I will do anything in my limited power to see you and your countrymen removed from this land—all of you at once or one at a time, if necessary, and as soon as possible."

"I know that, Rabban, but consider the following. While the Greeks are philosophers and Arabs have the corner on mathematics at the moment—although there are those who might argue—the important thing to remember is that Romans are pragmatists. Pragmatic people, Rabban, and behind all that devotion to your Law and your holy books and your feigned indifference to politics, you are as well."

Gamaliel started to protest. Whether or not the Prefect had it right or not, he resented being lumped together with these hated people.

"Tut. Let me finish. Because we share this characteristic, whether you want to admit it or not, you will eventually come to realize that I am no different from any of a hundred, a thousand men like me. You see how it is? Like it or not, if I fall from grace, one of them will replace me within days, possibly even hours. I assure you, if Cassia or any of the other members of the mission who have taken possession of my apartments and usurped my authority, were to replace me, the lives of your people would not improve one *unica*. Wouldn't you prefer the enemy you know to the one you do not?"

"May the Lord forgive me. You are all alike. Why am I not surprised?"

"Alas, yes we are. Well, except for Rufus. He is more like you. He harbors affection for doing the right thing by people, even those with no standing. Which is why, I tell him repeatedly, he will never rise very far in the Empire. You will like Rufus."

"Rufus? And you believe I shall meet him?"

"Oh yes, certainly. How else will you interview witnesses? Surely you do not believe my captors and colleagues will willingly submit to questioning by a non-citizen and a Hebrew at that?"

"I cannot believe that they would care an ass' ear what I managed to discover, even your innocence, should I prove it. You may be pragmatists, as you say, but you are also xenophobes and arrogant to boot. They will not care, Prefect."

"If I were not in the position I currently hold, would you dare to speak to me in that tone? I will answer for you. You would not. You would be choosing your words with great care. Mind you, you would have said the same thing, but you would have treaded only so close to the line you have just now crossed."

"That is very observant of you, Excellency. I cannot tell you how delightful it felt. I might ask for your forgiveness later. Then again, I might not. If I walk out of here now, it is a near certainty I will never see you again."

"I am counting on you not walking out and on receiving that apology later."

Gamaliel sighed. Pilate was right. If the Prefect could persuade him of his innocence and convince him that not acting on his behalf would bring about an injustice, he would not abandon him.

"There are other reasons why I cannot accept your commission, if that is what this is."

"Oh, yes, many. I am fully aware of the limitations placed on you. But do I have another choice? I do not. You, in spite of your stiff-necked religiosity, burn for the truth. If anyone can unravel this business, it is the Rabban of the Sanhedrin. Besides, none of my people will touch it with a barge pole. Yes, you will be severely limited. On the other hand, you will be free enough. Tell me what you need."

"I need nothing, Prefect. I cannot do this. Your people will not speak to me. How can I possibly interrogate them as to their whereabouts on that day? I cannot even roam freely about this building. My Law and yours will not permit it. If I can do none of these things, my hands are tied. You are expecting a miracle."

"I am expecting only that the shrewdest man in the land will do his best to uncover the truth."

"And if I fail?"

"My enemies and your countrymen will rejoice. Imagine. Finally they will have something in common."

"You are being needlessly cynical, Prefect. Your more immediate danger lies with me. It is clearly more in my interest to fail than to succeed. Why then would I try?"

"Rabban, Rabban, sometimes you are so innocent. You will only fail if you cannot, after applying yourself diligently to the problem, find the truth. It is your nature to pursue it as a dog will worry a bone."

"I have no familiarity with dogs or their worries."

"Your people regard them as pariahs, yes, I know. Too bad for you, but the imagery stands. It is your nature to do the right thing."

Gamaliel closed his eyes. He'd been had, no doubt about it, and the prospect of attempting to pry the truth from this race of self-satisfied despots would be nearly impossible. He tried once more to dissuade the Prefect from burdening him with the task which closely resembled farming the cracks between paving stones.

"Tell me, then, Prefect, with your authority usurped, how do you expect me to interview those who might be involved? How will your people take the news that I have discovered that one of them is a murderer, for example?"

"As to the latter, not well, I imagine. But in the end, they will accept it because they believe in the law and the untrammeled application of it. Then they will probably hound you to death."

"You are not making this easy for me."

"Very well. I will give you Rufus. If it appears that your investigation wanders down that particular path, then he—and not you—will have discovered it. It might save your life and would certainly garner him a promotion."

"I will need more than this Rufus as surrogate."

"Name it."

"To begin, I will need my friend, the Physician Loukas, to inspect the body. Can you deliver the corpse to me? Then, I will want him full time to assist me as well. He is sufficiently Hellenized to pass as one of you, and he can move about the Fortress without attracting the attention I would. I will send him to the place where the body was found as I need a full understanding of it. Also, his Latin is passable so he can help Rufus translate if your friends insist on speaking Latin instead of Greek."

"And also to make sure that Rufus translates accurately?"

"That, too, and I will need access to any and all who might shed light on the matter."

"Done. When can you start?"

"This afternoon. Now, I must go and find Loukas. He will not be happy. You will bring the dead man to some place where it can be viewed and brief this Rufus person on what is happening."

Chapter VI

The boy told him his name was Marius. "After Mars, the god of war," he'd announced. Gamaliel thought he did so somewhat too proudly. Romans and their love of conquest and violence, even when naming their slaves. Marius, Pilate said, would be his *dirige*.

"My what? Prefect, you know my Latin is spotty at best. What is this boy to me?"

"He is to be your guide. You may use him to send and receive messages. He will be, for the term of your investigation, your devoted servant."

"I will need a great deal more than this boy to do what you expect of me."

"At the moment, he will have to do."

Gamaliel and his *dirige* left the room and headed out to the fresher air of the Temple Mount. At least he hoped so. Gamaliel had no idea how to find his way out and left to his own devices he believed he would be lost forever in the lower reaches of the Antonia Fortress, his bones to be found after decades of fruitless searching. Who would search? His bones would never be found. They two had not gone more than ten steps when a figure loomed up from the shadows. So sudden was its appearance that Gamaliel's heart skipped a beat. The boy stumbled and dropped to one knee.

"Madam," the boy stammered.

Ah, it seemed the figure was a woman. Gamaliel could not be sure in the dim light and with many layers of fabric swathing the figure. Ignoring the boy, the woman stepped up to Gamaliel.

"You are Gamaliel, the Rabban of the Sanhedrin?"

"I am."

"I have heard of you." She glanced nervously over her shoulder. "He must not know we have spoken."

"Who must not know, the boy or the Prefect?"

"Cassia Drusus, who else?"

"My apologies, madam, but forgive me, you are—"

"I am Claudia Procula, wife to Pontius Pilate. Get up, boy. Rabban Gamaliel, I must speak with you but please, I…"

The boy stood but kept his eyes averted. Gamaliel shuffled his feet. "What is it you wish to tell me?"

This exchange made him uncomfortable. That he had been coerced into entering a pagan building was bad enough, but to speak to a pagan woman as well? He would have to think about all the transgressions now marked against his name when he spent time in his *mikvah* later that evening. This day seemed to be sliding downward at an ever-increasing pace. And it was still only the fifth hour.

"You must help him, rabbi. I have had a vision."

"A vision?" Gamaliel was no stranger to visionaries. In his capacity of Rabban he'd had to judge the veracity of many of them. Most were blatant frauds. One or two seemed to be connected somehow with the spiritual world, but he did not know how or why. At one time or another he had consigned to be punished or exiled nearly all purveyors of omens. Most had then recanted and taken up less parlous lines of thievery. A few remained whose insights still nagged at him. The King's companion, Menahem, for example, who'd shared his doomsday predictions of the Nation's certain demise a few years ago and had thereby ruined the better part of an afternoon.

"I saw who murdered Aurelius."

"You saw the murderer? Why did you not tell it to that person, what's his name, Cassia Drusus? Then I would not be—"

"I only saw him in the vision, Holy Sir. Cassia does not concern himself with visions. He is—"

"A pragmatist. Aren't you all? Very well then, tell me who killed your husband's rival? Have I got that right—his rival?"

"Rival? I suppose so. The murderer was a *Tribunus cohortis.*"

"A Tribune? I was not aware one such existed in Judea at the moment, aside from your husband, and you are not accusing him, surely. Is this Tribune a part of the mission that recently arrived?"

"Not him, not one of them, no…it is not clear…wait." The Prefect's wife stood still, her eyes looking off into the distance. Or the future?

"The party has one such, but he is not the murderer. No, it is not one of them, but another." She turned and disappeared into the shadows.

Gamaliel stared at the figure retreating into the darkness. "Well, my young *dirige*, what do you make of that?"

"They say she suffers from lunacy, Excellency."

"Boy, for the absolute last time, I am not 'your Excellency,' and it appears as this day unfolds she has plenty of company among the crazed. Get me out of this place."

Loukas practiced medicine in Jerusalem. It had taken him many years to find his way to the city of David. He'd spent his youth as a slave apprenticed to a Physician in Antioch. He'd come to Jerusalem, he said, to discover his Hebrew roots. Slaves were not permitted any religion other than their master's. Loukas' master had had none, which allowed Loukas to experience all. But it was not until he'd been freed and then inherited the medical practice that he seriously thought about anything remotely resembling the spiritual. Once begun, introspection led him to Judea, God's promised land, and he'd never left.

Gamaliel found him relaxing in his back court.

"Loukas, greetings in the Name. You are keeping well?"

"And to you, also. As always, Rabban, this is a pleasant surprise. I was just thinking about you."

"Good thoughts or bad?"

"In the case of the Sanhedrin's preeminent rabbi, I imagine only good. Is this a social call, a call regarding the state of your health, or have you become entangled in another mess that requires my assistance?"

"I believe the latter. What were your thoughts?"

"As it happened, I was thinking that it had been a while since we were engaged in anything out of the ordinary and wondering how long it would be before you'd come calling with another problem. Now I know. Tell me what bit of intrigue has managed to entangle you this time—murder, international conspiracies, illicit sales of potions, wayward princesses…what?"

"I was summoned by his Excellency, the Prefect."

Loukas waved him to a bench. "That can't be good. What did that terrible man want from you this time?"

"I could use some wine, Loukas. Once my mind is at ease, I will tell you, but you will not be pleased."

Loukas called for wine and some fruit and waited until his friend had settled. Gamaliel sighed—he found he did that a lot lately—and told Loukas of his predicament. When he finished, Loukas glared at him.

"He wants you to investigate the murder he is accused of committing. Have I got that right?"

"In a word, yes. You see my problem. How can I possibly do as he asks? I am a Jew. I speak practically no Latin, although they all speak Greek. None of his colleagues or his accusers will cooperate, in any event. The matter is to be adjudicated by their law, about which I know little or nothing. I am so limited that—"

"No. Rabban, excuse me for interrupting, but you are missing the main reason you cannot do this."

"Yes, yes, I know. If I take on Pilate's case, if I ally myself to him, so to speak, and even if I fail at it, I will be forever ostracized by my people—hated probably."

"That, too, but you still don't see."

"I am sorry, then. What is it that I do not see? I would have thought I covered all the terrible possibilities I face."

"No. Listen. You must ask yourself, what is the man playing at?"

"What is who playing at?"

"Pilate. Surely you do not believe he wants you to solve this murder, to exonerate him?"

"I don't? Why do I not believe that? I am sorry, Loukas, I must be very dense this morning. I do not understand."

"Drink some more wine and hear me out. Imagine you are Pontius Pilate. You are caught red-handed…that is what is meant by the phrase, isn't it? His hands are covered with blood when he was arrested, yes? So, as the Prefect, what do you do? Do you call on some Hebrew official to set you free? Don't be ridiculous. You are the Emperor's legate to the Palestine, as they insist this land be called. Therefore, you will either…" Loukas raised his hand and ticked off each point on his fingers, "…post your legionnaires and seal yourself off from further accusations until you personally root out the criminal. Or, you will contact the best Roman adjudicator in the Empire to handle your case, and/or you will promptly draw your short sword and eliminate your accuser and then forget the whole sorry business. If I know our Prefect, the last of these would have been his choice. In any event, you would not call on the Rabban of the Sanhedrin to solve your problem. To do so makes no sense whatsoever. So, I repeat, what is he playing at?"

"I had not thought of it that way. And yet…Loukas, you have a logical mind and I do not. I am a person who studies the Law and always it is to be understood within the margins of the human condition. The Lord is merciful in this way. I must look at this call from the Prefect in precisely the same context. As you say, he might have done those other things, but the fact remains, he did not. There must be a reason for it that we cannot see and…let me finish…it may not be as subtle or conniving as you would make it out."

"With respect, Gamaliel, I don't believe you are that ingenuous. I must conclude you are being stubborn."

"Perhaps you are right, but then I didn't tell you the part about his wife."

Chapter VII

When the door had closed behind Gamaliel and the boy, Pilate faced about and addressed someone sitting in a corner lost in the shadows. "Well, what do you make of him, Rufus?"

Rufus—for that was he, indeed, who had crouched in the dark throughout the meeting between Pilate and Gamaliel—stepped into the light. "Pilate, what in the name of all the gods are you doing? How can this Israelite bumpkin possibly help you?"

"Do not underestimate him. Whatever you may have been told about Hebrews, this one is not to be trifled with. I have witnessed him at work. Yes, he is typically stiff-necked. Certainly he is not like the Jews in Rome or Alexandria or the rest of the Empire who seem to have grasped the need to integrate their beliefs into society at large. Here, they take their peculiar religion seriously and undiluted. Nevertheless, I tell you, if he puts his mind to it, he will dig out the truth and will not care whose toes he treads on doing it."

"But, surely—"

"And before you ask again, what other choice do I have?"

"What other choices? You are…well, you were the Prefect and as such, the commander of the legionnaires in this place. Why on earth didn't you simply refuse to be intimidated by Cassia's swaggering and send your troops to block him?"

"You travelled here separately from Cassia's group, I believe."

"Yes, you know I did. I sailed into Caesarea Maritima and traveled down to Jerusalem with you."

"Indeed, then you will remember that the others entered the country through Joppa and marched up the hills from there. They arrived a day before we did. Therefore, you did not see who accompanied them."

"How is that important?"

"It is important because they were accompanied by a partial cohort of legionnaires of their own who were formerly assigned to the peninsula. Not an Italian cohort, but close enough, men who had been recruited out of the Empire. A Tribune of stature commands them. Understand it was they who stood at Cassia's back when he found me with Aurelius. They, not the local legionnaires, not my legionnaires, took me into custody. Furthermore, these same soldiers now secure the Fortress. I am not in any position to do anything. I have been outflanked. So, you see, I could not and I cannot force my will on anyone. You have another idea?"

"Send for a *zenam legisperitum* of your own choosing. Let him defend you, not this Hebrew."

"Believe me, it was my first thought. Unfortunately, the closest lawyer with any stature, that is to say one with any chance of succeeding at what I suppose needs to be done, resides in Syrian Antioch. It would take at least two weeks and a very fast horse to get the message to him and for him to make his way here to Jerusalem. Too late for me. In a little over a week, these eager men plan to haul me off to Rome. Any other ideas?"

"Let me kill Cassia, then."

"That is a tempting thought, but to do so would accomplish nothing. As I said, the power lies in Cassia's hands and backed to the hilt by that annoying Tribune and his legionnaires. Did I mention that they, while not Italian, are battle-hardened and considerably fitter than the mercenaries assigned to me? I did. So, killing that little man will not alter the course of events. Alas, Rufus, they have me boxed in."

"I did not know about those new soldiers. That is most unfortunate. Then it appears you are doomed."

"No, it is not the end, not yet. They do not know about Gamaliel."

"So, the funny little man in the dark robes and beard is all that is left to you? I am not encouraged."

"You should be. He is clever and I will employ him for the nonce. If he fails, I will try something else, something more muscular."

"An odd turn of speech, Pilate, but I understand the sense of it. So, you wish me to help this man?"

"Help him, but mostly watch him. He may not solve my problem, but in the process of trying, he may find us someone on whom we can lay the blame. Cassia and his friends are determined to bring me down, so we discover who killed Aurelius or someone we can convincingly accuse of killing him. Either needs to be a sure thing. They are not interested in my innocence. As you must have deduced by now, I am seriously short of supporters in this city."

"Not just in this city, Pilate. I brought letters from the Senate with me which I was instructed to deliver to you on your arrival in Jerusalem.'

"Really? And what do they say?"

"In essence they are inquiring into the numerous complaints they have received from the Jewish officials over the last several years. The Emperor is not happy. The Senate is not happy that the Emperor is not happy. And unless they have assurances from you that you are properly penitent…well, in a nutshell, the possibility of your recall has been discussed. You do understand the probability that this old man, who you believe can save you, is very likely among those who signed the complaints to the Emperor."

"I would be very surprised if he hadn't. What did the whiners say?"

"In the authorities' view, the behavior in question consisted of repeated and needless brutality and insensitivity directed at the Jews."

"It's about those standards I mounted around their Temple. I have removed them. The rest is nonsense."

"If you say so. Nevertheless, you cannot afford a slipup like this murder thing now."

"There will be no slipping, I assure you. Either way, you will provide me with a pair of 'innocent' ears."

A young woman entered Loukas' court bearing a fresh flagon of wine and some bread and cheese. Gamaliel admired her. Since his wife died, he had not noticed women generally but this young thing…well, there is beauty and then there are a few whose beauty transcends any norm. She had the olive skin which marked her as a woman of these parts and large sloe eyes that transformed her face into something beyond anything he'd ever seen.

He gestured toward the woman and asked, "You have replaced the poor dead Draco with this?"

"You approve?"

"Probably not. Having a young woman in your house with no other evidence of females in residence is a potential scandal, Loukas, not that you care."

"It is a scandal for you, perhaps, but not for me. Your Law has no flexibility. You are rigid to the point of paralysis, Rabban. Many of us—Jews but significantly less petrified—have seen the need for broader interpretation of the limits of the Torah. I know that is a sore point for you, but if you were ever to travel outside the city, to Alexandria, or Rome even, you would discover many Jews who have accommodated to the mores of the pagans. Not all of their practices are evil and damning."

"I am only too aware of this backsliding, Loukas. If you ask me, it is an excuse for slackness. And I will remind you that you do not reside in Alexandria or Rome. You live here, in Jerusalem, and here there is an expectation you will follow the rules as spelled out by the Lord."

"I know that. I do not wish to upset you, but this woman, whom you assumed might be my mistress…don't give me that injured look, that is what you thought and you know it…this woman, Sarai, is married to Yakob who is new to my service as well. I hired him. She was a benefit. He tells me he once served as a legionnaire, but I find that difficult to believe."

"She is married. I see. My apologies. Why difficult to believe?"

"If he had, why does he no longer serve? Plus, where did he manage to find time to secure so beautiful a wife? I intended to ask but am afraid I will offend, and I do not want to lose their services. She is lovely to contemplate, is she not?"

"You are in dire need of a wife, Physician."

"If you say so. At any rate, their story must remain a mystery, but their marital status should absolve me of any of your dark thoughts or condemnation. And shame on you, Gamaliel, for harboring old man's thoughts."

"I stand corrected and once again beg your pardon."

"Apology accepted. You were going to tell me about the Prefect's wife."

"Ah, the wife, Procula. I had a glancing acquaintance with her before."

"You know her?"

"I know of her. We have never met, but once, in another circumstance, she persuaded the Prefect to see me when it seemed unlikely he would. Some say she has visions, premonitions. Others believe her mad."

"And you?"

"I have no opinion. She is a pagan and I can only assume that status must encourage visits from all sorts of misguided spirits."

"Your extreme religious bias is duly noted. What did she say?"

"She said two things of interest. She said that I must help him, by which she meant her husband. And she said that she had seen the murder."

"Well, that should make your task simple."

"I wish. She saw the murder in a vision, so as appealing as that might be to some, it would never stand up as evidence enough to convict or exonerate anyone."

"A vision? Did she say who, in this dreamscape, the murderer was?"

"My Latin is poor and her Greek barely better, but I thought she said a Tribune. I was unaware there was one such in the city and wondered if he had traveled to Jerusalem with the party of officials who seem intent on bringing Pilate down."

"And?"

"And she said 'not one of them,' or words to that effect."

"That isn't much help. If not one of the party just recently arrived, who?"

"No idea, but it was a curious thing to say."

Chapter VIII

Sarai retreated into the brightly tiled room which served as an area for cooking and, in Loukas' eclectic living arrangements, for dining. Early afternoon sunlight streamed through the open windows as the aroma of roasting goat exited. She dropped a ball of dough on the table. She would knead it and roll it into loaves for the evening meal. Yakob sat across from her.

"Who is that man in the dark robes?" he asked.

"You do not know? It is the Rabban of the Sanhedrin."

"That insignificant-looking man is the chief officer of the Sanhedrin?"

"And the rabbi's rabbi, yes. His name is Gamaliel. Surely, you—"

"What is he doing in the house of our Physician?"

"You know as much as I do, husband. They are friends, although since our master is anything but faithful in his worship practices, I do not see how that is possible. The Rabban arrived an hour ago, and they have been drinking wine and talking about his visit to the Antonia Fortress. I heard the Prefect's name mentioned."

"The Rabban of the Sanhedrin visits the Romans, visits the Prefect? How can that be? I do not understand what the Rabban has to do in the company of our enemies unless it is to kill him. I know the Prefect is in trouble, but he is not dead...yet. So, what business does that old man have with our enemies?'

"Yakob!"

"The Empire and its agents are the source of our troubles. You know that. Everyone knows that. Why would he—?"

"Well, we know, but—"

"I have been away too long. No wonder the Nation stays under the Roman heel. Our own people, our leaders collaborate with them to keep us there."

"Yakob, you were a soldier in one of the Emperor's legions. Does that not make you a 'collaborator,' too? How is that any different?"

"It is not the same thing. They came to our homes and threatened to destroy them and our families if we did not serve. 'Jews,' they said, 'serve or suffer with your people.' They were going to burn us out, woman. I had no choice. These Temple people, these who shove the Law down your throats, these people have choices. That is the difference."

"But to serve for twenty years?"

"Woman, hold your tongue. You forget the punishment for desertion is death, a very unpleasant death. So, yes, I completed my years and took my severance and left. I wanted to live long enough to see this band of Roman murderers brought down."

"Brought down? Rome? Do you really believe that is possible?"

"Everything is possible. Judging if a thing is probable is the question. I am certain it could happen if enough people wanted it to."

"Even so, husband, you may be judging the Rabban too harshly. His reputation with the people is good, especially with women. Now, if you wish to talk about the High Priest that would be a different matter."

"The High Priest. That man wastes the air he breathes. All his posturing and posing, all his nonsense about finishing the Temple and keeping strictly to the Law. What Law? Moses'? Moses has been dead since the beginning of time. I tell you, King David himself, if he were to come back to life, even he would not follow this bloated person's idea of the Law. Times have changed, wife."

"Times may have, the Lord has not."

"The Lord, *Adonai, El, Ha Shem*. Why do you say it that way? Go ahead and speak the Name. You will not be struck down by lightning. This God person, I do not think even He cares about the Temple party's idea of Law."

"Yakob, be still. You must be careful how you speak."

"In Rome and in the other great cities of the Empire, Jews are not afraid to adapt, Sarai. You know that. And so far, not one of them has been struck down by God for lack of respect. You see? No angry roar from the heavens, no lightning bolts strike to tell them their God is unhappy. Do you think that maybe God is not as concerned with all this bowing and scraping as the Pharisees would have you believe?"

"This is Jerusalem and not any of those other places. We are in the Holy Land, the land given to us by the Name. In this place He is present and, unlike those other cities, He does not compete with pagan gods. Here He is Lord. He watches and listens. You survived twenty years as a Roman legionnaire. It would be a great tragedy if you come here only to die a blasphemer."

"Nonsense." Sarai's eyes filled at his scolding. "Oh, very well. For you, I will try to be discreet. But you should know there are many Jews like me who are coming together in this your Promised Land to do something about the Roman plague."

"Not my Promised Land—ours—our Promised Land. Please, I beg you, do not join with those people, those Zealots. Do not even speak of them. You, of all people, know that there is no force anywhere in the world that can defeat Rome. You served as a soldier. You know that. Those men are fools if they think they can do something where others, better equipped and better trained, cannot. I ask you as a soldier, what sort of army would be needed to defeat the legionnaires stationed here, and if you could raise it, how much bigger must it grow to when the legions sent from Rome arrive? Zealots with their knives and their boasting, what will they accomplish beyond shedding more blood? So, a Sicarii kills a tax-gatherer, and what then? Does your hated Roman shake in his boots, drop his spear and run? You know he does not."

"Every movement must start somewhere."

"Movement? What movement? You mean like Yehudah of the Galilee and his movement? His foolish attack on the Roman garrison ended in crucified men lining both sides of the road from Sephoris to Nazareth, rape and murder of women and children, and a city burned to the ground. All this because one old man thought there had to be a start? It was the mouse annoying the lion. That was not a start, that was a disaster. No, these new saviors of the Nation can only bring more pain and sorrow to the Lord's house. We have a good situation here, Yakob. Let us enjoy it. Leave war and plotting to younger, more foolish men."

Yakob scowled, mumbled something she did not understand, and left the room.

Pilate waved his wife to a chair and offered her his cup.

"I did not come here to drink, husband. You have seen the Jew?"

Pilate's eyebrow climbed a short distance up his forehead. "You know I did, Procula. You were lurking in the hallway as he left, I believe."

"Yes. Well, good. I told him what I saw."

Rufus who had been listening with half an ear sat up. "You saw Aurelius killed?"

"Yes."

"Pilate, we have no need for the Jew. Your esteemed wife can testify and—"

"She cannot."

"Cannot? But why? If she saw the man murdered and also who did it, why would she not speak to Cassia and tell him the real killer's name, tell him you are innocent?"

"It is not that easy."

"They would only laugh at me," Procula said.

"Laugh at you, but why?"

"It was a vision, Rufus. Procula came to me the day before and said she had seen Aurelius murdered and that I should not respond to a summons to the basement if one were presented."

"The day before? I don't understand."

"My wife has visions about impending events, Rufus. She sometimes sees things that will happen before they happen. She 'saw' the murder."

Procula shook her head and drained the Prefect's cup. "But you went down into the cellars anyway."

"You are not always right, as you know, and anyway, I forgot about the vision. I only remembered it when Cassia arrested me. Too late, alas."

Rufus slumped back on his stool. "Is there anything else I should know of this story which becomes increasingly bizarre by the hour?"

"Only this. In the past, when Procula urged me to employ services from an unlikely source, it has always worked to my advantage. Well, nearly always. Since, as we have just discussed, I have no other real alternatives, I called for the Rabban. So, now you know the secret of my success."

"I am stunned. With respect, honored lady, but you say your vision identified the murderer and then you had a second, ah… premonition that this Jewish official should be called to solve the Prefect's problem?"

"That is near enough, yes."

Rufus stood and walked toward the door. "It is time for me to throw in with Cassia. You are doomed, Pilate, and I wish to survive."

He closed the door behind him.

"Will he join Cassia, husband?"

"No. Rufus is not the keenest arrow in the sheaf, but he is a friend and will not betray me. That is why he will never rise in the Emperor's service."

"Never?"

"If you are unwilling to betray a friend, you will not stay long in any position of importance in the Empire created for us by Tiberius."

"Did you betray your friends, husband?"

"I *am* the Prefect."

Chapter IX

Loukas stared at his friend. Frustrated would not even come close to describing his expression. He had walked some miles with Gamaliel, shared danger and a few triumphs, but this new thing? No good could emerge from this morass.

"Enough, Gamaliel. If you insist on ignoring the likelihood that you are being duped by the Prefect, at least acknowledge the problem you face. It is not the difficulty you will encounter dealing with a hostile Roman officialdom, by the way."

Gamaliel shifted on the bench to gain more shade from an overhanging tree limb and sipped his wine. "Remind me. What would that would be?"

Loukas gazed heavenward and clenched his fists in frustration. "Sometimes you can be so exasperating. You said it yourself. If you throw in with the Prefect, you will be ruined. You will lose your position, you might be stoned to death, and most certainly you will become the latest target for these 'Dagger Men.' You must decline the Prefect's demand."

"Common sense and caution say I must, but I cannot and I need your help."

Loukas sat down. "Me? Sorry, but unlike you, I am not suicidal. I cannot conceive of any circumstance that would allow me to set foot inside that wasp's nest. Not even to help you. You want to clear a man from a charge of murder, a man the entire world agrees would be better off dead."

"Not all the world, surely."

"Your world, our world then. No, I will not do it. You are on your own."

"Then you must tell me what to look for in a corpse."

"A corpse? You're not serious. You may not touch a dead body much less study it. Do you honestly think you are capable of stripping a body, inspecting its various orifices—prod here and poke there? Rabban, have you gone mad?"

"You leave me no other choice, Loukas."

"I see what you are doing. You will not get away with this. This is extortion and I will not yield. If you insist on putting yourself in that position, it is on your head."

"Yes, yes, I understand. So, tell me what I must do. Pilate will arrange for the dead man to be available, and since you will not help me, I must proceed on my own. So, where do I start? Do I have to cut him open? Isn't that a violation of the law, Roman and Hebrew? I should start with his hands, right? I must look at his hands, nails and so on for…what exactly do I look for?"

"You are impossible. Very well, I will look at your dead man, but that is all. I will look, report, and depart."

"Thank you."

Loukas stood and started for the courtyard gate. "Shall we go to the Prefect now?"

"Now? Oh, no, not now. No, we will let the Prefect stew for a bit. It will do him good. He is far too confident he has caught me in his net. Let him wait and wonder. He has things to do and to contemplate in the meantime. No, you and I will take a walk about the city and listen. The murder in the Fortress will be common knowledge by now. We should move about in the crowds, stop at our usual places of refreshment and listen to what people are saying or gossiping about. Who knows? The solution may not reside in the Fortress at all."

Two hours mingling with the crowds, both the city's new arrivals and its permanent residents, and chatting with random passersby yielded an array of misinformation and the general sense that if the Prefect were to be deposed, no one would care. Rejoice, certainly, but not care. The tenor of the remarks and the evident glee over the idea that Pilate might soon depart forever convinced Loukas that Gamaliel should drop the idea of doing the Prefect's bidding.

"You see how it is, Rabban. Anyone who helps that despicable man will have the hate transferred to him. Don't you understand? You cannot win this one."

"I understand, my Physician, and I am listening, I promise. But a larger problem arises if I do not."

"Larger? How so?"

"Tell me, what is it we most hate about these people from across the Middle Sea? Is it their brutality? Perhaps a little, yes, but cast your mind back through our history and ask yourself this: Are they worse than the Greeks when the Great Alexander swept through here, or the Assyrians, the Babylonians? What shall we say of the Amelekites or King Saul's and David's Philistines? If you contemplate the sweep of our history, as much as it pains me to say so, by comparison Rome is a relatively benign oppressor. They allow the Sanhedrin to continue to govern. Admittedly this is done with severe limitations but not as onerous as they might be. The Temple still stands. Look, even now the smoke from the altar rises to heaven. It has not been looted or desecrated as it has been in the past. The Romans employ local people in any number of ways, not just to collect taxes, but as guards, workers, servants, and so on. They have enslaved people to a lesser degree than their predecessors. Consider Babylon and the Exile. Indeed, one could say they have bolstered the economy. Look to the north. Did you know that one third of all the salt fish supplied to their legions comes from the Sea of Galilee? We prosper in spite of the burdens they place on us."

"My friend, I am your greatest admirer, but just now you sound like one of their poets or historians. They are dreadful people and you know it."

"I do. I am only stating the obvious. We could be worse off."

"Bah."

"No, listen. To the east lie lands and a people who, if the rumors are even marginally correct, constitute a sleeping giant needing only a leader, enough greed, and the will to sweep through here like a plague of locusts. Look to the north. Beyond the sea that borders Cappadocia is a race of bearded men, the Rus, whose ferocity is legend. But, because the Romans are here, they are not. Suppose we were able to somehow persuade our current oppressors to leave, are you prepared for the consequences? Can we mount an army sufficient to resist the next Nation who covets our land or the next after that? Where will it end, Loukas?"

"But—"

"No buts. Too often we see only what is in front of our eyes, never what lies beyond. Those who would pillage and plunder are always with us and life is temporary. Only *Ha Shem* is forever. The virtues embedded in the Law, are forever. His promises are forever. Unless we would become pale copies of our conquerors, we will practice those virtues. Leave corruption and disregard for humanity to those who would rape and pillage the world. If we wish to survive and see our future, we must concentrate on the business of keeping the Law and all its requirements. If Pilate is innocent of this crime, I must prove it. If he is not, I must bring him down. Justice, Loukas, justice. Now, no more of this debate. I have precious little time to do this thankless job and two of those days are Shabbat. We have work to do."

"We?"

"Yes, we. Now let us see what this very dead Aurelius Decimus can tell us."

◇◇◇

Rufus had returned to what Pilate referred to as his prison.

"Back so soon? Please don't tell me you were unsuccessful in your attempt to join the forces led by Cassia. Surely not."

"You mock me."

"I am sorry. You are correct, I mock you. Rufus, you are a good man—too good for your own good, I might add. Cassia will never believe you devious enough to take into his confidence. Deviousness knows deviousness, and it is not part of your nature."

"I am both flattered and annoyed, Pilate. You seem to have that effect on most of the people around you, I believe."

Pilate shrugged and smiled. "Although it seems it's not working well at the moment."

"Where's your genius Hebrew? Shouldn't he be here sorting out the strands of your predicament by now? Has he had second thoughts and deserted you?"

"He is punishing me, if you must know. I forced him into helping me. He would rather not, given a choice, so he is making me sit like a naughty schoolboy. He hopes I will think of something helpful and, failing that, feel rueful. So far, I have done neither."

"He wants to have someone view the body of Aurelius. Where is Aurelius?"

"He is laid out on a slab one level down and is guarded by one of my legionnaires, so I have access to him if needed. Cassia thought that assigning my people to the less dignified tasks in the fort would add to my overall humiliation. Actually, it will help me. We have, if we need it, access to everything and every place necessary to investigate my problem."

"Except the principals themselves."

"Well, yes that is true. Cassia and his accomplices will not readily acquiesce to requests for an audience and to be questioned, but there is a way around that too. In fact, that is where you come in."

"Me? I thought you only needed me for—"

"Patience, my friend…Ah, I believe our sleuth has arrived. Enter, Rabban."

Chapter X

Guided by Marius, Gamaliel and Loukas entered Pilate's fetid cell. He did not stand to greet them. Gamaliel did not expect he would. Even in peril of his life, he would not give up his innate sense of superiority and official preeminence. Gamaliel pulled up a stool and sat without waiting for his permission.

"Do you suppose we could find a more salubrious place to do this, Prefect?"

"You do not find this room agreeable, Rabban? Every day you wander about the Temple Mount in a miasma of smoke created by the burning flesh of countless sheep, goats, birds, and bulls, yet you find this distasteful?"

"Yes, very. Is there?"

"I will see what I can do, but for the moment we must continue to meet here. Who have you brought with you?"

"This is my colleague and friend, Loukas. You have met once before, I believe. Among his many talents he is a Physician, and he is here to assist me."

"I did not bargain for more than just your presence, Rabban."

"Recall that I told you earlier I would need him and you agreed. So, here he is. He will inspect the dead man for me and also help with my poor Latin."

"I have given you the boy and Rufus for that. Why another Latin speaker?"

"As I said, it is not that I don't trust you, Prefect, but I suspect both the boy and Rufus will have a Roman bias. I am afraid they will hold back some of what they hear in the mistaken notion that it casts them or their allegiance to you in a bad light. Or they may decide that a particular bit of information is not important and leave it out. Besides, even I can tell the boy's Latin is barely better than mine."

"Redacting the conversations? Possibly, but shouldn't that be their prerogative?"

"No. I do not want my information filtered by their biases. So, I require my own check on their reporting."

Pilate twisted in his chair. "Did you hear that, Rufus? The Rabban thinks you might leave something out. Would you?"

"He would if he sensed it incriminating to you," Gamaliel snapped while Rufus composed his answer.

"I see. Well, that would please me."

"It might also doom you. Truth has many facets, Prefect, and if one only looks at those that please, you will miss it."

"Philosophy, as I pointed out earlier, is the purview of the Greeks. Do not burden me with it now."

"You must read the Proverbs in our Scripture. You will find that Greeks are not the only people who speculate on the meaning of life and how best to live it."

"Some other day, Rabban. Now you must be about the business of finding irrefutable proof that someone else, not I, killed Aurelius."

"Very well, I want Marius to escort Loukas to the body and then to the place where you found it. Loukas will need a great deal of light, so you might want to assign a soldier or two to be torch bearers. While he is busy with that, you will tell me everything that happened the day of the murder."

"Everything?"

"Yes, everything, from the moment you awoke until you found yourself confined to this terrible place."

"That may take a while."

"Then we need to begin. Loukas, follow the boy. Rufus, stand ready to correct the Prefect's account even if you think it makes him look bad. I must know everything as it happened and in the order it happened."

Gamaliel listened to Pilate's narrative, stopping him occasionally and asking him to repeat or clarify a particular point.

"When did the Centurion hand you the note to meet Aurelius?"

"Did I say the Centurion handed me a note?"

"It was implied."

"You misunderstood. A legionnaire reported the message to me orally."

"He spoke to you? I see. As there seem to be two separate sets of them, was this soldier one of yours or one that accompanied your visitors?"

"Is that important?"

"I should think it very important."

"One soldier looks much like another. I don't know."

"Surely not. Please concentrate. Yours or theirs?" Pilate only shook his head. Gamaliel slapped his hand on the table. "Prefect, please, could it have been one of theirs?"

"I don't know, perhaps, it could have been, yes. Satisfied?"

"Not even close. When did this exchange occur?"

"I thought I should honor the delegation from Rome. Actually it was my wife who thought of it. I proposed a banquet. They arrived a day earlier than I, as I told you, and as I had not been informed that they would be here, I needed some time to make ready."

"You did not know they were coming?"

"No."

"Is that usual?"

"Let us say that it is not unusual."

"I see. So, a legionnaire approaches you at the banquet—"

"Before the banquet."

"Before the banquet and gives you the message. What was the message, exactly?"

"It was to meet Priscus after the celebration was done."

"And Priscus is the Centurion? It cited a specific location?"

"Yes."

"Have you spoken to this Priscus since?"

"No."

"Why not?'

"Better question, Rabban, why would I? He sent the message."

"But he was not at the location when you arrived. Didn't that strike you as odd? He sends an urgent message but isn't at the scene when you arrive?"

"Not at all. I make it a habit of arriving early at meetings of that sort. I do not like surprises. I assume he practices that habit as well."

"You assume that. Were you early to this one and he was not?"

"This one? Let me think. No, as a matter of fact, I was delayed. He must have been as well."

Gamaliel closed his eyes and fought to suppress his frustration at Pilate's opacity.

"Another assumption and even so, you had a surprise after all. And this equally late Centurion, might he have arrived after Cassia found you and fled for fear of being implicated."

"It is entirely possible."

"But you have not asked him this?"

"No."

Gamaliel considered suggesting to Pilate that Priscus might have been party to the plan to implicate him in a murder and then thought it a better idea to wait and spring that on him later.

"I will need to interview him. Next question. You may not know the answer, but I wish you would venture a guess. How did Cassia come to be in that hallway at the precise moment you discovered the dead man? A moment sooner and you are in the clear. A moment later, you would have raised the alarm and been void of any incriminating evidence. But, miraculously, he appears at the precise moment when neither can occur. How did that happen?"

"I can only suppose he had been forewarned and followed me there."

"Yes, very interesting, but if he had been forewarned, by whom, and could he have not prevented the murder?"

"You believe he set the thing in place himself? That Aurelius was sacrificed for some larger political purpose?" Pilate pursed his lips and nodded. "It would be consistent with how the elite operate in the capital. Yes, very good, Rabban. Those were my thoughts as well, but I cannot prove them."

"I only think it is one possibility."

"Only one?"

"We have only scratched the surface here. For example, how well do you get on with this Priscus? Then, you say there is a Tribune of some note in the visiting company. Who is he and why is he here? Could it be that he plotted to be your successor as Prefect? Perhaps it was not Aurelius who lusted after your position but this man, or even Rufus, here. How confident are you that he is not plotting against you?"

Rufus bolted from his chair and moved toward Gamaliel, his sword half out of its sheath.

"Easy, Rufus," Pilate said. "He is only making a point. No one suspects you of anything. The Rabban is instructing me in the complexities of solving murderers. I take your point, Rabban. Why must you speak to the Centurion?"

"Why? Among other things, I wish to be certain that he did, in fact, send the message, not someone else."

"Rufus, fetch Priscus the Centurion here and then find that Physician. He must be finished with poor Aurelius by now. Anything else, Rabban?"

"Yes, where is the messenger?"

"Where? I have no idea. In the barracks, or standing guard, or patrolling. Who knows? I told you, it was not a written message, only delivered to me verbally."

"I want to speak to that soldier as well."

"I have no idea who he was. As I said, one legionnaire looks much like another to me. Theirs, ours, what difference does it make."

"A great deal. Listen carefully, if I understood you correctly, there are not two as I believed earlier, but three sets of legionnaires in play here. There are those who arrived with you from

Caesarea, those who form the permanent garrison in Jerusalem, and those who accompanied the delegation from Rome. Only the latter are beyond your control. Have I got that right?"

"Yes, I hadn't thought of it that way. I don't see why dividing the first two is important, though."

"Perhaps there is none, but you are not in contact with the garrison here on an everyday basis. They would be less familiar to you, wouldn't they? And that could be important. I do not know why at the moment, but it is something to be considered. At any rate understanding the shape of everything is important. One last question for now, but there will be others, many others, later on. Who had access to your dagger? Knowing that will limit the number of suspected killers if the people who might have taken it are few."

"Anyone with access to my apartments, my baggage, and my things could have stolen it."

"Obviously you did not wear it to the banquet?"

"No."

"Did you intend to?"

"It occurred to me, and when I couldn't locate it right away, I dismissed the thought. No one would notice."

"So you missed the dagger at the outset? That didn't upset you?"

"Things were still being unpacked and sorted. I was busy. I put the loss down to the momentary confusion."

"Which would make stealing it that much easier."

"Yes."

"And Cassia, even though he had arrived ahead of you by a day, recognized it as yours without your telling him?"

"Yes…now that is interesting. I hadn't thought of that. How would he know it was mine? Very good, Rabban. We are making progress."

"I wish that were so. All we have established is the possibility that you were part of an elaborate scheme to oust you from office. We have no idea why or by whom."

Loukas entered the room with Rufus who shrugged. "I cannot locate the Centurion," he said.

Loukas nodded to Gamaliel and jerked his head toward the door. Gamaliel nodded and stood. He glanced around the room as if trying to locate something or someone and then stood.

"Prefect," he said, "I will leave you now. Loukas and I must discuss what we have found and you will not be privy to the content of that conversation."

"I insist that I hear it."

"Sorry, not now, later perhaps. Young Marius, lead the way. Loukas and I need fresh air, and light, and time to think through what we've learned so far. I will need to speak to the Centurion, Priscus. Will you find him for me, please?"

Chapter XI

Gamaliel paid close attention to the route Marius took when they exited the dank lower reaches of the Antonia Fortress. He wanted to be sure that if he had to, he could extricate himself from its twists and turns without the boy's assistance.

"Where are we headed?" Loukas asked once they reached daylight.

"Some place where the possibility of being overheard by one or the other of the Roman's agents is limited."

"Whose Roman agents, Cassia's, Pilate's, or the mysterious Tribune and his legionnaires'?"

"Since we do not know the extent of any of their involvement, except for Pilate, all of them. We will go to the Temple. They dare not pass beyond the Court of the Gentiles. That includes Marius."

"You don't trust the boy?"

"Would you?" He pivoted in place and addressed the boy. "Marius, should I trust you to keep the things we discuss from the Prefect?"

The boy's gaze slid sideways. "Sir?"

"As I thought. To the Temple, Loukas, we have much to discuss."

Herod's Temple loomed against the skyline just south of the Fortress. Its sheer size nearly blocked the late afternoon sun and cast shadows halfway across the vast court that stretched between it and the Fortress. When they entered its inner courtyards, the boy became agitated.

"Stay here, boy," Gamaliel said. "This area is known as the Treasury. Don't look so hopeful, there is not much in the way of treasure, as you understand the word, but there is shade and if you behave yourself, one of the *kohen* might offer you a drink. The Physician and I will be over there." He pointed in the general direction of the Temple proper and walked away through the Court of the Women and through the Nicanor Gate. Once within the Court of the Israelites, he turned and faced Loukas.

"Tell me what you discovered from the dead man."

"Not much that you hadn't already been told. The killing was very efficiently done, a single dagger stroke directed downward and straight into the heart. Whoever wielded that knife knew exactly what he was doing."

"Someone trained as a soldier?"

"Yes, more than likely, or as a Physician."

"Which would include nearly any and all of the people currently in residence in the Fortress, including Pilate. I assume you are not putting yourself forward as a suspect."

"I am not. As to the rest, yes, except for the women."

"Not a woman? You're sure of that?" Loukas nodded his head. "That is not much help. Could it have been a suicide?"

"That is very unlikely. The dagger was, as I said, thrust downward from above. You cannot fall on your dagger positioned that way unless you begin by standing on your head. Ramming it home on your own would be both difficult and require a level of determination beyond most men. Were you seriously thinking suicide?"

"No, but if it were a possibility, it casts doubt on an absolute verdict of murder, you see?"

"I am afraid I don't."

"Roman law and, if I remember correctly, as ours, requires that a judgment of guilt in a crime of this seriousness must be based on evidence that meets the standard of clarity that allows no doubt. If I could make Pilate's accusers admit the man might have killed himself, that is, create even a sliver of doubt, they would have to dismiss the charge."

"You are planning a legal defense on the basis of *non liquet?*"

"If what you just said means Pilate's guilt is not clear enough to convict, yes. I am looking for a quick exit from this labyrinth I have been placed in. That sort of verdict would not have repercussions coming back to me, although it would not help much in Pilate's continuance in his position as Prefect. Is there anything else you can tell me about the wound, aside from the expertise in application?"

"I knew you would ask and yes, I noticed one oddity. I saw no evidence the man attempted to defend himself."

"His killer slips up on him and stabs him in the chest and he does not try to stop him. How does one do that? He must have been very quick, or Aurelius was somehow distracted."

"Perhaps, but here is the difficulty. Assume you are Aurelius Decimus and I am your attacker. So, I approach you thus," Loukas stepped forward and raised his arm as if to stab downward. "How could you not see me and then, what do you do?"

"I am sure I would at least put up my hands to ward off the blow. I might try to push my attacker away and failing that...I see what you mean. I would duck, twist, fight, do something to avoid being stabbed. There is no evidence he did any of those things?"

"None. I suppose it could be argued that the killer approached unseen. If some of the torches in the hallway had not been lighted or were extinguished beforehand, but—"

"It is unlikely he did not see his killer. So, we have another puzzle. Why did an apparently healthy and ambitious man not defend himself from an obvious attempt on his life, a successful one as it turns out? You are not making this any easier for me, Loukas."

"It does introduce an element of doubt, though."

"A small one, yes, but not enough to exonerate our client. If I read the situation correctly, those visitors to the Fortress seem determined to destroy the Prefect. It will take an argument the size of Noah's ark to move them from their course."

"There were other things that struck me as odd."

"Yes?"

"There were bruises under his jaw."

"Bruises. That's it? Not much to work with there. Might he have been drunk? If he was not in position of his senses, he might not have realized his danger and then was too late when he did."

"I could not tell, Rabban. He had been dead too long to test his breath for any odor of wine, and I could find none on his clothing. Then there is the nature of the stabbing."

"In what way is that a problem?"

"Why stab a man that way? If a person approaches another and lifts his hand up with a dagger…well, as we noted, he didn't try to defend himself, but with the dagger poised thus, unless the Roman stood stock still and allowed himself to be murdered, it makes no sense at all. Even a flinch, a move to the right or left, and the dagger could not have ever achieved such surgical precision."

"An extremely important observation. Have you an answer?"

"I wish."

"What have we so far? Aurelius Decimus, for reasons we can only guess at, goes into the underbelly of the Antonia Fortress and a figure looms up brandishing a knife. Before he can react, he is stabbed once in the chest, the killer flees, and Pilate arrives and stumbles over the body. Then, amazingly, Cassia, responding to a different call from a source at which we can only guess, comes on the scene in time to find Pilate with blood on his hands and his personal dagger in the chest of Aurelius. How does that sequence of events strike you, Loukas?"

"It is as odoriferous as the smoke rising from the altar over there. You think someone planned this whole sorry affair."

"I do. Stated thus should create a reasonable amount of doubt in the mind of his accusers. Unfortunately, the plot could well have originated with them, so they will not see it. We must find something else to attack them with."

"As you say. So, what do we do now?"

"Next, we retire to your courtyard or mine, refresh ourselves, and make a list of questions needing answers."

"Such as?"

"We know what drew Pilate to that corridor, but why did Aurelius go there? Was he sent? Did he receive a message similar to the one delivered to Pilate? If so, who sent these messages? Did Priscus send the one to Pilate and then retreat in a panic when he saw the officials arrest Pilate? Was the Honorable Priscus part of the plot? If not, where was the Centurion in all this? Alternatively, is it possible that he had a private motive for disgracing Pilate and is the man who killed our noble? How did Pilate's dagger find its way into the hands of the killer? What—"

"Yes, yes, enough. I follow you. Let's do the rest of this exposition in my court. I have been watching your *Kohanim*, and an idea just occurred to me about how the stabbing might have been done."

"What? How?"

"My court, fresh wine, some shade, and relief from this billowing smoke. What does your friend the old priest call it?"

"Jakob ben Aschi calls it Holy Smoke.

Chapter XII

Three separate sets of eyes tracked Loukas' and Gamaliel's movement across the Temple Mount. They had nothing in common beyond a need to know what had transpired in the Court of the Israelites. Of the three, one could have entered the court and attempted to eavesdrop if he had wished but had resisted the temptation for fear of being observed. One started after them until one of his attendants whispered in his ear. He seemed startled and then annoyed and held back. That man wore the short toga and insignia that marked him as an important Roman personage and not an Israelite, and thus barred from the Temple. The last was clearly not a Jew and then the High Priest arrived and pivoted right and left as if seeking someone specific. He spotted Gamaliel and stepped up to confront him.

"Rabban," he said, short of breath, "we have him."

"Greetings in the Name, High Priest. You have who?'

"And with you. Yeshua ben Josef, we have him. Now it is only a matter of time. I will expect you to make yourself available when we bring him in."

"You have lost me. What are you talking about? Bring him in? Where? Why?"

"You have not been listening to me all these years. The Galilean rabbi, I have him nearly in my grasp."

"Why do you...? Of course you do. So, how do you 'have him,' as you say?"

"One of his men, Yehudah, who serves a very important function and is a member of his inner circle, has agreed to deliver him to us."

"He will betray his teacher?"

"In a manner of speaking, although I am not sure that at this moment he believes his teacher is guilty. He has offered notes detailing what the man says. He thinks we will read them and be drawn to the heretics' cause. They are damning, Gamaliel, damning. You must study them. You will see. We expect that when the time is right, he will lead us to Yeshua. We will have this blaspheming rabbi in front of the Sanhedrin before Passover unless I am mistaken."

"High Priest, with respect, I am too busy right now with a much more important affair of State to be bothered with this rabbi and charges of—"

"Blasphemy, breech of the Law, violation of Shabbat. The list goes on."

"I see. Blasphemy. You're sure about that, because the last time we spoke we disagreed on the meaning of the word when applied to this particular rabbi."

"You cannot stop me with another discourse on the Law, Rabban. You know what I mean and I am serious. This man is a threat to the Nation whether you will split hairs over some fine point or not. I will have him."

"Yes, yes, I see that you will. Also, I do not care one way or the other about the possibility that some obscure teacher from the north has crossed one of your sacerdotal lines. I will dispatch my student Saul to monitor what you do and he will keep me informed. If and when it comes to a trial, you may be assured I shall preside. Until that time, I will be otherwise occupied. Now I must be off." Gamaliel and Loukas left an annoyed High Priest and headed for the Sheep Gate and Loukas' home beyond.

But first, Gamaliel turned to the boy. "Off with you, Marius. Report what you can to your master, and tell him I will join him at the fourth hour the day after tomorrow. I will expect him to have Priscus the Centurion available and also the legionnaires under his command."

"But Excellency, he told me to stay with you until I had—"

"Something to report, yes, I know. Tell him you will do better the next time. Now go, be off."

"But tomorrow? Shouldn't you be investigating or something tomorrow?"

"Tomorrow is Shabbat. I do not work on Shabbat. Tell him—fourth hour, two days."

Across from them, the toga-garbed man asked one of his attendants to identify who had just spoken to the pair of Jews. He was told that the man speaking to the Physician and Rabban was the Hebrew's High Priest. The official smirked and shook his head in disgust. He indicated to his men that they were to return to the Fortress. Aside from the fact they were both legionnaires and strangers to the city, they could have been twins. They had the fair skin and golden hair one associates with people from places like Germania or Britannia, and the ice-blue eyes of men trained as killers. He turned and signaled to a rat-faced man standing twenty cubits away. That nondescript person drifted off in the wake of Gamaliel and Loukas. He had every reason to believe his appearance would not attract attention. It never had before. It had served as his best insurance against reprisals. He believed no one would notice him this time either. He was wrong. There were others following the Rabban's progress away from the Temple. They would join in the procession toward the city's northern gates.

The rat-faced man would not return to his employer that day, or ever. His body, stabbed in several places and dumped in the Gehinnom Valley, would be found days later, presumably someone the Sicarii deemed a הלועפ ףתשמ. But this one, like a few before him, would go unremarked. Bodies of felons, victims of felons, and riff-raff generally were routinely deposited in the valley and added to the city's accumulated trash and offal. Unless someone was interested in them enough to inquire as to their whereabouts, they would be carted off and buried in what would later come to be known as the Field of Blood.

Loukas opened the gate to his courtyard and called for his servants. Gamaliel took his accustomed seat under the shade of a fig tree and grunted.

"In the Temple you said you had an idea to share with me later. Is it later, yet?"

"Perhaps." Loukas turned to a young woman. "Sarai, fetch our guest some food. The Rabban will take his evening meal with us tonight. He will need water to wash and a place to pray after a bit." He turned his attention to his other servant. "Yakob, I believe you were a legionnaire in the past. As such I assume you were trained in the art of assassinating the Empire's enemies. I will not ask you if you ever did that, but I wish to know about technique."

"Sir?"

"Sorry, I have not made myself clear. Very well, if you were sent to dispatch someone who did not know you were present, how would you do it?'

"I do not understand. We attacked, shield and sword, lance or whatever other weapons we found at hand. A dozen years ago I served under Germanicus and once dropped one of Arminius' troopers a with a tree limb."

"You miss my point. Let us say you are alone and your target is…I don't know…this trooper who had been standing guard. Your side has an impending raid planned, and you wanted to remove him lest he cry out and the element of surprise dashed. What would you do?"

"I see. In that case, I would wait until his attention wandered. Standing guard can be boring. When the time arrived, I would approach him from behind, grab his chin, and either slit his throat or stab him in the heart."

"Which?"

"The preferred method would be to slit his throat. That would eliminate any possibility he could cry out."

"What circumstances would require you stab him instead?"

"If you don't trust your blade. Sometimes, after a battle, it may be dulled. If you have not had time to hone it on a stone first, then slitting a throat is not so easily done. If the dagger has lost its edge, it will at least have a pointed end. Then stabbing is the option."

"Show me. I am your target."

Yakob stepped behind Loukas and pretended to have a knife. He put his left hand under Loukas' chin and pulled back. At the same time he bent his knees into the back of Loukas' which caused them to buckle and Loukas to lurch backward off balance. Yakob drew his hand across the Physician's throat.

"There, you see Gamaliel. Our killer must have lain in wait for Aurelius. When his back was turned he performed this maneuver. The place was dimly lit, and there were footprints deeper in the corridor. I am guessing that the Prefect's dagger was ceremonial rather than practical and so it would not have an edge. Thus, he stabs rather than slits Aurelius' throat."

"And you came to this notion in the Temple?"

"I watched the *kohanim* sacrificing a bull. They had to stand to one side or behind the animal to get at its throat. It came to me that such an approach would explain the lack of any evidence the dead man tried to defend himself. You saw how helpless I was just now."

"Man or woman?"

"Oh, surely no woman could execute that strike. Could she, Yakob?"

The servant shook his head. Sarai arrived with a flagon of new wine and some cakes.

"I am no soldier, but I wonder…Sarai," Gamaliel said, "let us pretend your husband there is your enemy. However, he does not know that. Also, pretend you carry a dagger up your sleeve. That is, you grasp it by the hilt but twist your hand so that the blade is next to your wrist. Yes. Like that. You smile and approach him…go ahead." The woman stepped up to Yakob. "Now, you slide your left arm around his neck. Very seductive…

good. Now you bring your right hand up along his chest…is he alarmed? No he is not. He is a man and he expects something of an amorous nature from you. He is smiling back. As your right hand rises, you unfurl the dagger and then, pah! You strike down. Sorry, Yakob, you are dead. There, you see, it could have been a woman, Loukas. I believe you are correct in assuming it was a man and the attack came from behind. However, that fact will not exonerate Pilate. Hypothesizing a woman as the killer might."

"It creates some doubt?" Loukas frowned and waved his servants away. "You are mad to take this assignment. Somewhere Holy Writ says, 'the wolf will lie down with the lamb.' There is no doubt which of you is the wolf and which the lamb. We are not at that peaceful place Isaiah envisioned and wolves are not known for their sense of fair play. In the end the wolf, I fear, will devour you."

"If I am to be devoured by the wolf, then it shall be so. I am set in my course and cannot turn back. Thank you for your offer of a meal, Loukas, but I will not linger. Tomorrow is Shabbat, and I prefer to be home when it begins."

Chapter XIII

Gamaliel drained his wine cup and rose somewhat unsteadily from his bench. "Woof," he said and steadied himself with his hand on the table.

"Are you not well, Rabban?"

"I am fine, Physician. You need not practice on me just yet. I suffer only from the effects brought on by a self-centered Roman official imposing on my time and conscience, compounded by the ravages of advancing age. I do not know which is more debilitating. My impression is it is the former."

"I will have Yakob accompany you."

"Yakob? Why would you think I need company on my way home? I said old age advances, not that it had arrived."

"I was not concerned about your supposed problems with aging. I know you too well to worry about that. My concern lies elsewhere. I am certain we were followed after we left the Temple Mount. I saw a man behind us when we cleared the Sheep Gate. If you are weakened, you will be vulnerable. Yakob soldiered for the Empire. Now he can protect one of its more illustrious residents."

"Your sarcasm is wasted on me and as regards lurkers in the street, you did see one. At first there were three, all armed, if the bulges under their tunics were what I suspect they were, but shortly afterwards two dropped off at the gate with a fourth man. I have no idea who that might have been, but I do not believe he had anything to do with the other three."

"You saw all that?"

"I stopped to pluck a fig blossom, if you recall, and I looked back. Alas, it is a habit I acquired only recently—looking for people who might be following me. It is a very annoying and late addition to my here-to-for peaceable lifestyle, if you must know, and yes, I saw them, three armed men who, by the look of them, could have served with Yakob. I do not think they are after me. Not yet, anyway. I believe they are only curious as to why I spent so much time in the fort in the company of our Roman masters."

"Why would anyone care about that?"

"The murder, as we discovered, is gossiped about everywhere. Curiosity is only natural, wouldn't you say?"

"I do not think that falls under the heading of idle gossip. I insist Yakob go with you."

"Very well, if it eases your mind. It would be useful for him to know where I live in the event you need to summon me or I you. I will take my leave until I see you on Yom Rishon."

As ordered, the boy, Marius, presented himself to Pilate who did not appear to be happy. Marius had nothing to report and feared the Prefect would be angry, even have him beaten.

"Boy, what have you to tell me? What is the Rabban up to?"

"We left here after you had your talk and went outside."

"Yes? And then?"

"Well, that was pretty much all. The Hebrew and his friend talked about how stuffy it is in here, and then went into that Temple place of theirs. I was not allowed to go with them. There is a rule or something about people going inside who don't believe the way they do. What do they do there? I mean—"

"They sacrifice animals to their god and chant and, I don't know, whatever people do in Temples. That sly old fox slipped into the Temple. He is on to you, boy. That was to be expected, but I had hoped he would ignore you because of your age and obvious stupidity. No luck with that. Pity. So, anything you hear from him will be what he wants me to hear. Did he leave a message?"

"Yes, Excellency, he said he would be to see you the day after tomorrow. He had something else in mind for tomorrow."

"Something else? What else could he have to do that is more important than solving this murder?"

"He said something that sounded like shbott. I don't know what language he was speaking or what he meant."

"Shabbat, their holy day. I forgot. I will not be able to budge him for a full cycle. Curse their ridiculous god and its idiotic rules. Did he say anything else?"

"He asked me to remind you he wished to speak to the Centurion and his men."

"Very well, boy. Go and eat your evening meal and quickly. I may have need of you later."

The boy scurried off, glad to be out of the presence of the man he, along with most of the rest of the servants, feared more than death itself.

Pilate drummed his fingers on the table. It was still early in the game, but he'd hoped for something tangible from the Rabban by now—a hint, a pointer.

"Rufus, you were there. What can you add to the boy's useless report?"

Rufus hitched around in his stool and grunted. "Only this. The Tribune who accompanied Cassia and Aurelius to Jerusalem was standing nearby and also seemed to be inordinately interested in the…what did you call him?"

"The Rabban of the Sanhedrin."

"Him, yes. The Tribune had two of his legionnaires with him. What do you suppose he wanted?"

"If I were he, I would first want to know what the Prefect was up to and then where the Rabban fit in. I am sure he has more than a passing interest in this business. Anything else I should know?"

"I had the impression there were others in the plaza with eyes on your Rabban as well."

"Who?"

"I can't be sure. It was just a feeling."

"Did the Rabban see you?"

"I don't think so…no I'm certain he did not. From the Fortress he moved very quickly to his Temple and when he emerged sometime later, he engaged in a conversation with the man I was told was the High Priest, whatever that is."

"Whatever that is? Rufus, he is the link between Rome and Hebrew governance. Furthermore, make no mistake, it is an exceedingly delicate link. If this Tribune, who came here uninvited and who is interested in my plight is, in fact, lusting after my office, as I must now assume, he had better learn a lesson or those letters you carry in your baggage which are directed at my performance will look like poems by Ovid or Horace, or one of our other idle aristocrats by comparison."

"I love Publius Ovidius."

"You can afford to."

Pilate stood and paced. He did so when the course of events he followed did not move as he wished them to.

"I have no time for the effete ramblings of the Empire's elite. My life has been spent serving the Emperor. My thanks for ridding the Middle Sea of pirates and putting down one insurrection after another is assigning me to this position in a country that sits like a boil on the Empire's backside. Perhaps I would have been better advised to take up poetry than soldiering, Rufus. Then I wouldn't have to explain myself to critics sitting in comfort thousands of miles away and happily ignorant of the customs, the challenges, and the innate frustrations that come with overseeing our conquered people in general and these Israelites in particular."

"But it is an honorable office, Pilate. You know it is. Why else would anyone covet it?"

"Point taken. Probably they do not yet realize it is a career ender. How could they know? It has an exalted title and produces decent revenue. Ambitious men are always on the hunt for those two commodities. It is only when you fulfill your fondest dream that you realize there is a reverse alchemy at work that often turns the gold for which you lusted into lead. The Tribune can have it if he wants it. Why can't I be lolling in the sun on Capri with the Emperor and his whores instead of sweating like an over-worked horse in this godforsaken sand dune?"

"You are bitter."

"You noticed. Never mind, ours is to serve, not to question. Since the Rabban will be absent for a whole day, we must do some investigating on our own. The Rabban wished to speak to Priscus. We can do that and his legionnaires as well. It might save time."

"What shall we ask them?"

"Ask them? Various questions, I suppose. What would you suggest?"

"I have no idea."

"Gamaliel would not be at a loss. What would he want to know? What do I want to know?"

"I am going to dine, Pilate. We can continue this tomorrow."

"Why did Priscus not show up at the meeting? That is what I would like to know. If he'd been there…or might he have been the one who wielded the dagger? Now that is a line I believe the Rabban should explore."

SHABBAT

Chapter XIV

Gamaliel's manservant, valet, and general do-all, Binyamin, had left him an ample supply of cold food for Shabbat and had taken off to honor the day in his own way. Gamaliel spent the morning in prayer and contemplation of the Psalms of Lament. They matched his mood as he thought of the consequences that could ensue from his involvement with the Prefect.

> *Ha Shem, please deliver me. O Lord, hurry to my side!*
> *Put to shame and confusion those who would seek my life.*
> *Let them be turned back and dishonored who wish to hurt me.*
> *Let those who murmur, 'Aha, Aha!' turn back from their*
> *   shame....*

Would his countrymen turn on him? He shuddered at the thought and tried to push it from his mind. Shabbat required that he not think about worldly things but concentrate on the Lord, on his blessings. It was one thing to be engaged in a project at the specific order of the authorities or to enlist their aid in resolving a problem that involved the good of the Nation. He had done that before, not always willingly, but with the understanding that the benefit was general and therefore justifiable, but try as he might, his mind refused to let go of the onerous task he'd agreed to take on. He had allowed himself to become the Prefect's reluctant ally and champion...or was it the Prefect's game piece? That was a thought for another day. Was he involved only in a complicated game played by Roman notables and one in which game pieces were brought into play and disposed of as circumstances dictated following some complex and undecipherable strategy—undecipherable to the pieces, anyway. He exhaled. Neither status sat well with him or with anyone else, except the Prefect. Whether he succeeded or failed, he would be the object of the Nation's scorn or Rome's retribution, possibly both.

> *Do not turn your servant away in anger, you who have*
>   *helped me.*
> *Do not cast me away, nor forsake me,*
> *Lord, you are my salvation! Even if my father or mother*
>   *forsake me,*
> *you will bear me up.*

It was no use. The psalms of David did not help. He pushed the sheets away and left his house. He would walk to the Temple and contemplate the glory of the Lord in His Holy place. A stroll like this had served him in the past and it would again. As he stepped over his door sill, he spied the boy, Marius. Unfortunately, the boy also saw him and before he could retreat into his house, the boy scampered up to him,

"Excellent, sir," he said, "my maser asks if you would meet him for a moment only."

"I cannot."

"He said that if you left your house, you would be walking about and what harm would come to your Holy Day if you were to meet him somewhere? He wishes to ask you a question."

"Marius, we are not having this conversation. It is Shabbat and I cannot meet, discuss, or in any way engage in the Prefect's problem. I have said too much already."

With that, Gamaliel turned on his heel, reentered his house, and slammed its door in the boy's face. He tried, but failed, to suppress his annoyance at the boy and Pilate. Even to yield to that would violate his strict observance of Shabbat. He took a deep breath and ate an early midday meal. He spent the remainder of his day parsing an Isaiah scroll sent to him from the community in Qumran. Their leader wanted a fresh pair of eyes on it. Copyists, he'd declared, sometimes left out parts of or attempted to improve on the text. Gamaliel had to admit that studying the scroll for errors bordered on work, but as it was for *El Shaddai*, he thought he could be forgiven if he spent the afternoon looking for a stray *neqqudot* or a missing word, either of which could change the meaning of a sentence or a whole passage. Surely, that would be deemed a worthy Shabbat enterprise by the Lord.

Pilate did not expect Gamaliel to interrupt his Shabbat. He had dealt with that particular bit of Jewish stubbornness before. He had hoped he might persuade him otherwise. He was now at loose ends. His Centurion, Priscus, had been intercepted by his accusers and had been closeted with Cassia and the ominous Tribune all morning. He did not like what that implied. Were they in the process of suborning his captain? When the boy returned without Gamaliel, he yelled at him but spared him the beating he'd promised if the boy failed in his assignment. Properly chastised and fearful, he'd sent the youngster back into the streets to watch for anything that might be useful.

"Look especially for the agents of the men who oppose me. Do you know who they are?"

The boy said he did. Considering the Prefect's obsession with the visitors to the exclusion of all others, he wondered if the Prefect did in fact know who his enemies were. Either way, he did not want to invite another session of invective being screamed at him. In truth, Marius had only a dim and confused idea of who Pilate thought they might be. He knew the man, Rufus, was probably on the Prefect's side and had been told that the men who were in the Fortress when the other two arrived were not. The moves and counter moves men made as they went about their daily routine were a mystery to him. He, on the other hand, had more serious worries. He guessed he should try to understand Pilate if he ever wanted to survive this low position on the social ladder and get the chance to return to his home rich and famous or, if not that, alive The latter, unfortunately, was not solely in the hands of the Prefect. There were the others. He shuddered at the thought. He knew now that he'd made a serious mistake in agreeing to their terms and feared he would never be able to correct it. He tried to concentrate on the actors in this odd drama playing out in the Fortress, those who had approached him initially and all of these new ones. He dismissed the Prefect's wife from his list. She could not be a party to any of it although the rumor about her being a mad woman did pose a question or two. And anyway, aristocratic women like her were not capable of stabbing a man. Everyone knew that. Once outdoors and in the spring sunlight, breathing became easier. The Prefect remained confined within the Fortress and could not track him here. Marius had not had his midday meal and he went in search of a place where there might be refreshment. He did so without success and it was at that point the extremes Shabbat entailed were made apparent to him.

Gamaliel's head began to ache. Evening had come and with it the end of Shabbat. Yet he still stared at the scroll in front of him in the flickering yellow lamp light. Binyamin had brought him a bowl of stew, but he had not touched it, so absorbed had he been in the words of the prophet. He rubbed his eyes and let the ends of the papyrus scroll roll together, but the words he'd read remained etched in his mind. Isaiah, prophesying about the fate of nations: Moab, Egypt, Babylon—did the prophet mean the Rome of the future, not Nebuchadnezzar's royal domain from the past? He hoped so. But what did these few lines mean. Peace for the Nation, his contemporaries all agreed. Hope for peace also meant the departure of the Roman presence, surely. Did it? Was it remotely possible that the *pax Romana* was what Isaiah meant? Never. *Ha Shem* would not allow it, would he? It was all too much, Rome, Israel, all the nations under the rule of Rome. Did they all, like him, wish to shed the Roman yoke? If not the *pax Romana,* then what? Will there ever be this kind of peace in the land and if so, when? Now? Soon? Ever? Or should he seek another, a deeper meaning? He pushed the two ends apart and read the words again.

> *...A shoot will rise from the stump of Jesse; from his roots a branch will bear fruit. The Spirit of the LORD will rest on him—the Spirit of wisdom and of understanding, the Spirit of counsel and of might, the Spirit of the knowledge and fear of the LORD—and he will delight in the fear of the LORD.*

That would be David. Jesse was his father, so...

> *He will not judge by what he sees with his eyes, or decide by what he hears with his ears; but with righteousness he will judge the needy; with justice he will give decisions for the poor of the earth. He will strike the earth with the rod of his mouth; with the breath of his lips he will slay the wicked. Righteousness will be his belt and faithfulness the sash around his waist.*

Solomon? David's son by Bathsheba, he could be a shoot from Jesse as well, once removed, and an arbiter of great skill.

> *The wolf also shall dwell with the lamb, and the leopard shall lie down with the kid; and the calf and the young lion and the fatling together; and a little child shall lead them. The cow will feed with the bear, their young will lie down together, and the lion will eat straw like the ox.*

This was hopeless. David, Solomon, world peace? Understanding prophesies was like fishing with a torn net. Just when you think you have caught something, the prize slips away through a hole. More importantly, did any of this bit of Holy Writ harmonize in any way whatsoever with his involvement with Pilate? *He will not judge by what he sees with his eyes, or decide by what he hears with his ears...* Good advice, that. I will do as Isaiah suggests, judge with righteousness and not be concerned with anything or anyone else. He would leave the remainder of Isaiah's prophesy for another day.

Gamaliel blew out the lamp and took himself to bed.

YOM RISHON

Chapter XV

Dawn. Yehudah, known as Iscariot, a surname he'd acquired, but not inherited, had not slept. He frequently had difficulty sleeping. Too many things pressed in on him, still unresolved issues from the past, but last night had been different. Yeshua's mad actions the previous day preyed on his mind. What had he been thinking? He ground his teeth. We were so close and then this nonsense with the ass and the parade down the hill. Why? Everyone knew that the city would be teeming with Roman legionnaires and collaborators. The last thing we needed to do was to attract attention. Yes, we should go to the city for Passover. It would be expected. Yes, teach on the Temple Mount. It would be expected, annoy the Temple party. It, too, would be expected. There was no danger in doing the expected, the predictable, or the acceptable if only marginally so. But Yeshua… with him there seemed no limit to what he would do to make trouble for himself—for all of them.

He'd been instructed to secure an ass, and he'd done it. He hadn't asked why. He doubted Yeshua would have told him if he had. Yeshua acted on some inexplicable instinct half of the time, anyway. It's possible even he didn't know why he wanted the beast. Not right away. So, he'd done as he'd been asked and with the others, gathered on the Mount of Olives. Yeshua sent two, Simon and Andrew, to fetch the animal. When the poor beast had been dragged over to them, he mounted and started down the hillside. He looked ridiculous, knees drawn up to his hips to keep his feet from dragging on the ground. The animal was too small and obviously not used to bearing the weight of a full-grown man, and it lurched and huffed down the slope. The rest of us formed a ragged procession. Yeshua seemed unconcerned at the spectacle we made. He'd made an entrance.

Madness.

Pagan gods make entrances, kings and conquerors make entrances. Important personages make entrances. Earlier, Pilate had made his own entrance into the city. But he rode a tall horse and wore his dress armor. He was accompanied by his entourage of soldiers and hangers on. The crowd lining the street had cheered. Most were coerced or purchased, but cheers they were nonetheless. It was the show people expected. And what do we do? Days later, on the Mount of Olives, here comes this great tall man riding down the hillside on an ass's colt. Did he intend to mock Roman authority? What was Yeshua playing at? It was a farce. Worse, the people on the hill joined in this piece of bad theater and began to chant. "Hosanna…" At least those who were not laughing did. They'd cheered and laid palm fronds and scraps of clothing in his path—a perfect parody of the triumphant entry Pilate had made. Nothing good could possibly come from this.

Later, Tomas told him that Yeshua's ride down the hill fulfilled prophesy. What prophesy, he'd asked. That the Messiah would be riding on a white colt and enter the city in triumph through the Golden Gate at his coming. Well, they had entered the city through that gate, alright, and had provided entertainment to many who witnessed it. But triumphal? Foolish, yes, dangerous probably. Now there could be no doubt, this journey they'd begun at the Jordan, years before, had wandered off the path. Where had it gone wrong? He'd believed, had wanted to believe, indeed had committed his very soul to it. And now this. Perhaps those officials from the Temple had been right. Perhaps it was time to move away from this man before too many lives were compromised, too many dreams dashed.

Yehudah sat with his back against the still cool stone wall. The others still slept within. He watched as the sun lighted the wall opposite. He remained there until he heard stirring within. His decision made, he stood and walked away.

It had been exactly one week since Marius had accosted him at his door step and taken him to see Pilate. Once again the youth waited at Gamaliel's door. He had not knocked. If he had, Binyamin had instructions to put him off until the fourth hour and in any case not to admit him. Gamaliel would not be denied his morning meal and prayers and, furthermore, there was something about the boy that disturbed him. He could not put his finger on it, but there was something not quite right about Marius. He consigned that thought to the depths of his mind where it would work its way through its myriad corridors and rooms in search of significance.

He signaled Marius to proceed and the two set off to meet Loukas at the entrance to the Fortress. Their conversation consisted of Marius' description of his early life and how he'd ended as a slave-servant in the Prefect's household

"Loukas, did you know this boy says he comes from far off and is the Prefect's slave/servant quite by chance. He says he comes to us from Gaul and elsewhere. What do you make of that? This is his first visit to David's City."

"Truly? From Gaul, you say, Marius? I had no idea."

They entered the building using the nearly invisible door that lead into the depths of the fort. Gamaliel made a point of checking their progress into the building. The last time they'd been there he'd memorized the route out of the building. Today he reversed his memories and was pleased that he correctly anticipated each turn to the cell occupied by the Prefect.

"Greetings, Excellency," he said and again drew up a stool uninvited. The Prefect's brows rose at his presumption, but Gamaliel did not care. He had not sought this task, had not wanted it, and felt put upon for having been coerced into taking it. He would bestow only the respect due the Prefect's position, or former position, and that as little as possible.

"I had no idea this place was so vast. It is like a small city. So, to business. Is the Centurion, Priscus, available, and also the legionnaires under his command?"

"Rabban. Sit down, please." The Prefect tried a bit of sarcasm but it was a poor effort. "Priscus is no longer with us. He has been transferred to the barracks in Tyre. He left an hour ago. I tried to dissuade him, but he had his orders. It doesn't matter, anyway."

"Doesn't matter? How so? I needed to determine the nature of his message to you."

"He spent most of yesterday in conference with my accusers. They must have turned him. Rufus asked him that question as you might have, and I am afraid he has betrayed me."

"Really? What questions did your friend ask, and how did his answers signal a betrayal?"

"Well, in the first place, Rufus asked who had he entrusted the message to and he said, 'What message?' You see? He denied ever sending a message. He has made me out as a liar and a fool. I maintain I went to the hallway at his request and now he says he never…he has compromised my defense."

Gamaliel helped himself to a cup of the Prefect's wine and offered a second to Loukas, who declined.

"Loukas, what do you make of all this?"

"The Prefect has a problem, it would appear."

"Yes, but what sort of problem? After all he has had one large problem all along. How does this news change things?"

"If the Prefect—" Loukas began.

"I am right here and can hear you, Physician," Pilate grumbled. "You needn't speak as if I were not."

"My apologies, Excellency. Very well, if your entire defense hinges on the Centurion's testimony that it was he that lured you to the crime scene, then you have lost a key piece of evidence, but I am guessing the Rabban has a different take."

"Different? How?"

Gamaliel cleared his throat and sipped at his cup. "Suppose the Centurion spoke the truth? Suppose he was sent away not because they wanted him to make you out a liar but because your accusers couldn't shake his story?"

"What? He spoke the truth? But I did receive a message from him."

"Did you? All you know is that you were told by the bearer of the message that it came from Priscus. Suppose it did not. Suppose someone else sent it in his name."

"Someone else? But that is absurd. He sent it. Why would you think he didn't?"

"Several reasons, the most important of which is, he said he didn't. Also, he was not in the hall when you arrived. You may have arrived early or late, as you said, but surely he would have arrived with or shortly after Cassia. He didn't. So why not?"

"I don't know. Why?"

"Because he never sent the message in the first place. Therefore, he had no reason to be there."

Pilate scratched his head and frowned. He shot a quizzical look at Gamaliel.

"Did anyone else see you receive this message, possibly hear how it was delivered?"

"I am at a loss, Rabban. What are you getting at?"

"Stay with me. I ask again, do you know if anyone else witnessed the message being delivered to you? If so, did he overhear any or all of it, particularly what the person said when he identified himself to you?"

"Identified? What do you mean? It was a legionnaire. I already told you that. What more is there to know?"

"Prefect! Please listen to me and try to concentrate. If a legionnaire approaches you and wishes to address you, he doesn't simply start talking, does he? He presents himself. He says something like…'Sir, I am so-and-so from such-and-such unit. I have a message from Priscus the Centurion for you.' Am I correct in this?"

"Yes, that is approximately what he might say. And?"

"And? What did this one say to you? Who did he say he was?"

"I can't recall."

"Yes, so I ask you once again, was there anyone there, beside yourself, who might have heard and who would remember?"

"Oh, I see. Let me think. Well, the hallway was crowded with people. If they had wanted to, any one of them might have heard it as well. Yes, and my good wife stood no more than two cubits from me when the soldier approached. Understand, Rabban, they are all alike in my eyes and since they are all assigned to me here or in Caesarea Maritima, I rarely pay attention to how a soldier appears before he delivers news."

"So you said. May I question your wife? You see the importance of this. If we can find the messenger, we can find out who sent the message. If we find out who sent the message, we will have our killer."

"You wish to query my wife?"

"I do."

"But her testimony, should she be called on to give it, would be discounted."

"Because she is a woman?"

"Because she is my wife. It will be assumed she would lie for me, so who will believe her?"

"We are not in court, and I am not asking for exculpatory evidence. I simply want to know what she heard. If she remembers who delivered the message and any details, we will be able to move closer to a solution."

"I have no objection, but there may be problems from the current authorities. She is under close surveillance. If she wanders in here and they discover you are interrogating her...well, there could be problems."

Gamaliel sighed and looked at Loukas who frowned and then nodded.

"Do you suppose she might be in the need of a Physician? The stress of her situation must have taken a toll on her humors." Gamaliel studied Pilate's face for a hint of comprehension.

"She is as healthy as a yearling calf. I don't see a need...oh, I see. You want your man to attend to her and he will ask the questions. Yes, that would work. It would be best if Rufus led the way. It would add a bit of credibility to the enterprise, don't you think?"

"Indeed. Off you go, Loukas. Don't forget your nostrums and powders."

The two men left, Rufus still digesting what he'd heard and what was now expected of him.

Chapter XVI

Gamaliel watched the Roman and his friend leave. When the door closed behind them he turned to Pilate.

"How long has Marius been a part of your household, Prefect?"

"The boy? I don't know. Marius, when did you come to us?"

"When?"

"Yes, when, boy. Speak up."

"Ah…It has been a little over three moons, Excellency, to the Fortress staff."

"Moons? Quaint. The Fortress has what seems an endless supply of these people, Rabban. They come and they go. Some are freed, some sold or transferred, some run away, few actually succeed at that. He is useful, if not very bright."

Marius stirred uneasily. Whether at the insult or because he'd become the object of attention Gamaliel could not be sure. Gamaliel smiled at him.

"There is nothing wrong with your Greek, is there Marius? Your Latin is as poor as mine, if I read your body language correctly, but the Greek is more than passable. Have you any other languages at you tongues tip?"

"Excellency…I mean, sir?"

"I am asking you if you speak anything else other than Greek."

"Latin."

"Sorry, we have already established that Latin is most definitely not one of them. Hebrew, perhaps?"

Marius blinked and looked away. "No, sir, I come from the other side of the world. Hebrew is not spoken anywhere but here, so I can't know it."

Gamaliel turned back to Pilate. "Perhaps we will have something to work with when Loukas returns. In the meantime, Prefect, try to remember anything that may have happened the day of the murder that, in retrospect, now strikes you as odd."

"I have already told you everything I know."

"Yes, so you say, but I find that when one is pressed to review an event or an important day, repetition of its particulars will often produce a small memory which at first might have been overlooked or deemed insignificant, but later acquires substance. So, I ask you again. Was there anything odd that day?"

"What do you mean by odd?"

Gamaliel gritted his teeth. For a man of unquestioned intelligence and perception, Pilate seemed annoyingly dense. "I do not mean weird or disjointed or completely out of the norm, Prefect. I mean something unexpected or out of place but not remarkable in itself."

"I still do not follow you. My days are routine. Except for ordering the banquet, I followed my daily rota—meetings with your people, listening to endless complaints, adjudicating minor disputes, ordering the crucifixion of a notorious bandit—"

"Barabbas."

"Yes, how did you know? Never mind. The Fortress has no secrets as long as we hire servants from among your people."

"You do. How many on average?"

"I couldn't say. You will have to speak to my steward about that. It is temporary work, you understand. While I am in the city, they work and draw wages. When I leave, it's back to the fields or shops for them."

"Or the street."

"If you say so. Is my hiring servants from among the locals important?"

"As I implied earlier, everything is important until it is not."

"I see. So, back to your question, anything odd, out of the ordinary, dislocated, or just not quite right, but seemingly unimportant at the time?"

"Yes."

"Let me think." Pilate cudgeled his forehead as if in deep thought. "No, can't think of a thing. Procula had something, but it was no concern of mine."

"Other than the vision, your wife spoke to you about a peculiarity?"

"Rabban, it was nothing, a trifle. You know how women are—scattered and unreliable and…well, you know."

"I do not know. Please tell me what the event or incident was, no matter how trivial it may seem to you now."

Pilate exhaled and rolled his eyes. "Very well, she said she thought she saw a woman in our rooms that she did not recognize as one of our servants."

"A stranger in your rooms and you thought that unimportant?"

"Operative word, woman, Rabban, a woman in the rooms. A cleaner, perhaps, or one of the temporary servants about which we just now spoke."

"But unexpected in that place at that time?"

"I guess you could say that. Anyway, she said later that after she turned it over in her mind, the face did seem familiar after all. You know her history. She sees things that are not there."

"But I have heard with great accuracy as often as not. So, she thought there was a woman she believed to be a stranger, but later, on reflection, she changed her mind. Why would she change her mind?"

"People do, Rabban. Maybe not your god, but mortals do and often. Remember, she is a woman, for all that. She had time to think about it and realized she did recognize the stranger after all and that's an end to it."

"I see. Anything else?"

"Nothing."

"When would this woman have been in the rooms un-announced?"

"I didn't say anything about her not being announced."

"But you did. Your good wife at first did not recognize her. Therefore, she noticed her. Had she been expected, no notice would have been taken. But she must have seemed out of place at the time. If she or anyone else belonged there, she would not have been, don't you see?"

"I'm afraid I don't."

"Well, think about it. Would your wife recognize this woman again if she saw her again?"

"I suppose she might. Gamaliel, what are you getting at? One woman more or less among so many women servants cannot be important."

"Maybe yes, maybe no. We shall see. I will have to have Loukas question her a second time at this rate."

"Bah. It seems to me you should be digging into the movements of my unexpected and unwelcome guests from Rome. You will find your killer there."

"It is one possibility. The problem is how do I approach their exalted personages? You know they will not stoop to being interviewed by me. Your friend, Rufus, might try, but will they respond to him? And, pardon me if I seem less than impressed, but I do not think your Roman friend could extract juice from a grape, much less the truth from your guests."

"Be careful, Rabban. You may have me in a tight spot at the moment, but I fully expect to be extricated from it, and then you and I will resume our respective positions."

"With respect, Prefect, you cannot be that slow. Haven't you just handed me a very good reason to fail at this task? Is it wise to threaten the very person who might be able to rid you of this curse?"

"Rabban, it is yourself who misses the point. Win or lose, I am still in a position to do you great harm. You have agreed to help me, but it does not alter our relationship, only tempers it. How long depends as much on your willingness to maintain it in a correct manner as it bears on me. You do see, don't you?"

Gamaliel did. Whatever temporary advantage he possessed at the moment would be swept away whether he succeeded in clearing Pilate or not. Either an angry Prefect would destroy him for failing, or the other Romans, equally angry at his success, would do the job. Life, he decided, under the thumb of these implacably brutal and coldly pragmatic people could have no good ending for him. He yearned for the bright hopefulness of Isaiah where the wolf and the lamb were at peace. Aesop, the fabulist, had a story about a wolf and a lamb. He couldn't remember the details except he was pretty sure that it didn't end well for the lamb.

Chapter XVII

Gamaliel sat back and focused on Pilate. Could he really be this stupid or was he playing a different game than the one he'd set up for Gamaliel—murder and redemption? Pilate had imbibed a considerable quantity of wine lately and that might explain his lack of perception, but he should at least have grasped enough to realize he needed to answer questions in a coherent manner.

Pilate raised his eyebrows and returned Gamaliel's stare. "What?"

"Forgive me, but I am curious about something, Prefect. You did not rise to the eminence of Prefect by being obtuse, yet as I consider your responses to my questions, you seem remarkably so."

"You say I am being obtuse?"

"In a word, yes. What is it about asking you to repeat the narrative, to fill in details, to forage about in your mind for answers or memories that has caused you to seem so slow of wit?"

"I remind you, Rabban, watch your tongue. My refusing to play your game of remembrance is what you call 'being obtuse?' It is you, Rabban who is obtuse."

"I?"

"Why do you waste my time with these simpleminded questions about daggers and legionnaires? I understand you have your methods, but this one seems unnecessarily dense."

"I, dense? Prefect, it is not I but you who—"

"Nonsense. You are squandering precious time on trivia. Who cares about the identity of a legionnaire or who works or does not work in the Fortress, or the status of the boy? The questions you should be asking are ones about the real perpetrators of this travesty."

"The real perpetrators…and who, might they be? I mean, if you know who committed this murder, please tell me now and we will be done here. I will go home and you can return to your duties."

"My visitors, my guests, the men who came to remove me from office, who else? Cassia Drusus and the Tribune Grex. They must be the co-conspirators of this whole sorry business. I have said so from the beginning and you agreed. They are the only logical answer to the question of who are the instigators, surely. Anyone not deep in the arms of Morpheus can see that."

Gamaliel slumped in his chair and studied his feet. This was impossible. He would never unravel this knot if the Prefect insisted on only one solution, the impossible solution. Why had he allowed himself to be talked into this fool's errand? Why hadn't he listened to Loukas? He sat up and fixed Pilate with as fierce a stare as he could manage.

"Prefect, if my method, as you call it, is insufficient, I will happily withdraw. Shall I? Clearly, I have nothing to gain and everything to lose here. Before you answer, consider the following. As much as it will pain you to do so, you must accept the fact that it is possible you are wrong about your fellow Romans and their intentions."

"Ah, that is where you are being obtuse, Rabban. Consider the following. Priscus sends me a message but denies it, thus betraying me to them. As a reward for his perfidy, for incriminating me, and also to keep him from unbiased examination, they send him away, thus removing important information needed to prove my innocence. Further, who gains from this crime? They do, you see? Or consider this, Priscus is the one who kills Aurelius and puts me in the position of accused."

"Priscus says he did not send the message. They believe him. Thus, in their eyes at least, you must be the liar and that is the incriminating bit."

"He denies it now, but—"

"Pilate, he says he did not send the message. I believe he did not send the message. Why would he lie? I have doubts about your adversaries being responsible for your plight, much as you might wish it."

"And the possibility Priscus engineered the murder?"

"It is one possibility, however a remote one. As to the others, no, probably not."

"But they are such obvious suspects. I do not understand how you cannot see it."

"Pilate, you have convinced yourself that this business can only play out a certain way. You dull your wits at my questioning because you think I cannot grasp that important point, correct?"

Pilate opened his mouth and was about to speak, but Gamaliel held up his hand. "Listen to me. Take a step back and consider. Put yourself in their boots. If you were to hatch such a plot would you do any of the following? Would you ask a Centurion known to be loyal to the Prefect to send a message that could lead to a murder for which he would later be accused? No, you would not. Would you use a legionnaire about whom you know nothing whatsoever to deliver such a message? Wouldn't it be wiser to use one of your own legionnaires? Finally, would you, either as one of your visitors or as your Centurion, hatch such an elaborate a plot? It has so many parts that could easily go amiss? Think for a moment. I am not privy to the inner workings of the Roman mind or the plots and plans you people hatch to acquire power and position, but what little I know leads me to believe that if these men wished you ill, they would have taken a much more direct, dare I say pragmatic, approach to do you in? A quick thrust of the short sword and a culprit to be identified later would be far more efficient and characteristic, don't you think? Or, better, lay trumped-up charges of treason at your feet and then clap you in irons. The word bruited about the Empire is that your Emperor needs only an accusation to produce a death sentence. So, why all this sneaking around in darkened corridors, dispatching secret messages, and ornate daggers? None of this makes any sense at all if ascribed to any of those men."

"But if not them…?"

"If not them, then who? I understand. Another point, if they are, in fact, the authors of this porridge of a plot, would I be able to question them, dig out the proof, and convict? I would not. They will not deign to be questioned by me. Since that avenue is closed to me and since it is an unlikely pathway in any event, it is my intention to chase down the threads of this mystery in the only direction left open to me, and that means I need you to concentrate on your answers even if you think they are not the ones you would prefer to give."

"They had nothing to do with this?"

"I don't know, but for the reasons I just stated, I don't think so. I admit I could be wrong, but either way—"

"You are stuck with what you have available." Pilate relaxed and shook his head. "Tell me this, then, if it turns out you are wrong and the guilt does lie with these men after all, will this line of investigation you are following eventually lead to them?"

"Oh yes, certainly. But I cannot guarantee I will be able to do anything about it. Bringing them to justice will require more than a non-citizen and a Jew at that. Perhaps Rufus…?"

"Rufus? Ah, Rufus, I see. Perhaps."

Chapter XVIII

Gamaliel stood to take his leave of Pilate. The room had become oppressive and he sensed his mental and physical state required fresh air and distance between the Roman and himself. His collar rubbed his neck and aggravated his already chafed skin. The Prefect started to object but Gamaliel waved him away.

"Enough, Prefect. I cannot go on just now. When Loukas returns, tell him to meet me on the Temple Mount. Tell him I will be with Jakob ben Aschi. He will know the place."

"I insist you stay."

"Sorry, your insistence carries the weight of a beetle's wing at the moment. As you say, win or lose, I lose."

"I never said—"

"I will call on you again tomorrow at the latest, perhaps later today."

The thought occurred to Gamaliel as he listened to the arrogant Roman official threaten him that the only thing that could save him from impending disaster would be for the Prefect to commit suicide. As that seemed unlikely, Gamaliel needed to escape. He wanted time to think, to contemplate his dwindling options, or at the very least to be alone for a while. He went to the Temple.

The *kohanim* had reserved an area adjacent to the Temple where they would congregate before they assumed their duties and where they could refresh themselves, put on or shed the blood stained leather aprons worn if they'd been assigned duties at the altar, or just to relax for a moment. There would be water available and company. Gamaliel had no need of either, but he also knew that none of the Romans assigned to monitor him would follow him into the area because of the certainty they would stand out like a tree in the desert. Blending in with the priests of the Temple would be difficult for an Israelite, impossible for even the cleverest of his nemeses. Gamaliel knew he would have privacy with the *kohanim*. He found a stool, greeted the few priests he knew, acknowledged those he did not, and waited. Loukas joined him an hour later.

"You bolted, the Prefect said. He is not happy with you."

"His happiness or lack thereof is not a condition foremost in my mind at the moment and anyway the unhappiness is mutual."

"If not his happiness, what is foremost in your mind?"

"It has been made very clear to me that win or lose, I cannot survive this exercise. If I succeed in exonerating the Prefect, I will bring down the wrath of those who oppose him, both Israelite and Roman. If I fail, Pilate's last act as Prefect will be to destroy me."

"But you knew that going in."

"Not quite. I knew only that failure might have consequences depending on the fate of Pilate and success would earn me the enmity of my fellow Hebrews. Now it seems either outcome will be the death of me."

"What do you plan to do, now that you comprehend the reality I tried to warn you about days ago?"

"There is nothing I can do beyond trusting *Ha Shem* and doing what is right. I must confess suicide occurred to me."

"You can't be serious. You would take your own life?"

"Not me, him. If Pilate would conveniently fall on his sword, everyone's problems would be solved—his, the Nation's, his enemies, and most certainly mine."

"Operative word, 'conveniently.' It won't happen, as you know. Now, would you like me to tell you what the wife of your wished-for suicide had to say?"

Gamaliel gave a vague wave of his hand and nodded.

"She did remember the exchange between her husband and the legionnaire. She seemed certain he was one of those permanently garrisoned in the Fortress. She said she thought that because they were all shabby in dress and decorum as opposed to those assigned to Caesarea Maritima who are much smarter in appearance and clearly more disciplined. But then when they, in turn, were compared to the soldiers accompanying the delegation from Rome, they came off as beggars. The soldiers with the visiting delegation, she declared, looked like they could be the offspring produced from an erotic encounter by one of their gods with women—beautiful Roman women, to be precise. I saw one or two of them and she's correct. They are eerily handsome in a Greek god sort of way. You could cover them with white powder and pass them off as statues in a pantheon."

"Fascinating. So, the messenger came from within the fort. That is useful, but at the moment, gives us nothing."

"It is another piece surely. Anyway, returning to your dilemma, have you considered leaving the city for a while—hiding out in the wilderness or seeking asylum at someplace like Qumran?"

"I am too old to survive the wilderness, and although I get along with the men at Qumran, I do so only from a distance. One afternoon's disputation with those people and I could add them to the 'men who would gladly see me dead list.'"

"You need to spend time developing skills at getting along with others."

"Yes, well, some other day. For now, we concentrate on the matter at hand. I need you to ask her another question. Pilate reported that his wife may have seen a strange woman in their quarters the day of the murder. He dismissed it and she recanted subsequently, but I would like her to tell her side of the story. I do not think the Prefect takes her seriously in matters he considers mundane."

"Querying her further will be a problem."

"How so?"

"The room where I 'examined' her was not empty. She kept glancing at one woman in particular. Rufus told me afterward that the woman in question was part of the visitor's entourage and had been sent to spy on her. I had difficulty getting the few bits and pieces of information that I did."

"She does not wish to be interviewed again?"

"I wouldn't say that. She wants to help her husband, but does not want the interview to occur where she might be overheard. She thinks…she is sure that there are watchers and listeners assigned to her."

"If I were the visitors sent to spy on Pilate, I would not leave her out of the equation either, whether he is involved in a murder or not. She is an important personage, irrespective of her husband's current status, and she will not be allowed to venture out unchaperoned."

"Perhaps she will want to visit one of their temples, one reserved for women."

"Fine, but then how will you approach her, or will I?"

"Neither. We will recruit a woman to ask the questions of her in our stead."

"A woman? Who? I do not know many women whom I could entrust with such a mission—or any other to be truthful."

"What about Sarai."

"Who?"

"My servant, Yakob's wife. Sarai is not stupid and she is one of us, so to speak. More importantly, while she is faithful and moderately orthodox…don't look at me that way…she would be willing to enter a pagan Temple if you would provide an excuse, a dispensation."

"It is a thought, Loukas. First we must get a message to the Prefect's wife. That may not be so easy, and then she may not wish to be questioned again under any circumstances. She struck me as a skittish person."

"We can try."

"Yes. I am tired, my friend. I wish to go home and contemplate all the sins I must have committed that landed me in this morass. You talk to Sarai and see if she is willing to serve as our agent. We will meet again at the seventh hour and tackle the Prefect once more."

"And importune the wife?"

"Yes, that too. By the way, do you notice anything unusual about the boy, Marius?"

"Unusual? Only that he is rather tall to be still unbearded, but he may come from one of those places that breed giants. I doubt it was Gaul, though."

"No, not Gaul. The accent is all wrong. You think him a budding *Nephilim*? Precocious or retarded, it is hard to tell which, but no, I do not believe he possesses a gigantic future. Very well, until later, may *Ha Shem* be with you, Loukas."

"And with you, also."

Chapter XIX

Gamaliel met Loukas on the Mount several hours later. His immediate return to the Prefect's murky lair was momentarily diverted by an irate and very red in the face Caiaphas, who bore down on him like a trireme whose drummer beat an attack cadence.

"Rabban, it is too much. Now you must act. This time he has done us in."

"Who has done what to whom, High Priest? You did say us?"

"The Rabbi Yeshua ben Josef. We are in very deep trouble."

"I dispute the 'we' and what exactly has he done now that has you so exercised, High Priest?"

"What? He has made a mockery of the Prefect's very person, that's what."

Gamaliel closed his eyes and prayed for patience. "How is that a problem? And who hasn't mocked the Prefect or at least thought to? I say good for him. The Prefect is and will always be the object of scorn, mockery, and derision as long as he and his band of bullies remain in our country. So what exactly has Yeshua ben Josef done that you believe will result in the downfall of the Nation?"

Using all the detail he had been told, Caiaphas took a deep breath and described how Yeshua had summoned his followers and directed them to fetch a donkey tethered to a ring in the wall a few paces from the path leading down from the Mount of Olives, how the spectators had cheered him along as he descended the path toward the Temple and through the Golden Gate.

"And all this concerns you how, High Priest?"

"I know the power of Rome firsthand. They are not a light-hearted race. They do not possess a sense of humor when it comes to ridicule and, whether Yeshua intended it or not, they would take it as such. That means trouble, my friend. Now do you understand?"

"What is to understand? I suppose some of them recognized the procession, meager as it was, as a thing they had witnessed elsewhere."

"Many who witnessed this foolishness laughed. They assumed this Yeshua was putting on a show for them, creating a bit of theater, a comedy, and making fun of the Roman Prefect."

"Let us hope that was all he had in mind. To do otherwise raises larger questions about his ambitions as a leader, but that would be of no interest to our Roman oppressors. Anyway, we do not often get a chance to laugh at imperial power, High Priest. My friend Loukas, here, might even call it therapeutic. If I were a local Roman official, I would turn a blind eye to this. Anything that brings a smile to the oppressed should be encouraged. Their playwrights do it all the time."

"Nonsense. Many may have laughed because they saw something they thought was simply ridiculous. A great, tall man sitting on a colt, knees all tucked up and riding down the hill. For them, it was a charade, a farce."

"But you suppose it will rile the Prefect to anger, and he will punish us all for the folly of a few?"

"Did you not hear? 'Hosanna,' they cried. 'Hosanna in the highest,' Rabban. Don't you see?"

"No, I do not see. No one will topple an empire with a dumb-show like that. Surely you don't think anything serious will come of it."

"He made a parody of the Prefect's entrance that those pilgrims witnessed earlier. Yeshua is no fool. If he did this thing, he did it for a reason."

"I am pleased that you now acknowledge that the man is no fool. I hope you will soon see that he poses no threat to the

Nation either. I have said it before and I repeat it now, drop this peculiar vendetta and leave him be. This business had to do with a claim to be messiah, not to ridicule Rome. Since we know he is not the Messiah, I predict that in a season, a year at the outside, he and his minyan will dry up and blow away like chaff on the threshing floor. The more you pursue him, the greater his reputation grows. I warned you before, if you are not careful, you will make a martyr of the man. Trust me, you do not want to do that. Besides, I know for a fact that the Prefect is currently too occupied with other matters to be bothered by a bit of foolishness on the hillsides."

"I know the power of Rome where you do not. They exile their poets and their critics and those who satirize them. Whether Yeshua intended to ridicule them or not, they will take offense. That means trouble. What thing preoccupies the Prefect?"

"I am sorry, but I cannot elaborate. Caiaphas, if the Prefect has heard of this at all, he has dismissed it, although, I cannot say the same about some of the others currently occupying the Fortress. With them, you may have a point. I will see what I can find out on that score. Either way, it is too late to do anything about it. He has put on his show for whatever reason and it cannot be taken back. The best plan, it seems to me, would be to pretend it never happened. After all, do these pilgrims have the government's ear? Will they report it? Do the Romans solicit their views on anything? Would a person traveling here for Passover take the time to wander into the Praetorium and describe this event and its implications? You know they will not. Let it go, High Priest. Let it go."

Gamaliel watched as Caiaphas spun on his heel and marched away, his face a shade redder than it had been when he first confronted him. He assumed the High Priest would take his less than enthusiastic support back to his allies in the Sanhedrin. He shook his head and motioned to Loukas to come along. It was past the ninth hour and time drew short.

Loukas turned and stepped off with Gamaliel. "The High Priest is obsessed with that rabbi. Why do you think it is so?"

"Alas, he is not alone. At first, this preoccupation was exclusively Caiaphas'. Lately, I am hearing from others who have been brought into it. It is regrettable. There is so much more that needs our attention, but there seems no end to the need the High Priest and his supporters have to persecute this man. I cannot figure out the why of their intensity. Obviously, the cause is not easy to tease out of the rhetoric, but it seems to pivot around the nature of this city and its inhabitants. In the cities you like to throw in my face, Alexandria and so on, Rabbi Yeshua and his view of the Law would not pose a problem, but this is the Holy City, the City of David. Here we are rigid and unbending in what we take to be the 'way.' Outside these walls, as you have often lectured, the Faith is more flexible and accommodating. But here the teaching of Yeshua ben Josef, taken at its face value, supports similar ideas. As such, they feel threatened. For them and for me, I have to add, if I am to be honest, it worries us. This parade he created on the Mount of Olives, for example, could be interpreted as a declaration of his messiahship, a fulfillment of prophesy. What will the Lord do when his people, the people he chose above all others, stray too far from the path He has laid out for us? Think of Moses in the wilderness for forty years. Forty years to reach the land promised to them because the people he delivered out of Pharaoh's hand wanted a more comfortable deity."

"*Ha Shem* does not change his mind? He can't, say, alter the rules here and there?"

"No."

"Pity."

Chapter XX

The two men turned and made their way toward the Antonia Fortress, neither with enthusiasm and both with trepidation. Loukas broke into Gamaliel's thoughts.

"She will not do it, she says."

"Who will not do what?"

"Sarai. She will not be our agent to question Procula. She refuses to enter a pagan Temple. I tried to explain the importance of the task, but all she could do was purse her lips and mutter darkly about how 'the Rabban of the Sanhedrin could sanction such an unholy and dangerous act.'"

"She said that? She's right, how could I? I would not do it, why should she?"

"Would not the Lord understand that a small transgression in the pursuit of a greater good is more than justified and forgive her?"

"I do not like being put in the position of abandoning my principles on the altar of expediency and, apparently, neither does she. It was wrong to ask. It is enough that I have to find ways to salvage the reputation of a man who on his best days can only be described as misguided—"

"Misguided? Surely you are playing the fool. He is, on those best days of which you speak, a brutal, conniving—"

"Enough. Vituperation will earn us nothing. We must push on. I do need to hear about the Prefect's wife's thoughts on the strange woman."

"But why? Didn't she say she'd turned the whole matter over in her mind and now she recognizes the woman?"

"She did."

"And you are still not satisfied?"

"I am not, and before you ask why, I don't know. It just smacks of…it's odd, that's all. And it's important that I find out why she changed her mind."

"You will be the death of me, Rabban."

"Quite possibly."

They made their way into the Fortress without the aid of Marius who, once dismissed, seemed to have permanently disappeared. Pilate stood when they entered. His face fell when he recognized Gamaliel and Loukas.

"Oh, it's you. Where is Marius? How did you get in here?"

"Answering your questions in reverse order, we walked in following the path I finally memorized. As for the boy, I don't know. Who were you expecting just now?"

"What makes you think I was expecting someone?"

"Well, you stood as we entered. In all the time we have known one another, you have never risen at my appearance. It is not something you do for any but your Roman equals or betters. I am flattered, by the way. Also, your expression registered a noticeable level of disappointment when you saw who we were."

"Very well, I was expecting someone else."

"May I inquire who?"

"No, you may not. The boy, he was instructed to never leave your side."

"Well, I sent him away earlier, and now it seems he has decided to stay away. Prefect, we have discerned his real purpose for being assigned to us and we have not said nor will we say anything that, reported back to you, would be useful. I assume he reports to you. If he has other ears to fill, they will learn nothing of importance either. So, we do not need or want him anymore."

"I see. Nevertheless, I will have him with you. I will send a guard or two to find him."

"You trust him then not to be in contact with others—people whose interests do not coincide with yours?"

"Don't be ridiculous. He is a slave. If he is caught selling his loyalty, he will die. He knows that, and so he would not dare."

"As you wish. I have a more pressing problem to discuss. It is very important we put some questions to your wife again. Our thought of having one of our women meet her in the Athena Temple has fallen through."

"The Temple of Athena? I was not aware she had any plans to go there, so that will not be a problem. Why did you want her to go there? She wouldn't have agreed to go in any case. Tomorrow is her day for the horses."

"Horses?"

"The hippodrome, Rabban, she is a great admirer of the race horses. Not the races, mind you, she thinks they are a form of cruelty to the animals, but she loves the beasts themselves. When she is near a hippodrome, she invariably marches off to the stables to visit her four-legged friends with tidbits to feed them. This week the chariots and the courses will be idle in honor of your Passover. There will be no races. Tomorrow she will go and chat with the horses. She talks to them. Don't ask me what about or if they answer. I have never had the courage to ask."

"Does she have a favorite?"

"Yes, Pegasus. That is the name of a horse our gods—"

"I know what Pegasus is."

"You do? I didn't think you were allowed to read any theology save your own."

"You would be surprised at what I read. So, let me get this straight. Tomorrow she will travel to the stables at the hippodrome to talk to the horses."

"Exactly."

"And Pegasus will certainly be one she will spend some time with."

"Yes."

"Loukas, tomorrow we should acquaint ourselves with the horses in the hippodrome's stables."

"She will be watched. If you approach her, they will know and she will have to answer for it," Pilate said.

"How good are you with horses, Loukas."

"They terrify me."

"Truly?"

"Equinophobia, Rabban. Since I was kicked and had a leg broken as a child, I do not willingly spend any time with them nor do I allow myself to even approach them. Why do you ask?"

"We are going to the stables. I had hoped you could hide in the stall of the famous Pegasus and when the good lady made her visit, you could ask her a few questions without being seen by her watchers."

"Rabban, I will accompany you to the stables, but the instant one of them exits his stall, I will be on the move. If anyone is to hide in the stalls, it will have to be you."

"You might use the boy," Pilate said.

"But it appears he has vanished, and besides that, I don't think I would trust him with the task. The other problem with the boy is he is as recognizable as I. No, it will have to be me. Tomorrow we will sally forth to the stables early. When will your wife make her pilgrimage?"

"Midday."

"Fine. Tell her it is important she spend some time with Pegasus. Now that is all we can do today. I would love to interview your guests, but I suppose that is out of the question. Can you ask Rufus to make a few discreet inquiries with them? I would dearly like to know why and how Cassia knew to come to the basement precisely when he did. I would like to know what business this mysterious Tribune has in the city. And, if he can cut their purse, so to speak, I would like to know where they were in the hours prior to and after the banquet."

"I can ask Rufus, but…"

"I understand. Anything he can discover will be a blessing."

◇◇◇

"Are you really going to stand in the stall with the horse?"

"If I must, yes."

"Those horses are very high strung, Rabban. They are as likely to kick you to death as look at you. I have treated some of the handlers from the hippodrome brought to me with serious injuries. A few are killed now and again. What do you know of horses?"

"Absolutely nothing, but I know a Physician who will make for me a sop of some sort that will calm at least one of them down so he behaves like an old donkey rather than a prancing stallion. You can do that?"

"I can though I doubt the owner will be happy to find his favorite steed wobbly about the knees."

"You heard the Prefect. There is no racing for several days. He will recover in time to drag a chariot and an insane driver around the *termai*. Now, come with me. I want to speak to Agon, the jeweler, and I want you to hear what he has to say."

"You are buying jewelry?"

"No. My interest is in the jeweler, not the jewels. Agon, although a Jew, was a legionnaire at one time, like your Yakob. I have a feeling I need to know more about that peculiar combination."

Chapter XXI

The Antonia Fortress' southeast tower provided a panoramic view of the city to the south and west. Below and to the south, smoke from the Temple's altar drifted across toward the Mount of Olives. Beyond that, in the old City of David, people scurried about preparing for the day's conclusion. To the west, Jerusalem spread like a gaudy carpet, filled with activity, buying, selling, and bartering. The two men watched as Gamaliel and Loukas disappeared into the crowd.

"There they go. Tribune, it appears the Emperor's fortune-teller, or whoever it was who got his ear this time, had it right. I deem that as near a miracle as anything I have experienced. I would like a denarius for every time some charlatan pulls the fleece over that old fool's eyes."

"If I were you I would bridle that tongue of yours, Cassia. To whom the Emperor listens is something one should criticize only with great care and not openly."

"There are only the two of us."

"I have found that in places like this, where servants and slaves seem to jump out of the wall when you least expect them, there is never 'just the two of us.' Cassia, we are friends and have been for a long time, but with this Emperor, who is given to abusing anyone who seems to look at him cross-eyed, discretion is not just the better part of valor, it is essential if you wish to survive. I don't think you want to be tossed off a tower by the Emperor.

Even a hint of disloyalty, no matter how facetiously stated, could send you sailing."

"I see no foreign ears way up here, and we are a long way from Capri and Imperial sycophants, Grex, unless I am to count you among their number. Would you report me?"

"Not unless it came to choosing between saving my life or yours. At that point, self interest would displace friendship. I expect you would do the same if our positions were reversed. I said it only as a caution. I do not wish to lose you. Not with so much in flux. Tiberius can't last forever. Who will replace him, do you think?"

"Replace the Divine Presence? One can only guess. Who is your choice?"

"If I had a choice to make, I would have tapped Germanicus were he alive. Someone like him would do nicely, but the Senate will not want another Julius. The betting is on Germanicus' son, Little Boots."

"Not Claudius?"

"Apparently not, but then who can say for certain which mistress', or former wife's, or rival's son, or surviving cousin, nephew, or general, might eventually emerge as our newest Caesar? It is best not to choose or at least not to show an interest in favorites."

"Returning to our Prefect, Tribune, it seems clear he colludes with the Jews, and even with a death sentence hanging over his head, he persists. Why do you suppose that is?"

"It is possible he believes that the god of the land, this strange Jewish deity, can catapult him into power. Maybe he has Marc Antony ideas and wishes to be the King of Judea and all surrounding states."

"That, or something equally grandiose or why would he go on?"

"Perhaps it is all he has left."

"Do you have someone watching that strange person…what's his name?"

"He is called Gamaliel. He holds an honored place in their governing body, the Sanhedrin. We must handle him with discretion for the nonce, and yes, I have him in sight at all times."

"Will your discretion have a terminus?"

"That will depend on what our soon-to-be deposed Prefect tells us. Now, it is enough to keep him in sight. Happily for us, you found Pilate with a murdered Aurelius. His business with their god is now no longer relevant."

"But may be needed later."

"True enough and either will guarantee we have him in place until we deliver him to Tiberius. Then he will either learn to fly or end his days on the rocks of Capri, and we will have disappeared from the Emperor's view. I hope permanently."

"Pilate has a well known capacity for survival. That is one horse I want in the stall before I cease betting on it. Did he really believe Aurelius lusted after his office?"

"Possibly. What he believed or what he did not believe, no longer matters. We have him and we will deliver him. Then, the gods willing, we will be clear of this quagmire into which the Emperor has dropped us."

◇◇◇

"Where are we going? Did you say a jeweler's shop?"

"Agon crafts jewelry and is an old acquaintance of mine. I had his son as a pupil briefly. Nice boy, but a trifle thick. He has decided to take up something less demanding of his powers of reasoning."

"I see."

"Probably not, but you shall. Agon owns a shop in the Souk. He specializes in creating items from precious metals and stones, usually on order although he has an array of pieces to sell for the occasional drop-in. More importantly, he once served as a legionnaire in Cappadocia. He was badly wounded and very nearly died. The legions of Rome have no use for cripples and particularly alien ones, so they abandoned him where he fell. Somewhere along the way, he found refuge and healed and then learned the jeweler's trade. He has become skillful enough at it to attract the wealthier segment of the city who desire to have individual, one-of-a-kind, pieces. He manages to support himself and his family comfortably with his shop."

They pushed their way into the narrow store. Loukas, a man Gamaliel knew had a keener nose than most, tested the air. He nodded. "He plates as well as forges."

"He does. Greetings in the Name, Agon."

"Rabban. *Ha Shem.* It has been some time. Have you another puzzle for me?"

"Not a puzzle this time. I seek information."

"What sort of information? The word on the streets or what the mysterious Tribune, Grex, is doing in the city? Or maybe the latest on the Prefect's troubles? I have all sorts of gossip. How much is truly news and how much is news that is true I cannot say."

"I will have it all, but most pressing at this moment, I would like you to tell me about Hebrews serving in the Imperial legions."

"You need to know this because…?"

"Because my friend Loukas, here, has a new servant who once served, because it seems the city is currently overstocked with legionnaires, and because I wish to know the who, the what, and where of them. Finally, I wish to know because something has become dislocated in my mind and I cannot reconnect it."

"Something is…you lost me on that last one. Are you saying you have a feeling, a tickle, that there is a connection between Hebrew legionnaires and whatever problem you clearly have but are keeping to yourself?"

"Yes, that is it exactly. There, you see, Loukas, wisdom drawn from experience and surviving to a reasonable age. How are your old wounds, by the way, Agon? Loukas here is a Physician. He has been known to work miracles. Perhaps he can restore you to the man you once were."

"That is a happy thought, but unless he can reverse time, it will not be possible."

Loukas studied the jeweler for a moment. "You received a severe wound in your leg?"

"Yes. How can you tell? I haven't budged since you arrived."

"But you did as we entered, and your posture tells me you still suffer from the effects. If it involves sinews and the internal scarring is not too deep and extensive, I might be able to restore something. It will not be a miracle, however, just practical medicine."

"Physician, you should know that miracles are claimed by the recipients, not by the performers. Maybe, when the Rabban has finished with me and the problem that obviously is eating at him, you will have a look."

"There, you see, Loukas," Gamaliel said with a smile. "You should stop complaining about having to work on our problem. I have brought you a paying client. Now, Agon, tell me about Jewish legionnaires. Oh, and if there are any, Jewish mercenaries."

"There is a difference?"

"Point taken. And Pilate? What's the latest on our Prefect? What do you hear?"

"Ah, that is a great mystery. Always in the past, the news leaks from the Fortress like water from the mythical Danaids' sieve. But beyond the original news that there had been a murder and that Pilate is implicated, nothing new has emerged." Agon seemed uncomfortable as he spoke.

"What is it you are not telling me, my friend?"

Agon waved his hand dismissively. "It is nothing, but—"

"But?"

"Rabban, there are some who say you are in the Prefect's employ. That makes no sense, but you have been seen coming and going from the Praetorium. Are you part of a plan to cover up the crime? I know it is foolishness on their part, but people will gossip and the truth will suffer. Your visits raise dangerous questions in people's minds."

"And well they should. Do not worry, Agon, if I am seen going in and out of the lion's den it should be understood in terms of the book of Daniel. It is to be party to the Lord's work. I am not changing my allegiance from *Ha Shem* to *Panthera leo*. Also, you may tell your friends that Loukas has been called to attend the Prefect's wife. Thus, we are both seen for different reasons."

"I was sure it would be something like that."

Chapter XXII

The sun hovered above the western walls as Gamaliel and Loukas left Agon's shop. Most, but not all of the hours they'd spent there had been taken up with Agon's lengthy discourse on legionnaires in general and Hebrew ones in particular, the delegation and the latest rumors concerning Pilate. To the first, Agon declared most Jewish legionnaires had been recruited from the Italian peninsula. Recruited, he said, did not accurately define the process, however. They joined rather than be harassed and/or persecuted. The few survivors of twenty years of war and hardship usually scattered throughout the Empire seeking a respite or at least a measure of peace in their declining years. It would not be usual for them to migrate to Jerusalem.

When Gamaliel had asked why, Agon explained that few, if any, were recruited from Judea, much less Jerusalem. Most recruits came from the more distant enclaves of the Empire. Further, they spent the bulk of their adult lives living more like pagans than Jews. They would have no immediate connection with either the city or its people. In addition, when the practice of their beliefs, however marginal to begin with, was proscribed, they would find it difficult to enter the rigidly structured society the City of David required.

"Even so, some do come to Jerusalem," Gamaliel said, "Besides yourself, and Yakob, how many others would you say there are?"

Agon thought that it would be difficult to estimate an actual number. At best he could only venture a guess. He received visits from old legionnaires now and then, most of whom might have been Jewish at one time or another. Gamaliel had snorted at "might have been" and explained that as a practical matter, if one were born a Jew, he or she was a Jew forever. It was not something one could shed like an old cloak. Whether orthodox, observant, a High Holy Days-only believer, or if he had decided to reject his heritage altogether and pour out libations to Pan, when the Empire mounted a program to persecute Jews, as they sometimes did, no one would escape no matter what he or she declared about their Jewishness. A Jew's reality is simple. It is bestowed by *Ha Shem* and it is indelible.

Loukas started to say something and then thought better of it. He was no stranger to Gamaliel's lecturing on the topic and he knew better than to interrupt. It would be useless to bring up the enclaves in the Empire's other great cities again. Jerusalem served as an island of faith in the midst of heterodoxy elsewhere, as Gamaliel had often remarked, and nothing could shake his friend from a conviction that those other adherents to the Lord were but a temporary aberration, soon to disappear when the Lord saw fit. On the other hand he felt his friend was probably correct about the inclusiveness of the race when a persecution was launched. Agon smiled his agreement at the Rabban's lecture and agreed that he was probably right. He also said he thought this opinion was shared by a majority of the city residents. That sentiment would be sufficient to persuade many war-weary, fall-away Jews to seek to settle elsewhere.

Gamaliel wondered how in spite of this, Agon had settled in Jerusalem. Agon shrugged and said, "Family." He did not feel the discomfort some of his colleagues did in the presence of a smothering orthodoxy. Gamaliel had bristled at "smothering" but let it pass, although it had cost him to do so. Agon said there were others like him here, also. The question then was, if there were any other attractions beside family ties which would induce men to settle in Jerusalem.

There could be a few reasons, Agon suggested, but knowing the mind of a particular person was never easy. A few might wish to reconnect to their roots, so to speak. There is something about being denied a particular thing that makes one want it the more. Then there were the deserters. The thought that some of the renegade legionnaires might be deserters had not occurred to either Gamaliel or Loukas because they had been told that desertion was extremely rare, that deserters were severely punished. So severely that few attempted it, fewer succeeded. Agon said they should look around them. If a son of Abraham deserted his post wouldn't it follow that Jerusalem would be the only place he could go and not stand out. A Jew in Rome would be noticeable. In Jerusalem, the reverse would be the case. In David's city a Jew on the run could effectively disappear from the authorities and, more importantly, they would not bother to look. Finally, a man without a country or a real home would most likely gravitate to the one place he'd believe safe and feel familiar, if not comfortable.

Where did those whose arrival did not involve family disappear to, Gamaliel wondered. Agon thought some settled into society and found work. Others, he did not know how many others, found an outlet for their lingering animosity toward the Empire by joining one of the scattered groups which opposed Rome's presence in the Promised Land. They might turn up with Barabbas in the wilderness or with another band led by someone like him. They'd bring their skills as disciplined soldiers to such a group, and for that they would be welcomed.

Gamaliel pointed out that Barabbas was in prison, a fact Agon did not know.

"Truly?" he said. "For how long?"

"Forever, I should say. You do not imagine he can escape from the Antonia Fortress?"

Agon shook his head and said that no, alone he couldn't, but he had many followers and some of them had skills which might make it possible. As former legionnaires, they would not try storming the Praetorium, but they could abduct or imprison an important Roman official. Then, they might negotiate an exchange with the threat of death to the hostage if Barabbas were not released.

Gamaliel realized that that explained the flinty-eyed legionnaires guarding the visiting Tribune and Cassia Drusus. Agon reminded him that there were groups besides the bandits in the wilderness which had similar designs. Zealots would be happy to recruit a disillusioned legionnaire as would the *Siccori*. Where did he suppose those assassins came from? They were not part of the culture until very recently.

"Ah, that is a very interesting thought, my friend." Gamaliel said and shot Loukas a look.

Before they left, Agon entertained them with the news he'd gleaned from a traveling merchant who'd bought a gold chain with his profits which made transporting his earnings back to Corinth safer, as he could hide it under his belt. They listened with dismay at the retelling of the merchant's tale about how Tiberius had taken into his head that *Ha Shem* posed such a threat to his Gods that a delegation of high-ranking officials was to be sent to investigate. Presumably they were to report back to the Emperor with a plan to depose *Ha Shem*.

"Can you credit that?" Loukas said, later.

"Certainly not. Surely the merchant misheard."

"More than likely. You know how news travels by word of mouth. Each set of ears hears a different story from the reporting mouth, and the distortion strays further and further from the truth like a ship which sets off just a hair's breadth off course and continues on to the wrong port."

Later that night, as he sat alone staring at, but not seeing, the papyrus sheets in front of him, Gamaliel wondered if his lies to Agon would be the last straw that would finally bring the Lord's wrath down on him. Was he really doing this investigation because of an overriding need to see justice? Did the Lord expect him to impose his righteousness on everyone else, and moreover, was it necessary to apply it to a pagan culture which routinely ridiculed and despised it? He did not often yield to self doubt, but in this instance, he questioned his basic premise. When should one's own code of conduct be applied to others, particularly those who did not share it? He cherished the Law as a lover cherishes his beloved, but the Roman Empire operated within its own set of strictures. Could he justify the use of Hebraic practice to exonerate one of them from a crime, particularly one as serious as murder? Was he on a path of self aggrandizement, and if so, wouldn't the Lord be right to bring him down for it?

He shook his head. Sometimes he was stubborn as an ox and pestered by flies of doubt. Right or wrong, he had committed himself to this undertaking, and doubts notwithstanding, he would see it through. The Lord would decide his punishment or reward. What he needed now was sleep. He blew out his lamp and took himself off to bed and uneasy rest.

YOM SHENI

Chapter XXIII

Loukas met Gamaliel at the head of the street that led down to the hippodrome, the Circus, the Romans would call it. He carried a sack and appeared annoyed.

"You are out of sorts, Physician. Is there a problem?"

"And you look like you could use another three hours of sleep. Yes, there is a problem. As you requested, although I do not remember you actually asking in the usual sense. You said 'Loukas will prepare a sop,' or something like that. You never said, 'Loukas, my esteemed friend, will you be so kind as to make me something that will render even the fiercest chariot horse tame as a lamb?' As I say, I did not hear that. Perhaps you did and I missed it."

"So that is why you are so testy. Yes, well, you are right. I sometimes take you for granted. I am sorry."

"There is no 'sometime' to it, Rabban, and yes I have your sop, two of them, in fact. After I left you I visited the Souk and bought a few apples. I cut out a core of one and filled the hollow with a potion that induces sleep. Horses, they tell me, love apples, and so there will be no difficulty inducing Pegasus to eat it. The problem arises in the dose. I know how much will put a man to sleep, but a horse? I also assumed that we only wanted to make the animal drowsy, not knock him out. That made the problem more difficult. I guessed this Pegasus must be the equivalent of twenty men, so I put in twenty times the normal dose I would use to induce sleep."

"That should do it. So, what is the problem?"

"I have never dosed a horse. Do they respond to drugs the same as people? What if they are more sensitive to the potion and instead of making him docile and drowsy, I accidently killed him?"

"Ah, I see. That would be a tragedy. You said you had two sops. What was the other?"

'I took a second apple and prepared it as the first with half the dose."

"That was very wise of you. Which is which?"

"I tied a thread to the stronger one."

"I don't see a thread."

Loukas grabbed up the apples and turned them over, first one, then the other. "I swear to you I—"

"Loukas, rest easy. The thread has been lost. Perhaps it is a sign that we should let the Lord chose. He will not let us down."

"Bravely spoken. You do not believe that anymore than I do."

"Do not presume, Loukas, if I said it, I believe it. We will have to trust whichever apple we use will do the job. How long will the dose last?"

"I have no idea."

"Well, this is turning out to be a good beginning. Very well, it can't be helped. We must be off. We dare not be seen by either Procula's entourage or anyone else lurking about and keeping tabs on her."

"Or us."

They made their way down the cobbled street to the enormous structure that the first Herod built for his Roman supporters. As he had ruled at the sufferance of a distant and often fickle Caesar, he thought it necessary to offer blandishments such as this huge hippodrome along with an amphitheater and several pagan temples. He'd patterned his hippodrome after the Greek model but made it grander and bigger, a characteristic of the way in which Roman culture absorbed the Greek. Bigger and grander, but rarely better. This Circus had been built into the hillside which allowed the earth that had been removed to make one end of the flat racecourse available for the construction of the opposite. The stables were located below the viewing stand at one end, and it was there that the two men hurried.

Loukas was uneasy in the presence of so much horse flesh. Thirty cubits away from the stalls, the aroma of manure nearly stopped him in his tracks. Gamaliel sent him to a vantage point well within his line of sight with instructions to signal when Procula appeared. He found Pegasus' stall. Stable hands had not yet arrived, and he found himself alone with the horse. He seemed docile enough. Gamaliel wondered if he'd need Loukas' soporific apples after all. When he lifted the latch and took one step into the stall, the horse's nostrils flared, as he reared up on his hind legs and waved his forehooves in his Gamaliel's direction. Gamaliel retreated. He would need the apple after all. He fished one from his pouch, prayed it was the correct one, and offered it to Pegasus.

"Here, my handsome beast, look at what the Rabban has brought you."

The horse walked stiff-legged to the stall gate, snuffled, and took the prize. He bit down, chewed, and the apple disappeared down his gullet. Gamaliel waited. Nothing happened. Gamaliel could detect no sign of weariness or drowsiness. Time passed and still no signs of sedation. He had to assume that the drug needed time to be absorbed. The horse continued to stare at him in what he took to be a hostile manner. He murmured soothingly to the beast, the way he'd done when his boys were colicky or restless. A long time ago.

"So, Pegasus, time to sleep, yes? Shall we lie down now? Good horse." Gamaliel wasn't sure if horses slept standing or if they settled onto the hay. Horses were something he knew about only from hearsay, but he had a vague remembrance that they slept standing. "Or just close your eyes, there's a good boy."

He was conversing with a horse. He felt like an idiot. What other humiliation must he endure before he was done with this onerous assignment? Loukas called out and signaled that Procula had turned into the street and would arrive at any moment. In desperation, he produced the second apple and handed it to the horse. Loukas waved at him again, this time more urgently. There was no time to lose. Either Gamaliel must enter the stall and hope the horse did not kick him to death or he would have to abandon the plan altogether. He lifted the latch and stepped into the stall. The horse glared at him and pawed at the ground, apparently its wits not yet dulled by Loukas' potion. Gamaliel shushed Pegasus, who shied to one side, but made no other menacing moves. He wondered if just buying the horse's amity with the apple might have been all that had been needed. He didn't have time to work that out. He flattened himself against the wall to the left of the stall gate and made more cooing sounds. Positioned as he was, he could not be seen from the corridor. The horse continued to glare at him. Gamaliel smiled back, he hoped, encouragingly.

Procula paused at the stall gate and spoke to the horse.

"Pegasus, my beauty," she murmured and offered him an apple as well. He clopped forward for it, and Gamaliel pressed harder against the rough boards of the stall. Pegasus now stood perilously close. "How are you this lovely morning? Rabban, are you in there?" The latter said in a softer voice.

"I am."

"My husband, the Prefect, tells me you wish to ask me questions."

"I do. Only a few, but the answers might help. I am curious about the strange woman who entered your chambers the day of Aurelius' murder. Do you remember?"

"I remember saying something to my husband at the time. Then, after I had thought about it, it seemed to me that I had, indeed, seen the face before. She would have been one of our company. After that I gave it no further thought."

"I see. Do you think you would recognize her again if you were to see her?"

"Oh yes, certainly. Pegasus, you poor dear, are you not well? What is the matter with the horse, Rabban?"

Pegasus had started to sway.

"He seems fine, Madam, but then I am no expert. Another question about the woman, how would you describe her?"

"Describe?"

"Tall, short, plump, hair color…that sort of thing."

The horse had swayed only slightly at first, but now he seemed to be staggering a little from side to side and threatened to pin Gamaliel to the wall.

"He looks very distressed, don't you think?"

"He? Who? I thought we were discussing a woman."

"The horse, Pegasus. He seems to be—"

"I believe he is dreaming, Madam. They do, you know. Past races, past glory. I would not worry. Description?"

"Oh, yes, the woman. Tallish. Now that you mention it, yes, very tall and, dare I say it, homely."

"I see. Have you, in fact, seen this woman since?"

"Seen? I…umm, perhaps, I can't be sure. There are so many… Oh dear, I fear the horse is ill, don't you?"

"As I said, just little drowsy. Perhaps some bad fodder, nothing to concern you. So, you're saying, yes, this woman has been in your company since that day?"

"In my company? No, not exactly but…he is more than just sleepy, Sir. Oh yes. Bad fodder you say? Really? No, I haven't seen the woman although I sometimes think I have. But then that is frequently a problem for me. I see things, you know, visions. Often I cannot separate what's real from what is not."

"Would this woman have had access to your baggage when you saw her?"

"Access to our baggage?" The horse jolted to its right and to Gamaliel's relief, away from him. "Yes, now that you mention it, she might well have. Is that important? Oh, poor Pegasus, you are ill! He is sick, Rabban."

"Important? That would depend on the location of your husband's dagger at the time. One last question, when your husband, the Prefect, received the message from the soldier to meet Priscus, was there anyone else nearby?"

"One or two of our visitors were there." Pegasus coughed and drool dripped from the corner of his mouth. "I believe I must find this horse's owner. There is something seriously wrong with the poor thing."

"Madam, if I may—"

"No more, Rabban. The horse is ill, perhaps mortally so, can't you see?"

Procula dashed off, and Gamaliel stepped to the stall gate. He turned to look at Pegasus. The Prefect's wife was right to fetch the owner. The horse gurgled deep in its throat, huffed three times, crossed its eyes, and collapsed with a crash. Gamaliel had no idea a horse would be heavy enough to shake the earth when it fell. This one did at any rate.

Chapter XXIV

Gamaliel waved at Loukas to follow him and started up the hill toward the Temple and away from the hippodrome. Loukas caught up with him.

"Did the sop work?"

"Oh, indeed."

"Do you have an idea which apple did the deed?"

"Absolutely."

"Really? Which?"

"Both."

"You gave the horse both apples?"

"He was hungry."

"Hungry?"

"I had to. You called. Procula was on her way and the beast had yet to show the slightest sign of the drug's efficacy. I gave him the next one. That seemed to do the trick."

"You didn't."

"I did. Listen, I know how much horses upset you. We need to be away from this place, Loukas."

"Upset me? You might have killed that horse."

"I believe after several hours of deep and restorative sleep, Pegasus will rise up refreshed and strong enough to pull two chariots. Come along, Loukas, we have more work to do this morning."

"You will leave it, possibly to die?"

"Do I have an alternative? You are the healer. Are you suggesting you would like to go back and tend to it? Shall I fetch your bag of medicines and tools? Will your potions work any better on the horse this time?"

"You are correct. We have other more pressing things to deal with this morning."

The two men hurried up the hill and away from the Circus. Gamaliel, gasping for air, raised his hand to signal Loukas to stop.

"You need some conditioning, Rabban. You sound like one of those horses after it has run the course."

"And I feel like poor Pegasus must at this moment. The Lord only knows if and when he will run that course again and, like him, I am about to collapse."

They found a shaded shop which offered them new wine and bread and cheese.

"Collect yourself, Rabban, while I attempt to remove the odor of horse manure from my sandals. Why did I let you talk me into this foolishness?"

Gamaliel caught his breath. "Even the offal disturbs you?"

"Anything equine, my friend. So, what did you learn from the wife of our esteemed Prefect?"

"Not much that we did not already know. After having given it much thought, she is certain that the mysterious woman who popped up in her rooms that day did belong to the household. She was vague as to how, exactly. I presume her household is large and has a turnover as slaves and servants come and go. Still, if the woman traveled down from Caesarea with the Prefect's party, she would have been noticeable. Also, she said she believed she would recognize the woman again if she saw her. Now, here is the interesting part. I asked her if she remembered seeing the woman since that one encounter, and she cannot remember ever seeing her."

"I see. Rabban, that makes no sense. If she is certain the woman is part of her household, what has happened that no one sees her for days?"

"As I said, it is an interesting point to consider. Perhaps she is ill, or left service, or visiting family. Oh, and one last thing. There were several people in the vicinity of the putative legionnaire when he delivered the message attributed to Priscus."

"And you do not believe the Centurion sent that message?"

"No, I do not, but who knows? Anyway, enough of that. Let us review what we do know."

"We know practically nothing. What is there to review?"

"Oh, I am not so sure about that. We know a few things. We do not know how or if they connect to Pilate's predicament, but we know them. There is always something, you see. We do this summing up as both a discipline and in the hope that the thing we need to move us along will leap out at us at the utterance."

"You mean that if you or I articulate a bit of trivia, it may take on significance in the presence of something else we've said?"

"In a nut shell, yes. So, what do we know that may touch on our investigation? We know that there are some former legionnaires in the area who also happen to be Israelites if not born here, at least are Jewish. How many we cannot say."

"I can't see that is important beyond a possible link to the radical groups in the area. Useful for the Roman establishment to know, but not for me."

"Do not dismiss a detail, Loukas, simply because you do not see where it fits the story. You may be right, but I am drawn to the fact that prior to this week, I only knew of one, no, make that two, Jewish former legionnaires in the whole of Judea and the Galilee. Now I find there may be more than you can count on your fingers, perhaps several times over. I find that knowledge surfacing when it did most interesting. Then, we have the mystery woman. Pilate and his wife dismiss her out of hand. Perhaps they are right to do so, but we only just heard about her and I am curious about her single appearance. As you pointed out, if she is part of the household, where did she disappear to and why?"

"Well, I will grant you that it is a mystery, but I don't see the connection of either of these points to the murder in the basement."

"Nor do I, but I can't dismiss them. Finally..."

"There is more?"

"Quite a bit, but for now, I am curious what has happened to our guide, Marius."

"The boy? He has undoubtedly found a better way to waste his time than to traipse around Jerusalem with us. Besides, you said you had no use for him"

"That part is true enough. For the rest, you forget he is supposed to be a slave, Loukas. A slave does not choose how he wastes his time. In fact, he is not allowed to waste time at all. Either Pilate has found other duties for him, or he has run off, and more the pity if he is caught. Then, there is the possibility that he is not a slave at all, but holds some other position in the palace about which we are being kept in the dark. Either way, I believe we will require his presence before we are done."

"Not a slave? The boy seems nice enough, but I saw no evidence of duplicity. Why would anyone pose as a slave if he were not one? What other position could he possibly have beyond what he has now? Maybe we should query Pilate as to what has become of our shadow."

"Not just yet. I need to think about it for a day or two."

"A day or two may not be available to us. Passover approaches, Rabban, and failing exoneration, Pilate's removal to Rome soon after that."

"Two Passovers if the Essenes among us have their way."

"Pardon, two?"

"Our friends—I use the term loosely—in addition to believing the Temple is false and should be relocated to some holier place, employ a variant calendar. For them tonight is the Passover."

"That's awkward."

"Only for those with friends or family who have joined that sect. It will mean two meals of remembrance for some of them. Come, we must press on."

"Where to now?"

"Back to Pilate. I thought he failed to appreciate his position, and then I thought he was just dense."

"Which are you thinking now?"

"That he is considering his position, and that he knows something he is not telling us. I do not know whether he withholds it deliberately or innocently. Luckily for us, I have memorized the path to that fetid hole he currently inhabits."

"Do think he would object if I were to burn some incense?"

"Probably."

Marius stood not quite twenty paces away, screened by an awning's flap. He had been following them. He wiped the sweat from his brow. Dashing up the slope from the stables to the shadow of the Temple Mount had caused as much strain on him as it had the Rabban. He wished he could sit in the shade with Gamaliel and the Physician and enjoy a cup of wine as well, but not now. Not today. If he'd had any doubts before as to the Rabban's intentions, they were now wiped away. Against all common sense, he seemed bent on investigating and possibly clearing Pilate's name. Why would he do such a thing? Surely he knew that the Hebrews would celebrate the removal of this man who everyone detested. He had to know that, yet he pressed on. Worse, because of the old man's stubbornness, Marius would never be free of the men who now owned him.

At first, he'd assumed the Rabban would simply go through the motions, investigate the murder, make a suitable public effort to ward off any punishment the Prefect might have planned for him had he refused to do so, and move on. Then later, when the Tribune and his men carted the Prefect off, Gamaliel would celebrate with the rest. But Marius had been wrong. The Rabban was serious. Worse than that, if what people said about him were true, he might succeed. The Greeks, the boy believed, called what he was feeling as being "caught between Scylla and Charybdis." He did not know who or what those two things were, but grasped the sense of it. What should he do? Where did his loyalties lie? More importantly, could he muster the courage to act on his own and perhaps stick a knife in a man…or two? He looked down the street toward the looming hippodrome he'd just left. Should he tell the stable master who poisoned the horse? Would that solve a problem or create a new one? Certainly, it would distract the Rabban, but for how long? He decided to wait and see.

Chapter XXV

Loukas led the way from the shade and comfort of the shop back out onto the street. Gamaliel heaved himself up with a grunt.

"Tell me, Rabban, can you remember a time when the country could fairly be described as the land promised to Moses, the land they traveled to for four generations after the first passing over? I cannot think of a time when we have not been an oppressed Nation. My study of the King's Book suggests that except for David and Solomon and perhaps briefly with Solomon's immediate successors, we have been subject to invading tribes and nations or subject to the whims of a despot for what seems forever."

"Your reading is superficial, yet near enough. What is your point?"

"Point? I am not sure I have a point. It simply occurred to me that this business with the Prefect is but a small itch on the giant backside of our history and we, mostly you, are taking this call to justice far too seriously."

"Small or large, victim or villain, justice is never trivial, unneeded, or to be set aside because in the broad sweep of history it will be deemed insignificant. You take Caiaphas' obsession with Rabbi Yeshua. He would have him cast away, even stoned. To do so would be, in my opinion, an unjust act, but will it affect history? It won't. People will just say 'the removal of one itinerant rabbi more or less cannot make a difference' and they would be right. Yet, to fail to provide justice or fairness to him or to anyone else, denies it to us all. Justice cannot be arbitrary. It cannot be granted to some but not others because we don't like them, or we think they are foolish or unworthy."

"You are the Rabban. You are trained to think that way. However, there are times, my friend, when you would benefit from a little Roman pragmatism."

Gamaliel snorted and the two pressed onward. They picked their way through the crowds busy with their preparations for Passover which for some would begin soon. The rest were occupied with making similar preparations for the High Holy Day two days hence. There were meals to prepare. Those pilgrims relegated to tents outside the city walls would have to improvise settings suitable for the occasion. That would not be easy. They would have to attempt to set up trestle tables on the steep hillsides surrounding the city. Even low ones, with the strategic placement of wedges and stones to level them could tilt and spill the evening meal on the ground. Some of the city's merchants, recognizing that and seeing an opportunity to profit from it, had cleared their shop floors and rented space to the influx of pilgrims either as dormitories or meeting rooms. For the latter, they set up trestle tables and couches which they then leased for a fixed period of time to anyone seeking a place to hold their Passover. Depending on the available space, several tables might be set up and more than one family might be celebrating at the same time. The early time periods brought the highest price.

A few elders in the city grumbled about this practice and the increased price for food and drink, lodging, and simple services that characterized Passover in Jerusalem. It seemed crass that people should seek monetary gain from it, but as yet, no one had had the temerity to call the merchants out. Every year Gamaliel was besieged by those holding negative views to find the passages in Holy Writ that would put a stop to it. He had not obliged them, believing that keeping the tradition should take precedence over presumed legalisms about how it should or should not be done. So, the Essenes had their Passover two days early. He wished that they kept to the calendar prescribed by the Sanhedrin, the one derived from the Nation's long history, but felt that a wrongly timed Passover was better than no Passover at all. And it did spread out the strain on the city's resources.

They continued on their way pushing through the crowds and making slow progress toward the Fortress. Gamaliel wondered what had possessed the first Herod, the father of this mouse who currently held the title of King, to build the Fortress so much larger than the Temple. Was he making a statement about his own spirituality, currying favor with his then Roman ally, Marc Antony, or did he see the rule of military might as the only way to secure his immortality? In any event, he'd been wrong on all counts.

Pilate was not in his subbasement cell when Gamaliel and Loukas arrived. A servant greeted them and said that Cassia had granted the Prefect's wish to return to his apartments on the condition he agreed to the terms of house arrest. The difficulty with this new arrangement lay in the fact that Gamaliel now had no access to him. He sent a message by way of the servant appraising Pilate of that fact and that if he expected any further help in clearing his name, the Prefect would return to the room immediately or establish another meeting place. The servant looked startled and then left to deliver the message.

"Take it as a sign, Rabban," Loukas said. "You are to move on from this folly."

"The only 'sign' I see emerging from this latest change, is the fact that the Prefect is supremely self-centered, and he had no thought what his need for the comforts of his rooms would have on anyone else. It is the nature of despots to justify their actions irrespective of the consequences."

"If you say so. Do you believe he will meet you here?"

"I hope not. I hope he will find a nice sunlit space outside this monstrosity of a building where we can sit and relax and enjoy fresh air and a view that is not four stone walls."

"How long will you wait for an answer?"

"Not long. If he still wants my services, he will answer immediately. If not, we will know in less than an hour."

Loukas began a slow pacing of the perimeter of the room, counting out each step in units which Gamaliel recognized as Arabic enumeration. "When I have circled this room five times," he said, "either Pilate will walk in through that door or I will walk out."

"Fine. I wonder what happened to the horse."

The door burst open and Pilate entered. "By the horse, I suppose you mean Pegasus. My good wife reports that he is comatose. I don't suppose you know anything about that, do you?"

"Is it important if I do?"

"Not to me."

"Then, I would rather not say. Pilate, we need to come to an understanding. I am trying to tease out the threads of this mystery for you. To do that in a timely manner, by which I mean, before you are shipped off to Rome in chains, I need access to information. You are the only access point I have and you are not telling me everything I need to know, yet you desert me at this critical moment."

"Desert you? Do you mean because I have abandoned this sewer? I have answered all your questions, Rabban. What else is there to say? I assumed that after you interviewed Procula, you were finished with us."

"Surely not. I need you to go over your recollection again."

"Not again? Why?"

"Because with each telling something new may emerge. As you repeat the story, the immediate details come to you automatically, and you no longer have to think about them. Then the smaller bits and pieces surface in your memory. So, tell me again. What happened that day? Tell me right up to the point you found yourself relegated to this dank cell."

Pilate sighed and repeated his story. Gamaliel interrupted once or twice to prompt him into thinking about one or more details.

"Picture the room in your mind, Prefect. Now, in your mind's eye, look around you. Who else is there? What are they doing? Is anything out of place? Is anyone looking at you—not looking at you. Where is your dagger, for example?"

"My dagger? It should be in the great trunk in the corner."

"Is it?"

Pilate's face darkened as he concentrated on the image behind his eyes. "No, by the gods, it is not."

"So it was removed the previous day?"

"It must have been."

"That would have been the day your good wife thought she saw a strange woman in the apartments. There, you see, Prefect, you still have much to tell me."

Chapter XXVI

Pilate poured three chalices of wine, kept one and pushed the other two toward Loukas and Gamaliel. Loukas reached for his and smiled his thanks. Gamaliel hesitated.

"Not just now, Prefect, I need a clear head."

"And I don't?"

"No, actually I believe a little wine might make you a little less 'pragmatic' and a great deal more loquacious. Please, drink up. Have some more."

"You are mocking me, Rabban. Be careful. I do not like to be mocked."

"No one does, and I assure you, making fun of you is the furthest thing in my mind." Gamaliel thought he heard Loukas cough. He hoped the Prefect had not. "It is a simple truth that men's tongues are eased with wine. I need you to be at ease. I believe you will be more likely to remember details outside the mainstream of your story if you are. Where were we?"

"We had decided my dagger had gone missing the day before the banquet."

"Exactly. A mysterious woman appears, disappears, and a dagger goes missing. No one has seen or heard from her since, at least we don't think so, and your weapon ends up in the dead man's heart. It is too much of a coincidence to ignore. Go on with your story."

Pilate continued, and once again, Gamaliel interrupted him from time to time to probe a memory, to force him to "look around" the room and describe a person or an event.

"When the legionnaire handed you the note—"

"I told you, Rabban, there was no note. He reported to me in person and delivered the message. No note."

"Sorry, yes, you did, but you see, if not, that presents a problem."

"May the gods forgive me, Rabban you are the most exasperating man on the face of the earth. What kind of problem is created by a legionnaire speaking to me?"

"I misspoke."

"Well, at last. The genius of Jerusalem admits he made an error."

"Indeed. It presents not one problem, but two. Listen carefully and tell me what I may have misunderstood. The soldier approaches you, makes some sort of acceptable greeting and delivers this message, 'Excellency, the Centurion Priscus sends his greetings and asks that you meet him in such and such a place. He has something to tell you in confidence.' Have I got it approximately right?"

"We have been through this before. Yes, yes, close enough."

"Good. Why, if it was a meeting that included something of such importance that privacy and confidentiality were required, would Priscus have entrusted it to a lowly soldier and not at least have written it out? I keep thinking there must have been a note because there should have been a note. Soldiers, as a rule, cannot read. Therefore, sending the message by way of a note assures secrecy or at least confidentiality. But delivering it to you orally means the entire barracks could have known of the meeting. You can envision the ramifications that possibility creates. That is the first problem. The second stems from that premise. If Priscus thought his information was important enough that you meet privately and in secret, why have an intermediary deliver the message at all? Why didn't he just approach you and tell you himself? I have heard of the Roman fascination for intrigue and note passing, but common sense—pragmatism—would dictate a direct contact, don't you think?"

"He might have been busy or away at the time."

"'Might have been?' He attended the banquet, did he not? So he was not busy and obviously not away anywhere."

"Very well, it wasn't important enough to require the level of security you describe."

"With respect, Excellency, that makes even less sense. He claims that he never sent the message in the first place. No, the obvious conclusion is, someone else recruited the legionnaire to deliver the message. He wouldn't have written it for fear the soldier would read it—"

"You just said soldiers cannot read."

"I believe that is true for the most part, but the writer might have been sufficiently unfamiliar with this particular soldier or barracks to know who did and did not and therefore could not take the risk. The more important thing here is who can write and if he can, in what hand? You might have recognized the writing or the source of the papyrus. In any case, he could not risk being found out. Remember, you received the message just as you were about to enter the banquet so that you could not easily confirm its contents with the Centurion. Am I correct in believing he left shortly before the official ending of the meal?"

"Now that you mention it, yes he did. At the time, I assumed he went to our meeting. You believe that to be significant? Rabban, you are right. This is far too convoluted even for me and decidedly for them, as well."

"So what do we know or think we know?"

"You tell me."

"Yes, well…we know that your dagger was stolen a day early. That means the murder was premeditated. We know that the nature of the message delivery means that all the legionnaires on duty that night could have know its contents…or not. That leads us down a different pathway. Is it possible that it is the legionnaires who wished a man killed, perhaps even Priscus, and all the rest is smoke and mirrors?"

"I had not thought of that. You might just have it, Rabban. Now, how do I convince my visitors that is what happened?"

"You don't. In the first place, they do not appear to be interested in your innocence at the moment, and this is only speculation. Furthermore, the Centurion has been sent away and cannot verify what, if anything, happened after the dinner. Did he go to the meeting? He claims to not have sent the message, therefore he wouldn't have gone to that dark corridor. I believe he tells the truth. Therefore, he did not go. Further, no one can identify the legionnaire who delivered the message much less which of the hundred or so legionnaires currently in residence may have held a grudge against Priscus. Calculate the chances of discovering the facts about this? Then there is the difficulty of the dagger."

"The dagger?"

"If you are an angry legionnaire and you hear about an opportunity to dispatch your Centurion that afternoon, how do you manage to steal the Prefect's dagger the day before?"

"Oh."

"We must dig deeper, Prefect, but I assure you we are making progress."

An hour later and two hours past the time Gamaliel had his noon meal, the two men emerged from the bowels of the Antonia Fortress. Gamaliel seemed deep in thought, Loukas serene and detached. Neither noticed the High Priest bearing down on them like a heavy-laden merchant ship riding a following wind. He pulled up in front of Gamaliel and jabbed the Rabban in the chest with a stubby finger.

"We will have him this day," he announced.

"*Ha Shem,* High Priest, dare I ask who is to be had?"

"The Galilean, Rabban, Yeshua. As I predicted, one of his men has sold him out."

"A triumph for you, no doubt. This concerns me how, exactly?"

"A trial, Rabban. We will try him and you must preside."

"Very well, but that can't happen for days, weeks even. The Law ascribes certain rights to the accused, to counsel, for example, and there must be witnesses who are reliable. You know the lesson from the Book of Susannah. And then there is Passover to celebrate. It will be a week or two at the earliest before any of this can be done."

The High Priest looked crestfallen. "That long? Surely not."

"Absolutely."

"But by then, the Prefect will be gone."

"Gone? You think they will have him off to Rome. Not if I can help it."

"Rome? Whatever are you talking about? He will have returned to Caesarea Maritima. I need his judgment now."

"His judgment? Whatever for? The transgressions you accuse the rabbi of fall within the jurisdiction of the Sanhedrin, not Pilate's."

"What? Yes, well, never mind. Now that I think about it, I believe that a preliminary hearing would be more in order."

"A hearing? What sort of hearing?"

"The Sanhedrin can hear about the blasphemous things he's accused of and then proceed in an appropriate manner."

"I see. In any event, you will call on me if and when the time is set for a trial?"

"You may count on it."

The High Priest did not sound very convincing. Gamaliel cocked an eyebrow. The High Priest scurried off.

"Well, let's hope that this is the end of conversations about what's-his-name, the itinerant rabbi from the Galilee," Loukas said.

"Yeshua. Yes, let us so hope."

YOM SHLISHI

Chapter XXVII

Yehudah had come to be known to his comrades as the Thief. For some it meant only that he had an uncanny way of producing large results at small cost. Later it would carry a darker connotation. He had not slept, and the sun glimmered on the edge of the horizon. Another dawn to contemplate, only this time from a crude cell in the depths of the High Priest's dwelling. Perhaps this dawn would be his last. Somehow, everything he'd worked on, his plans, hopes, certainties, had soured like wine to vinegar. What had he missed? Clearly, there were people of influence who wished to help. He thought he'd understood them. He'd been wrong—dangerously wrong and instead of helping, he had brought on the destruction of the one man, the only man, who'd ever called him friend.

After the fiasco with the ass on the Mount of Olives, Yeshua had proceeded to cause a near riot in the court of the money exchangers. It had been awful, outrageous even. Yehudah smiled at the memory. Coins had clanged and skittered across the stone floor and into corners. Opportunists scrambled after them shoving and cursing one another. Tables overturned, doves flapped to the ceiling, lambs bleated and Peter, whose years of hauling nets has given him arms like posts, tossed anyone with designs on the Master out the door like so many barrels of salt fish. His own contribution had been less dramatic, but he'd gotten in a few good licks and had managed to escape in time to avoid the Temple Guards and avoid arrest. It had been an amazing departure from Yeshua's usually serene nature. It had been exciting. In retrospect, it had been ill advised. It seemed Yeshua was determined to provoke the Temple party. Had he wanted them to arrest him all along? Why had he done those things just now when the movement seemed to have gained momentum? Such a stupid waste. Well, he had done so and the consequences followed as day follows night, or the other way round in his case. They were here in prison waiting for the officials to determine their end. Exile, proscription, a trial for blasphemy he'd heard the High Priest mutter.

In spite of assurances that his name and role would not be revealed, he'd been forced to lead the Temple Guards to the olive grove and betray Yeshua. At the last moment he'd hoped that, with the second sense Yeshua seemed to possess, he would feel the approaching threat and escape. Wouldn't you think a man who could raise the dead would be aware of impending danger? If he had, then all this crashing around in the darkness would have been for nothing. But that had not been the case. Rounding a clump of figs, there he was. Yeshua had looked right at him and knew. "Yehudah, is it with a kiss, then, that I am to be handed over?" he'd said and added, "Do what you must do." So, almost as if it had been preordained, he'd kissed Yeshua, and the guards seized his arms. Some of the others rushed in and there for a brief moment chaos reigned. Peter drew the sword he kept tucked in his tunic and took a swipe at one of the guards. Had the old man really believed that he could lead a group of fishermen and their odd-lot companions and beat back armed and armored guards?

Yeshua had raised his hands and everyone froze in place. "Why here, High Priest?' Yeshua said. "Why this way? I have been out and about in the city and in plain sight. You could have asked anyone where I might be found and arrested me. Yet, here you are in the dark and in the small hours of the morning when darkness is deepest. And so the dark, not the light, is your preference, is it not?" It had been a very good question, but the more important one would have been, "Why, Yehudah, why you and why now?" Indeed, why had it been him and not one of the others? Any of them could have fallen into this trap the Temple people laid. Why not Simon, the hot headed Zealot? He would have been the logical choice, or Tomas, whose belief in the mission seemed to waver from one crisis to the next. But no, it had to be "the Thief." So now all sat waiting for the doom Caiaphas has planned. Yehudah couldn't bring himself look at Yeshua.

The middle of the week and Gamaliel had reached a point in his investigation only marginally closer to solving the murder than when he'd started. Progress made certainly, but new questions to be asked. What do the wits say? Two paces forward, one back. Still, one thing seemed certain, the visitors from Rome had an interest in taking the Prefect back with them in a few days time. Before they parted, Loukas said he would have a good think on what he had heard. For Loukas, a "good think" usually involved large quantities of wine, so the probability of his arriving at the meeting place on time seemed slim.

The High Priest called on him early. Not a welcome sight. Binyamin ushered him in, and Gamaliel offered him some cool water.

"Good morning, Gamaliel, *Ha Shem*. You will be pleased to know we took the Galilean into custody last night."

"What makes you think I am pleased at that? I am not. I have disputed this point with you for nearly three years. I could not have been clearer. The man is radical and unorthodox, but at the same time, harmless. So now what? You have him you say? I do not care, High Priest. I have important things on my mind at the moment truly and—"

"Gethsemane, Rabban, you should have been there."

"No, High Priest, I should not. If you are planning to put this man on trial in a few weeks, then I, as one of his judges, should not have had any contact with him and certainly not have taken part in his arrest."

"Nonsense. You are splitting hairs, as usual. You need to know this. You know Gethsemane?"

"No."

"It is one of those newly planted olive groves in the Kidron Valley. Because the cuttings are still tender, the owner of the plot does not allow pilgrims to camp there, so it remained mostly deserted. When we arrived—"

"High Priest, I do not wish to hear this."

"Bear with me, Rabban. You will see. My telling will help you understand."

"But I do not wish to understand."

"Only the Yehudah person…that's the disciple I told you about, the one who sold his teacher to us for a year's wages—not that he will ever get to spend it—only he seemed to have any idea where to find Yeshua. "

"High Priest, I am sure that this is very interesting to you and others who share your dislike of Rabbi Yeshua, but it does not interest me. I have important things to attend to and must be off."

"Wait. Hear me out for a moment longer. Yeshua looked straight at me and said, 'Why this way? I have been in plain sight for days. No, here you are when darkness is deepest. You could have found and arrested me then.' I must confess to have been momentarily flustered by his scolding."

"As well you should have, and it is a pertinent question. Why *did* you wait until dark and so late to arrest him?"

"Prudence, Rabban, I was exercising prudence. He has many followers and at least one of them is a known Zealot. They are like rats. You see one Zealot, you have a hundred more lurking about nearby. So, we waited until most of his people were asleep, not dancing attendance on their hero. Now we will wring a confession from him that even you, Rabban, could not refute."

"You might and you might not. I will be surprised if he is so obliging. If you want him dealt with in any real way, you will have to do better than that."

"You can't know that."

"He does not strike me as just another of your wild-eyed radicals. He has *gravita*s, High Priest, and that distinguishes him from the rest."

The boy stood in the archway of a shop, ignoring the glare from its shopkeeper, watching and waiting. He had been tracking the Rabban for days now. Just when he thought he had the man's intentions figured out, something happened to cause him to hesitate. The High Priest had arrived, and they were having a long conversation about something. What was it between the High Priest and the Rabban? Were they both in it together? He'd been told the High Priest could not be trusted, so he guessed the two of them together made sense. He would have to report this.

The Rabban came out with the High Priest, but they set off in different directions. He followed Gamaliel. He did not fear being spotted today. There was no way the old man would guess who dogged his heels, not in this crowd, not dressed this way. His own mother would not recognize him today.

The Physician waited for him at the Hulda Gates. Where were they off to today? Pilate again? Should he try to reengage with the Prefect? How could he manage that? He really needed to find out what the two men had uncovered. He hesitated, glanced around, and in that brief moment of inattention, lost his prey in the crowd. He hurried in the direction he'd last seen them headed.

They were gone.

As Gamaliel suspected, Loukas showed the signs of a misspent night. His friend glared at him, so he said nothing. Loukas turned and jerked him into a shop and signaled for him to sit.

"What's this?"

"In spite of what you are thinking, I did not spend my evening with a skin of wine."

"I wasn't thinking that."

"You were."

Loukas proceeded to tell him of his relatively early night which had been interrupted in the early hours by a group of men seeking medical attention. Yakob had woken him and he'd spent the next two hours attending the group of men who'd fled up from the Kidron Valley where they had been involved in some sort of fracas. There had been an incident involving the Temple Guards they said. Some of the men had bad abrasions and cuts. They'd told him that guards had attacked them when they tried to defend their teacher or something. Loukas said he did not have the details as he was too busy applying poultices and bandages to listen. By the time they'd left, the sun was nearly up, and he'd given up hope of resuming his rest. Yakob had made him an early meal, and he had spent the rest of the morning trying to make sense of what Pilate told them the day before, and Gamaliel should not jump to conclusions based on his fatigued look.

"You don't believe me, do you?"

"Oh, but I do. I know what happened in the valley and why. Some of Rabbi Yeshua's minyan ended on your doorstep last night."

"Yeshua?"

"Caiaphas' favorite, yes. He had him arrested last night and there was a scuffle. So there, I do believe you. We must move on, Physician. I need to revisit Agon, and then there is one more stop I wish to make. What do you know about Greek drama? *Clytemnestra* for example"

"Greek drama? You jest."

Gamaliel shrugged and stepped into the crowd.

Chapter XXVIII

Three men sat in a rough semicircle and stared at the boy. *Menacing* would be the best descriptor. They told him to sit down and be still. He'd done so and now occupied a stool opposite them, mouth shut tight. The room had no window and only a small doorway let in air and light. Today, a rough fabric curtain covered it limiting both. A lamp set to one side on a plain plank table provided the only illumination. Its wick had been improperly trimmed and it sputtered and smoked. The air was close and reeked of unwashed men and burning oil. The boy pulled his frayed cloak closer in spite of the heat. He no longer knew what these men wanted or expected of him. He had done everything they'd asked yet he sensed he'd somehow failed them. How their failed plan could fall to him, he did not know, but he'd discovered that these men were not reasonable. Either way, no good could come from this gathering. The men murmured among themselves as if he were not sitting in front of them, as if he did not exist. Lately he had become accustomed to being treated as if he were invisible by men who ruled his life. But unlike the Prefect and his Roman friends, these men were not rich and powerful. They were hardly more elevated than he in the layered society in which they all struggled.

The discussion swirled around the effectiveness of assassinating one or more additional men. The boy assumed they were speaking of Gamaliel or possibly the High Priest. He wondered why those two. He could name half a hundred men, and a few women, who were more deserving of this group's justice. He'd spent enough time in the presence of the Prefect and his people to know who could and who could not be labeled a collaborator. But his opinion would not be solicited by these angry men.

He heard his name spoken and tuned his ears more sharply. They argued about his abilities. Could he be entrusted with a new assignment? What if he were captured? Would he betray them to the Romans? What assignment? Then he understood. They were arguing whether he could be trusted to slip a dagger into one or the other of the men about whom they'd just spoken. Was it the Rabban they wanted dead? Could he stab Gamaliel? Could he stab anyone? It is one thing to pretend to be someone else, to lie, steal, or arrange a meeting, quite another to assume the role of assassin. This had started because one of them had treated him with kindness—a rarity for someone like himself—but then it had spiraled out of control.

When Gamaliel reached the Souk, he sent Loukas off to the amphitheater with questions for the person who managed it. Loukas started to object. He had no interest in the theater. He considered it a poor substitute for the world of letters. He could not imagine how one could possibly mount the *Odyssey*, for example, on the stage or why anyone would want to. The stories that were acted out were either low comedy or bloody tragedies. *Clytemnestra*, for example, why had Gamaliel mentioned that piece? Murder and revenge. Gamaliel reminded him that because of his affectation in Greek dress and manners, he could pass as a pagan and gain entry to the inner workings of the company, and he had a question or two he wanted answered. Loukas heard him out and shuddered at the thought of mingling with people he considered lower in status than gladiators and tax gatherers, both of which he despised.

Gamaliel, in turn, entered Agon's shop once more. The jeweler's delight at seeing him soon disappeared when he heard what Gamaliel wanted from him. They argued for nearly an hour and then the shopkeeper relented and produced a wax tablet and began to write. He glowered at Gamaliel after each entry. Gamaliel merely shrugged and repeated his apologies for having forced the information from him but assured him it was for Israel and not Rome that he asked.

When Agon finished, Gamaliel thanked him. The jeweler nodded but said nothing. Gamaliel asked if he knew of a blade-smith, particularly one who specialized in creating dress daggers, the knife Romans called a *pugios*. Agon thought a moment and then gave him directions to two. Gamaliel once more reassured him that he had not betrayed anyone and might even have saved a life. He failed to mention that the life that might be saved was the hated Pontius Pilate.

The first bladesmith said he did indeed know the Prefect's dagger. He had fitted new leather to the hilt a year ago, but, no, he had not made it. He thought it might have come from His-pania originally. Gamaliel next asked if he were commissioned to do so, could he reproduce it and was told he could but he would need the original to copy, and he couldn't guarantee the quality of the iron. The bladesmiths in Hispania had secrets when they worked the iron that so far no one else had been able to replicate. Bronze, on the other hand, he could match easily. He couldn't remember from which metal the Prefect's *pugio* had been fabricated.

"How long would it take? If I had the original to work with, two weeks, perhaps sooner."

The second bladesmith told him the same thing. Two weeks? That would require more than short term planning. No clear answer to the time of premeditation. But the question remained: who lifted the original from the Prefect's effects? Gamaliel thanked him and went in search of Loukas.

The boy relaxed. They weren't asking him to kill anyone, only to maintain his surveillance. They were not happy that he had lost Gamaliel and the Physician, earlier. He was told to resume his post that evening and stay on it until he heard from them.

There was no mistaking the consequences that would follow if he were to fail again. The room was now filled with smoke, and the boy suppressed the urge to cough. It would not do to attract attention.

The fact that the boy had not known what the Rabban had planned for the hippodrome they thought most unfortunate, although the fact that the Rabban had apparently killed one of the Roman's favorite horses pleased them. The Roman's horses, women, and riches were hated equally. One of their number reported what the Prefect had told Gamaliel the previous day. The boy had not known that his ears were not the only ones busy in Pilate's lair. Pilate had revealed to the old man that the dagger, his *pugio*, went missing the day a woman visited his apartments. Did the Prefect know who took it and why? If he did, there would have be no meeting here this day. Multiple crucifixions, but no meeting.

Loukas had less luck with Mordekay, the amphitheater manager. He turned out to be one of those men who, despite his very Hebrew name, had suspect origins as to his birth and lineage, and whose affected demeanor bordered on the insufferable. No cast members were about when Loukas arrived. He found Mordekay lounging in the staging area inspecting some masks. He did not look happy. Loukas supposed he did not like the condition of the masks which were badly worn, one or two past redemption.

The manager started at the sight of Loukas. Jumpy sort of man, Loukas thought. Jumpy people, he believed, were usually guilty of something. What did this gilded lily hide, he wondered. He asked him about players and if any were missing. The man hesitated and then said, no there weren't any missing players. Loukas knew he lied. His knowledge of the theater might be thin, but he knew that players were always going missing. Loukas asked about the night of the banquet. Had any of his players been hired to perform, perhaps? Were any hired the day before, perhaps, to amuse the Prefect's wife. No? Could Mordekay suggest anyone else in the area who might supply players, singly or in a group to entertain at a banquet? No, he could not. Would he like to have a talk with the legal authorities about these matters? Was there anything he would rather not come to light in that regard?

The man's panic was very real, and Loukas tried to exploit it and asked his questions again. He received the same answers. Loukas realized Mordekay, quite out of character, told the truth. He shifted to the other topic Gamaliel wanted him to explore. Were any trappings, costumes, that sort of thing missing? Mordekay hemmed and hawed and then conceded that yes, some items were, but that was not unusual. Actors, he said, were never far from their craft. They would turn up eventually. Any that he might have noticed especially? A pause and eyes rolled right to left—a bad sign—finally, yes, some outfits that might be worn to designate an upper class servant and a soldier, Anything else? Another pause accompanied with the glazed look that signified another lie and a shake of the head. One would think an actor would be a more accomplished liar. At least he had something to tell Gamaliel. Loukas thanked his reluctant witness and left for home. Gamaliel would most likely be waiting for him in his courtyard.

The sun had nearly set when he exited through the Sheep Gate and made his way down the hill to his home. As he'd expected, Gamaliel waited for him in his usual place under the olive tree.

Chapter XXIX

Cassia Drusus reclined on his couch and contemplated his supper. Its aroma resembled nothing he'd experienced and differed in ways he could not describe but which, nonetheless, caused him to tilt his head up and to the side to move his nose away from his plate. The dish held food he preferred not to identify even though he recognized it for what it was—goat, lentils, and some sort of glazed fruit. Even the local *garum* didn't help. He'd already sent the young fig leaves sautéed in olive oil away. Jerusalem did not have access to the sorts of delicacies he'd expected. These strange people abhorred so many things that normal people savored. For example, he hadn't seen, much less tasted, an oyster since he'd left Rome, and you could forget anything even resembling pork. They ate goat and mutton, chicken and beef—peasant food, and they expected him to eat it. A swan…now that was a meal, glazed with fruit. Some eels washed down with a decent Ligurian wine—that was dining, not this overcooked country fare. The local wine tasted like rotten fruit or tree bark, that is, if it hadn't already turned. The bread would break a tooth if you weren't careful and the rest… he shook his head and grimaced.

The Tribune occupied the couch opposite and swirled wine in his cup. "You are not happy, Cassia. Is it the food, the company, or the place?"

"All of those and the idiocy that brought us here, Tribune."

"We cannot do much about any of them and especially not the 'idiocy.' The Steward tells me, that during the feast to their god, or whatever it is they are about to celebrate, there will be no women available either. The place is worse than Germania in the winter."

"Or Britannia in any season."

"I don't care how long these people have existed as a Nation, I have had more comfortable evenings in a tent, in the winter, eating bear meat and roots than in this dreary Fortress."

"That sums up the greater portion of my problem, Tribune, but not all of it."

"What then?"

"This celebration they have, Passover, is nearly on us. The Prefect is here to represent the Emperor. We have removed him from public view."

"And? He is arrested. He murdered Aurelius Decimus. What is the problem?"

"He has certain ceremonial duties to perform. If he does not appear at whatever time and place where he is expected or, worse, never appears at all, questions will be raised. Answers will be suggested. Rumors will fly and people may think that because the Emperor's representative is absent, the Empire is somehow vulnerable."

"That is nonsense. They have only to look around them. We have legionnaires out in full force. How does that make us vulnerable? No, you worry too much, Drusus."

"I don't think so. These people place great store in events progressing in predictable ways. If the sequence is altered or broken, they become restless. The more radical among them will form a wrong impression about the state of things and we could have violence. It is of no importance that our soldiers are deployed in force if a riot starts. You cannot tell me that those icy men you brought with you will hesitate to thrust their swords into the belly of anyone who so much as frowns at them. That can only make things worse. We dare not allow bloodshed on their holy day. You saw the letters Rufus carries. The Senate is angry at Pilate for allowing things to get out of hand in the past. Imagine what those patricians will say if we, acting in lieu of the Prefect, allow it to happen in his stead?"

"What are you suggesting?"

"Pilate is not going anywhere. There is no easy flight path off this hill. We should allow him to perform his duties in the days ahead. Then, if anything goes wrong, if confrontations or violence occurs, he, not you or I, will be to blame."

"That is very clever of you, Cassia, but will Pilate go along? He is not brilliant, but he is not stupid either. He will see right through it."

"As you say, he is not stupid and, more importantly, knows the limits he can go to with these people. He is a proud man. He will acquiesce because not to do so will deprive him of one more chance to strut in front of these wretched people. Oh, he will do it, never fear. He will not be able to resist."

"Then set that in place, but he is not to leave the Antonia Fortress. We will assign two of the men you describe as 'icy' to be with him at all times."

"Done."

"I am not finished. Tell him also that in four days time we leave for Rome, and barring a miracle, he will be in our company."

"What shall we do if he is able to find a surrogate to shoulder the blame for the murder of Aurelius?"

"He goes anyway."

"On what charge?"

"We revert to our original orders."

Gamaliel made his way homeward in the twilight. Lights flickered through the windows of the Great Hall of the Sanhedrin. He wondered what that meant. He had no knowledge of a scheduled meeting and no one had approached him about there being one. Something was afoot. He brushed aside the thought that formed in his mind as to what that might be. He had his own problems to attend to. He shrugged and moved on.

Loukas walked with him a ways and reported his findings about the missing bits and pieces at the amphitheater and the possibility its actors had gone missing. Gamaliel had expected as much, although he could not say why. The missing dagger, he told Loukas, meant that the patrician's murder had been premeditated and over time. He filled the Physician in on what he'd learned from Agon and from the bladesmiths, which pretty much confirmed his notion that the murder had been premeditated. Finally, as the sun began to slip behind the city walls in the west, he'd bid Loukas goodnight. He would send a messenger if they needed to meet on the morrow. At the moment he needed time to think. He needed to study the branches on the thorny tree of information that had sprung up in the last days and then do some judicious pruning. They suffered from having too little and too much. A proper paradox.

He greeted Binyamin who scolded him for his lateness and laid his meal. It had turned cold, but Gamaliel hardly noticed. He picked at his food and for the hundredth time that week wondered if engaging in this business with the Prefect had anything at all to do with the Lord's will for him—for either of them. Was he really *iustus* as Pilate claimed, Gamaliel the just man, or had he succumbed to the sin of pride? He pushed away his plate and retired to his reading room. The Isaiah Scroll still lay on his desk. It had come partly unrolled. He glanced at the exposed passage.

> *Behold my servant, whom I uphold; mine elect, in whom my soul delights; I have put my spirit upon him: he shall bring forth judgment to the Gentiles. He shall not cry, nor lift up, nor cause his voice to be heard in the street. A bruised reed shall he not break, and the smoking flax shall he not quench: he shall bring forth judgment unto truth. He shall not fail nor be discouraged, till he has set judgment in the earth: and the isles shall wait for his law.*

Gamaliel frowned and reread the passage several times. Though he would probably never admit it publically, he believed that a prophet's writings were to be understood situationally. That is, the book's words were to be understood by their reader to the extent that the circumstances which occupied his thoughts and energies at that moment resonated with the teaching. Passages that did not match them, did not do that. And frequently a passage that fit one set of circumstances on one day would miraculously fit a diametrically different set on the next. He could not teach so flexible an interpretation of Holy Writ to his students or state it publicly. Indeed, he hesitated to think it himself. But he held to it.

Since the scroll had been rolled shut earlier, but now lay open to reveal that passage to him, he wondered what the Lord intended. Obviously, He wanted him to see it. The possibility of the scroll opening by itself never occurred to him. He had fastened it himself. Binyamin had no interest in scripture and no reason to enter the room, much less unloose the tie. Gamaliel pressed his palms to his temples. What did it mean?

Justice. Whether he wished to or not, whether he would suffer for it or not, whether he succeeded or not, his calling was to pursue justice irrespective of the consequences to himself or the Nation.

He stood like that for a long moment and then retired to his bed chamber.

YOM REVI'I

Chapter XXX

Binyamin woke Gamaliel early. A visitor, he said. An important person waited and insisted on seeing the Rabban at once. Who? Binyamin muttered a name which Gamaliel did not catch. Binyamin left before he could ask him to repeat it. Gamaliel eased out of his bed and did his best to make himself presentable. He should have gone straight into the house and berated Binyamin for disturbing the morning routine. He had not had his morning prayers, his breakfast, or his ablutions. What sort of visitor could demand his immediate presence? Who stood in such a lofty position that Binyamin would disrupt the day in such a manner?

Josef of Arimathea waited for him in his great room. He looked worried.

"*Ha Shem,* Josef. This visit must be of great importance for you to be up and about so early. Can I offer you some refreshment? I have not had my morning meal. Will you join me?" Without saying so, Gamaliel wanted the old man to know he'd inconvenienced him.

"My deepest apologies, Rabban, but it is a matter of great urgency that brings me here. I pray the Lord and you will forgive me."

"Urgency? What has happened?" Gamaliel had a feeling he was not going to like the answer. He did not know why, but in his experience bad news never traveled alone. He had Pilate's problems and he guessed he was about to be handed another. A vision of the High Priest flashed before his eyes. Rabbi Yeshua had been apprehended and the High Priest said he had a plan.

"Caiaphas has arrested Yeshua. He is—"

"I know who he is, the rabbi from Nazareth. The High Priest has been bending my ear about him for years. I know he arrested him. What new information do you have for me?"

"That is just it. He has no grounds. The arrest does not conform to the limits of the Law. He is acting alone in this. I warned him and he—"

"Slow down, Josef. First, he can detain anyone if he believes the person in question has crossed the line in terms of blasphemy, for instance. I believe he does in this case. I have told him I believe he is mistaken, but he will not hear it."

"There, you see. He intends to put Yeshua on trial today."

"Josef, I take it, listening to the passion in your voice, that you are a supporter of this rabbi?"

"Not I alone, Rabban. There are others."

"Very well, then know this. Caiaphas cannot try anyone. That is the business for the Court and I, with a panel of senior rabbis, must preside. Also, even if there were to be a trial, it cannot happen in so short a time. There is evidence to be gathered, witnesses to be interviewed, and the accused has the right to representation and time to prepare. No, Josef, there will be no trial anytime soon. Caiaphas told me he would only have a hearing. He can do that, if he wishes."

"He maintains it is a trial, and he will have it today. You must come."

"I cannot do that, Josef. If there is to be a trial, I must sit as judge. To hold a trial on this kind of notice would make it and any findings forthcoming invalid. As such, it violates the rule of Law and because of that, I will not attend. Also, if I were to attend this gathering which Caiaphas bills as a hearing and if there were to be a trial later, I would not be able to judge the merits of the case impartially. I must not have my judgment biased by what is said in the hearing. Since a hearing is the only thing he can authorize, I am limited. So, no, I will not attend."

"What shall I do to stop the High Priest?"

"Again, speaking from my experience with the man, you can do nothing to stop him. You should remind him of what I just said about the rights of the accused, and if you want more leverage to slow this thing down, remind every witness he produces about the penalties perjury carries. That may soften or alter some of their testimony."

It took Gamaliel another half hour to calm Josef down. He finally left to attend Caiaphas' trumped-up hearing. Gamaliel did his best to reorder his morning into something approaching the norm. When he had finished, he set out for Loukas' house. He'd originally planned to send a messenger to Loukas and ask the Physician to meet at his home, but time had slipped away from him and the possibility of endless interruptions by Yeshua's or Caiaphas' supporters demanding he render an opinion or a judgment, attend the gathering, or some combination of the two, convinced him he should make himself scarce. He told Binyamin that he should inform all callers the Rabban was neither available nor at home. If they insisted on seeing him, they were to wait in the garden. He made sure Binyamin had the instructions firmly in mind and left.

Gamaliel ran into Loukas in the street, apparently on the way to Gamaliel's home.

"*Ha Shem,* Loukas. You are well met. I cannot stay at my house today."

"Cannot, why ever not?"

He explained the difficulties created by the High Priest's actions. Loukas smiled and shook his head. He found Caiaphas' antics concerning the Galilean rabbi a constant source of amusement. He suggested to Gamaliel that it might make a good farce for the theater company, and perhaps they should drop by the amphitheater and suggest it to the players. Gamaliel did not share the Physician's sense of the humor.

"Rome already has a low opinion of the Nation. More ridicule in their theater could only make things worse. Besides, you said yourself that there are no players in residence."

A legionnaire stood at the portal which before had provided access to Pilate and to the Fortress. He held up his hand and refused the two men entry. Gamaliel explained he had a commission from the Prefect himself. The soldier only stared and repeated his refusal. Surely, Gamaliel thought, the Prefect had not been removed from office and locked away somewhere. Worse, was he already on his way to Rome?

"Let us retreat and regroup," Gamaliel said and turned to leave.

Loukas stared up the steps that led to the wide plaza that faced the Temple. "Don't you want to know what has happened to the Prefect?"

"Certainly."

"Look up, Rabban. Our Prefect is in place. Something has happened and he is set free. You can simply climb the stairs and there you are."

"Now that is interesting. I would like to know the how of that, but to approach him in an open manner could compromise both our investigation and me. Our best advice would be to bide our time. If the Prefect has been exonerated by some other device, so much the better, and we are done. If all is lost, we are also finished. It only matters if his situation somehow sits at the midpoint."

"Sits in the middle of what?"

"Exoneration or certain death. We must wait until we know which it shall be and that, in turn, will tell us what to do next. Now, Loukas, without drawing attention to yourself, I want you to scan the Temple Mount and tell me if anyone is acting suspiciously."

"Pardon? Suspicious?"

"I have the impression we are being watched. I cannot say why I believe it, but I believe the boy is tracking us like a lion following a herd of sheep."

"The boy? You mean Marius? I would hardly call him a lion."

"Point taken, like a lamb looking for his mother, but tracking nonetheless. Now your back is to the Fortress. Just scan the crowd and tell me what you see."

"You're not serious."

"I am. Tell me."

Loukas sighed and let his gaze pan across the crowded Temple Mount. "You do realize the futility of this exercise. The place is choked with people. How can you expect me to pick out a suspicious person in this melee?"

"Crowds can distract you, but you must learn to discount them. Most of these people are here for a reason. They will move purposefully. They head to the Temple with their sacrifices, or they return. They engage in conversations or listen to one of the numerous rabbis on the porches. What you are looking for is someone with apparently no purpose at all. He, or maybe she, will be alone or mixed in a crowd but clearly not a part of it."

"I see. With that in mind, I have four candidates for you. None of them is the boy."

"He will have altered his appearance."

"If you say so. Very well, here are your 'suspicious' people. First, there is a woman by the wall over to your left. She is not looking at us. She seems to be absorbed in one of the guards. A plausible occupation for one so young, I should say. Second, about halfway to the Temple on a straight line from here there are three men who appear to be someone's servants pretending to have a conversation. And finally, ten cubits further along, there is a tall legionnaire who seems out of place. He looks too old to be in the Emperor's service, and why would a soldier be lounging against a fountain instead of patrolling or standing guard?"

"There, you see, you can sort through a crowd and spot possible problems. Now let us wander into the Souk and see if any or all follow us."

Chapter XXXI

Pilate could scarcely believe his good fortune. One day he suffered the humiliation of house arrest in the depths of the Antonia Fortress like an ordinary felon, and the next he was fully restored to his position. True, the Tribune had qualified his return to the bright light of respectability with stringent conditions. He could not leave the Fortress. He could not speak to anyone outside his official duties. He had not been cleared of the charge of murder and because of that, assuming no evidence of his innocence would be forthcoming, he would soon be placed on a ship bound for Brundisium and thence, via the Appian Way, directly to Rome or, more likely, to Capua, Neapolis, Capri, and thence to the Emperor. Either way, his future did not look bright. But for the moment, he could revel in his restoration.

Any other man would have been humbled by this arrangement, but as he'd announced to Rufus after the Tribune left, he'd "marched down that road before." He'd added, "After all, skirting compromising situations defined how politics at the highest levels usually played out in Imperial Rome."

As a man trained in the military, he understood a flanking maneuver as well as the next. Somehow he would need to find a way around this current mess. Luckily for him, his enemies did not know his arsenal held a secret weapon, Gamaliel, the Hebrew with the genius for solving complex puzzles. That crusty old man would untangle his mess. He stopped short—Gamaliel.

He wouldn't know about the change in his status. He needed to get a message to the Rabban. Where was that boy? Where was Marius? By the gods if he found him he would give the ungrateful little….well, he'll get a thorough beating when he turned up. In the meantime, he had to contact Gamaliel. But how? The Physician. What was his name? Procula would know. He sent for his wife.

◇◇◇

Procula's maid shook her awake. Lately, the Prefect's wife had had trouble sleeping. That is, she could not find rest at night and because of that, dragged through the day in a daze, napping occasionally. When this happened and if the nap lasted more than an hour, she seemed barely sentient on awakening.

"Madam, the Prefect asks for you."

"What?"

"You have been summoned by your honorable husband."

"Summoned? By whom?"

"The Prefect."

"Who?"

"Your—"

"Yes, yes, I know. Don't be stupid. I know. Why does my husband want to see me? You do not know, do you? No, you don't. Where is he?"

"He is in the Great Hall, madam. He is meeting a delegation from some foreign place at the moment. He says to come in the east portal and wait on him there. Egypt."

"What?"

"The foreigners are from that place, Egypt, where they say there are huge horses that live in the rivers and will swallow whole boats if they venture too near."

"Don't be ridiculous."

"One of the new legionnaires told me, and he was posted there once."

"And you believed him. Legionnaires lie, Drusilla. It is their nature. That reminds me…What am I thinking about?"

"Madam?"

"Never mind. It would be wonderful if my husband had left a hint as to why he wishes to see me in the middle of the night."

"It is already the fifth hour, madam."

"For you it may be, but for me it is the middle of the night. Very well, fetch me something to drink. Some fruit juice, and make sure it is freshly made. If you don't consume it immediately, everything in this fly-blown country turns to wine or vinegar inside an hour."

The servant scurried off mumbling about Equestrian women and their peculiar tastes and what was wrong with apple juice which had fermented a bit? It added a tang that most people found quite pleasing.

"Have any of the Hebrews tried to contact him?" The Tribune leaned against the cool stones of the Great Hall wall and watched as Pilate greeted the newly arrived envoys from Egypt. He had to hand it to the Prefect, whatever else might be said about this man, he did know his job.

"Not so far. Do we care? He is as good as dead for the murder. Will Tiberius care very much why this man is destroyed?"

"Yes, the Emperor will. You must understand the man, Cassia. His reason for dispatching us here may seem bizarre, but we are speaking of the current Emperor and when he gets a thing in his head, it will nag at him until it is resolved. Some new, more pressing concern may push it aside, but he will not forget. So, irrespective of the murder business, it's best if we continue with the task he set for us initially."

"The whole idea is absurd, you know. And if we fail in that?"

"Well, I do not plan on visiting Capri's seaside rocks, and certainly not by falling on them from a great distance. If we must, we will invent something that will please the Emperor."

"There remains the possibility that there is no substance to the accusation."

"There is that. If we take that tack, it will be important we have incontrovertible proof."

"How likely is that?"

"We will say he murdered Aurelius because he had the necessary evidence we were sent to find. We could find a witness or two who would, for a few denari, testify to that as instructed. I would rather find something certain here, as unlikely as that may seem, but either way, we cannot risk displeasing Tiberius."

"Then we will have to keep looking. I have posted men outside to track that Jewish official. He may lead us somewhere yet. Did you hear the rumor that he murdered one of the horses stabled in the hippodrome? They say he called on that god of theirs and the horse just dropped dead in its tracks. These people do not approve of the races, I know, but that seemed a rash way to say so."

"Nonsense, their King built the hippodrome. How can they not like the races? Which horse?"

"Pegasus."

"Ah, just a rumor then. I visited that beast this morning and it is fine. The keeper said it had an attack of food poisoning—ate a bad apple or something—but it has recovered. That is the problem with trying to rule these people. They are so full of myth and mystery, one can't sort out reality from fiction."

Procula waited for her husband to complete the formalities with the Egyptian delegation. When he looked her way, she motioned to him. He excused himself from the crowd and strode over to her.

"What is his name?" he snapped.

"Whose name?"

"That Physician who came to question you."

"The Rabban's friend?"

"That one, yes."

"Let me think. It was a Greek name, I remember that. Lou... Lou...Loukas Something. Why don't you ask the Rabban the next time you see him?"

"That's just it. I can't ask him. Not officially, and I need to get a message to him somehow."

"Send that tiresome boy, what's-his-name."

"Marius has disappeared."

"Send a legionnaire to the Rabban directly."

"I am afraid all my troops are momentarily compromised. It seems this pair of hunting dogs the Emperor has set on me is relentless. I dare not use anyone from the Fortress."

"Well, Loukas is all I know. He told me he lived outside the walls past the Sheep Gate, wherever that is."

"That's a start. Send one of your women to the Sheep Gate and have her ask around. When she finds the Physician, have her say that the Prefect's wife wishes to see him."

"But I don't."

"I need to send the Rabban a message, woman, and I cannot be seen contacting him directly. The Physician will come to you, and you will deliver it to him, and then he will deliver it to the Rabban."

"Why not just give the girl the message to deliver and save the Loukas person the trip to the fort? Calling him in is not part of your Passover routine. It will attract notice."

"Very well, I will write it out. Send a servant who can't read."

"None of my servants can read. I can't read. Are you certain the Physician can?"

"He must write all the time. If he writes, he reads. Send the girl."

Chapter XXXII

As they turned the corner into the Souk near where three spice vendors plied their wares, Loukas stopped and stared straight ahead. Gamaliel pulled up and waited for an explanation.

"Now this is something new," Loukas muttered. "We've been followed before, a great many times, if you recall, but this has to be a first."

"As you say, we have been followed, many times. We have been followed, stalked, and observed, and by friend and foe alike. We could teach a short course in the art of being followed. If I didn't know better, I'd say following one or both of us has become the National pastime. Beyond that, I am sure you just said something meaningful. Are you telling me that we are under surveillance now?"

"More than that, not only followed, but we are being anticipated."

"Can we move along? If I am exposed to them for any period of time, some of these spices, especially the pepper, make me sneeze. What do you mean, we are being anticipated?"

Loukas stepped off. "We have someone who is not in our train, you could say, but rather he walks in front of us. I recognize him from the Temple Mount."

"A coincidence, surely."

"I don't think so. If you think about it for a moment, what better way to seem uninterested in a person's destination, than to walk in front of him?"

"I cannot see how that would work. Suppose we turned down this side street. How would our 'anticipator'…um, anticipate such a move?"

"Wait."

Loukas paused again and feigned an interest in some fabric hanging from a rack. He turned the material toward the light and glanced down the street behind them. He shook his head at the seller before he ventured out of the stall to negotiate a sale. He cleared his throat and resumed his stroll up the street.

"There is one behind who would take his place. We can test it, if you like. If we turn here, the one behind will work his way up to and then pass us. We will naturally assume he has had no interest because he has walked by. At the same time the one formerly in front of us will take up his position at the rear."

"That seems to be an inordinately complicated way of keeping us in sight. Who would go to such lengths?"

"These men have been tasked with this sort of thing many times, if I am not mistaken. Shall we see if I am right?"

"We turn here."

The two men made an abrupt turn down a side alley. Within moments a man brushed by them. He did not make eye contact.

"Not so skilled as I thought," Loukas said.

"How so?"

"If I were that man, I would have at least glanced at us, excused myself for having bumped into you and so on. As it was, he made himself noticeable by not doing so."

"You have become devious in your thinking lately, my friend."

"It is the company I keep."

"Aha. What else should I be seeing?"

Loukas repeated his act of inspecting some fabric. Gamaliel did the same.

"There, you see? The man who preceded us has now taken up the rear."

"And there is more. Behind him appears another very familiar face. Who is that woman and what interest has she in us?"

"Where?"

"Opposite the potter's stall. She faces away now."

Loukas risked a quick glance down the street. "It is the woman from the Mount as well. This is very confusing. Why would she want to follow us?"

"Perhaps she doesn't. Maybe her interest lies not with us, but with the men who follow us. Now, as long as we are busying ourselves with this dance of fools, is there anyone else in the mix? Where is your out-of-position legionnaire, for example?"

"That is a problem. Unless he is still in full regalia, I could not recognize him."

"Why ever not?"

"It is an axiom of observation that the most salient feature a person displays will be the recognition point. A beard, a hat, a limp, and so on. The legionnaire wore his *galea, greaves,* and *baldric,* for example. If he threw a cloak over that and left the helmet behind, I would not know him. A quick look in his direction back on the Mount meant I only saw the descriptors, you could say."

"His *caligae*? I can see how he might discard his headpiece and cover the rest, but surely he would not have had time to shed his boots and change his footwear."

"Point taken, but unfortunately in this crowd it is difficult to see feet. I will keep watch, though."

"With this much company it will be difficult finishing our business here. Who do you suppose these people report to?"

"I would venture to guess that the skillful observers, the alternating front and rear watchers are from the Fortress but not sent by Pilate. That leaves the visiting dignitaries. Why are they interested in us?"

"Perhaps they are not. Alternatively, maybe we are the point for their visit in the first place?"

"Sorry?"

"Is it possible that we have this all wrong, Loukas? Maybe the visit and the murder of the Roman official are coincidental. Suppose their real interest is to investigate us…me?"

"You? With respect, Rabban, what interest would they have in you?"

"I admit, it is unlikely, but consider how Pilate's problem plays out if we remove them from consideration."

"I see...or perhaps I do not. Are you saying we are nowhere in our search for the man's killer?"

"Not nowhere. We were nowhere before. Now we have fewer nowheres to consider."

"Does that even make sense? Never mind. What you mean is, we have eliminated several suspects."

"And more. We will rub out all sorts of plots and counterplots. Roman politics is about intrigue, Loukas. If we can steer clear of all that, perhaps we will have a clearer view of what really happened."

"This assumes you are the interest the visitors have, not Pilate."

"Maybe."

"But you just said—"

"I didn't say they were not interested in Pilate. I am sure they are. Why else would they be here? No, what I said was that the murder of Aurelius Decimus was coincidental, not part of the original equation. They are after Pilate for something. I just don't know what and somehow I am part of that interest. If I am correct, then the murder came as much a surprise to them as it did to Pilate."

"Very well. I will have to accept your assessment as I have no idea what you are talking about. Where are we going, by the way?"

"We were going to visit Agon again, but with this entourage of curiosity-seekers in our wake, it would be best if we find an alternate destination. Shall we visit the theater? I am certain that will make at least one of our followers very agitated."

"It will? Who?"

"One of them. Perhaps more than one as I muse on it. Come along, Loukas. We have work to do. Not the task I thought to do initially, but this is better."

◇◇◇

The two men made their way through the Souk, still crowded with visitors, pilgrims and a few in the crowd who held less than honorable notions about what was to happen over the next few days. Loukas trailed Gamaliel out of the side street and toward the amphitheater. It would be something of a walk as they were on the opposite side of the city. Gamaliel, he thought, puzzled him. How could he have not grasped the intricate following arrangement he, Loukas, had uncovered and then intuit that the theater would disturb someone behind them?

"The theater? I have to assume you have a reason, beyond agitating one of our pursuers, for going there." Gamaliel shrugged and smiled. "So, why did you ask me about *Clytemnestra* when you sent me there earlier?"

"I do not know much about Greek theater and less about the Roman version. It all seems rather decadent to me. However, I have an interest at the moment. That play, it's about a woman, isn't it?"

"Yes...well, not really. It is about Agamemnon's wife who murdered him and his prize, Cassandra, after his victory at Troy. According to the story, Zeus appeared to a girl, Leda, in the form of a swan, seduced and impregnated her. No easy task, but then it is a story. So, then she produced four offspring, Castor and Clytemnestra, and Helen and Polydeuces—"

"From two eggs. Is that right?"

"Ah...that sounds right. Greek mythology is a little complex and I don't quite know if the eggs were actual eggs or simply signified twins or...Never mind. Agamemnon and his brother married the two daughters: Agamemnon wed Clytemnestra, and Menelaus, Helen. Then Paris—"

"Enough. I don't need to hear the story, Loukas. I am sure it is fascinating in an absurd Greek way, only that Clytemnestra was a woman and there are other women in their plays?"

"Yes, certainly. Why would there not be? Women have a different status in Greek society than in ours. So, yes, there are many women in their dramas. *Antigone*, for example, is Creon's daughter and—"

"Yes, yes, but what do all those women have in common?"

"Well, they are tragic heroines. Their stubbornness or hubris leads to…well, not all are tragic. *Lysistrata* is a comedy about women who—"

"That is not what I am asking. Who plays these women in the theater?"

"Who?"

"Yes, who?"

Loukas shrugged. Sometimes, he thought, Gamaliel could be infuriatingly obtuse. Who indeed? "Shall we try to lose our friends?" he said and nodded at the street behind them.

"No. I don't think we want them to know that we know."

"Then to the amphitheater."

"Yes, but for a brief visit only. A comprehensive one will have to wait for another day. Let us take our entourage on a tour of the city. We will end at your house but by a circuitous route."

Chapter XXXII

Gamaliel and Loukas descended the gentle slope from the city toward Loukas' house. An agitated Sarai stood at his gate. She shifted her weight from one foot to the other, and looked up the street toward the Sheep Gate. Once she had them in sight, she rushed forward.

"Master, the Prefect's wife needs you to attend her. She sends a messenger with a scrap of papyrus." She handed him a crumpled and yellowed note.

"There is nothing on this."

"No sir, there is not. It seems the woman was so nervous the dampness of her hands washed away the script, but she said the message was very important and though she could not read, she heard the urgency in her mistress' voice."

"Urgent, how urgent? What has happened?"

"The messenger could not say. All she said to me was that you should go to the lady immediately."

"That is strange. Think. Rabban, we have been in the company of agents from the Fortress all day and no one approached us with any message."

"Not so strange. The message from the Prefect's wife and the surveillance are obviously neither related nor connected."

"Do you think the message is from Pilate and he uses his wife as a subterfuge?"

"That would be my guess. Off you go, then, Loukas. I do not think I will wait for you here. If our trackers are still in play, it would be best if they did not follow you to the Fortress. I will leave first. I am now persuaded they are interested in me, not you. I will take them along with me to my house. If the news is important, you can stop by tonight and tell me what it is. Otherwise, I shall call on you tomorrow. Delay a few moments." Loukas frowned. "Recite a psalm and then leave. Better make it a longish one. I am weary and the route to the Sheep Gate from here is all uphill. I need to sweep all of our new found friends into the city before you leave."

"And if they do not all go with you? What if their interest turns out to be me instead of you, or both of us? What then?"

"In that case we will at least divide them. Don't forget there were more than one set of them behind us today which implies several people wish to know what we are up to. And all of them still wait for you, or me, or both of us. Nevertheless, I am reasonably sure it is I who interests them. Still, you may be right. We will soon find out. Remember—recite a psalm."

Gamaliel turned and climbed back up the hill to the Sheep Gate and disappeared through it. Loukas began to mumble.

> *O God, the heathen are come into your inheritance;*
> *they have defiled your holy Temple; they have laid*
> *Jerusalem on heaps. The dead bodies of your servants*
> *have they given to be meat unto the fowls of the*
> *heaven, the flesh of your holy ones to the beasts of the*
> *earth. Their blood they have shed like water round*
> *about Jerusalem; and there was none to bury them…*

When he reached, *we will show forth your praise to all generations,* he stopped and glanced back up the street toward the gate. Except for a few people he recognized as his neighbors or at least local, the way to the gate was clear. Gamaliel had it right. Whoever these people were and whatever they were after, it concerned only the Rabban. He sent Sarai back into the house and retraced his steps up the slope and into the city and thence to the Antonia Fortress. It was time to find out what the Prefect needed to tell him, assuming it was he who bid him come and not his wife.

◇◇◇

Gamaliel did not hurry home. He knew Binyamin would not have his supper ready for another hour and he wanted time to pray. He would make a trip to his *mikvah* and then he would eat. He felt the presence of his watchers as he walked. He managed to ignore them. Surely they could not be happy about their day's work. He and Loukas had led them to the amphitheater, inspected the tower at the Joppa Gate and what was alleged to be David's tomb. They wasted at least two hours at that and then took their shadows to the Water Gate, the Golden Gate, and inspected at least a mile of wall. While he and the Physician could enjoy an occasional stop to visit a colleague or have refreshment, the men lurking behind them had to keep constantly on the alert. Loukas had them make another quick turn which forced the men who were working in tandem to change places once again. They debated and then discarded the idea of spending the afternoon doing that maneuver.

"If we do it too often," Gamaliel said, "they will know that we have found them out, and I really don't want that to happen. I want them to think we are sublimely ignorant of their presence and their work. I believe that if they deliver a message to their master or masters as the case may be, it will be that we were wandering about aimlessly, and they will find that suspicious because they have determined that we are up to something."

"What? Why would they think that?"

"Why else follow someone except you suspect they are about to do something revealing. Therefore they will assume that all this traipsing about has a significance that they must now decipher. It will keep them off balance for hours. So, walk on. We need to give them some things to discuss."

Gamaliel had finished his supper when Loukas arrived. He refused Gamaliel's offer of some lamb and greens but accepted a chalice of wine.

"What news from the fort?"

"It is confusing. As you suspected, Pilate sent the message, not his wife. Pilate, it seems, has been restored to his position, but the charges of murder have not been dropped. He may not leave the premises except to perform his official duties. His tormenters, the Tribune in particular, made it clear that he will be going back to Italia with them in a few days. Pilate, oddly, seems perfectly content with this arrangement. It is a puzzle."

"Indeed. Did he have a message for me? Did he remember anything useful? More importantly, have we been dismissed from our investigation?"

"No, to the last. He wonders what happened to Marius and if we knew anything about the boy's disappearance. His wife, on the other hand, seemed quite animated and queried me at some length about that horse. I claimed we knew nothing about the beast. The horse lives, by the way, no thanks to you."

"We will celebrate the horse's resurrection later. I know the Latins do love their animals, even dogs, which is incomprehensible to me. Indeed, only Arabs seem to hold horses in higher esteem. So, he doesn't know what happened to the boy either. That is interesting, don't you think? Why do you suppose he ran away?"

"The boy? Who knows? Too many beatings, too little food. I can tell you from personal experience that slavery is a hard life even when your master is kind. I can't imagine that life in the Prefect's house could be easy."

"I know you are acquainted with slavery, so tell me, did that boy seem to be living a hard life, as you understand it?"

Loukas sipped his wine and stared hungrily at the side of lamb on the plate.

"Perhaps a slice. Do you mind?" Loukas cut a generous slab from the haunch and chewed a moment. He swallowed and emptied his cup. Gamaliel refilled it.

"No, he did not look like someone who had had a particularly hard life."

"No, I would have guessed the same. Not easy, but not hard either. Another question for you, who would be in charge of the servants in the Fortress?"

"If Pilate's house is managed like any other, he would have a steward. That man would manage all of the household accounts and keep track of the servants."

"When the Prefect arrives in Jerusalem, his household staff would be merged with the local one, that is to say, the Fortress staff, would it not?"

"Yes, undoubtedly."

"So, in the confusion of his arrival and the additional chaos caused by the arrival earlier of the entourage from Rome..." Gamaliel's voice trailed off. He poured himself another small measure of wine and drank. "I wonder."

"Wonder what? Are you suggesting that in the confusion one of the Tribune's men, or in this case, the boy, managed to infiltrate the Prefect's household?"

"That is one possibility, yes."

"One? There are others?"

"Oh yes, several."

"And they are?"

"Too soon, Loukas, my friend. I need to think about it some more. So, what did we learn about the theater this morning?"

"It was nearer noon and the answer is we learned nothing except that drama, whether Greek or Roman, is not popular in this city and the theater itself is used primarily for lectures, large meetings, and speech giving."

"That's all?"

"What else should I have learned? Dare I ask?"

"Actors, players"

"At the moment, there are none to speak of. A few itinerant players who must maintain themselves with other employment, the nature of which I'd prefer not to discuss."

"Yes, but picture how the plays are presented when they are performed, Loukas—the broad *pulpitum* and the *scaena* behind it, the *auditorium* in front, and the actors, actors in their costumes. A purple costume means the player is supposed to be a rich man while a red costume indicates a poor one. Boys wear striped togas, soldiers short cloaks. A yellow robe means the character is a woman and a short tunic means the player is a slave. Then a yellow tassel means the character is supposed to be a god. So very convenient. It's easy to identify your friends and your enemies in the theater. Then there are the masks. Think about it, in the play, it is one's appearance and mask that defines character, not the person wearing them, or in the case of the mask, holding it aloft. I find that most interesting, don't you?"

"You know something, don't you?"

YOM CHAMISHI

Chapter XXXIV

Caiaphas stretched and contemplated the dawn of a new day. A day in which he would revel in the success of the previous night and plan the next steps. The hearing had not been easy. The Yehudah person had made a poor witness. He'd been happy enough to accept the silver, but hesitated when it came time to betray his teacher. And then, there was the usual second guessing by revisionist thinkers, dithering in uncertainty. "What is Law?" they had asked, as if it were debatable. He'd listened to the undecided among them and some others as they wavered and questioned protocol. He'd let them. It was all part of the plan. He had time on his side, time and history.

If there was one thing Jews live with every hour of every day, it is their history, that nagging sense that the Lord is constantly watching and judging them from time eternal. They are convinced that if they err from the path He has set for them, judgment will follow, sooner or later, perhaps, but inevitably. Caiaphas believed that if reason failed, the sweep of history would convict. One way or another he knew he'd succeed and he had. He'd only to wait until everyone had their say and then he'd stood and addressed them, relieved that Gamaliel was not there to interrupt him or sway the meeting away from its necessary conclusion. For, it was necessary that the Galilean be taken care of. Of that he had no doubts.

When the meeting had worn down and the participants were

weary with what seemed endless testimony and debate, he'd begun his summation.

"We are given leave by our overlords, the Romans, to practice our faith as our fathers have, as we have through history. We may continue our sacrifices, our feasts, and worship, enforce our Law. In return, our conquerors maintain the roads, keep the peace, and protect us. For this, they collect taxes and extract tribute. It is not a situation we like or wish to continue. But the reality is, they are here and they will be here for a long time to come. Moreover, if they wish to, they could crush us like eggs. All of you have witnessed their willingness to strike out for the most trivial cause."

Here he'd paused and pointed at Yeshua.

"Now, along comes this misguided man, besotted with messianic zeal. He started a riot in the holiest place on earth, in the Temple itself." That part, Caiaphas knew was a stretch. The riot occurred in the area somewhat removed from the Temple where the money exchangers plied their trade. Still, he liked the image it evoked. "He threatens to bring the Temple down. He says 'Not one stone will stand on another!' He makes a mockery of the Prefect by entering the city riding on an ass with a reed for a scepter. Hundreds joined him in this foolishness. Do you suppose the Romans will put up with this? For how long? Is it even likely? You know they are a race with little patience for acts of disrespect and none at all with civil unrest. What this Pilate, whose reputation for cruelty is legend, is capable of. Even now Jewish blood stains the pavement outside these very doors, spilled by him and his soldiers."

At this point in his speech, Caiaphas had travelled the length of the room and stood directly in front of Josef of Arimathea. Fixing him with a glare he hoped others would view as righteous anger, he continued.

"But, as great a threat as that is, there is an even greater one we must address."

Caiaphas paused again, hearing his words resound off the stone walls, hoping they would carry the day. No longer was he to be seen as just a persecutor of country rabbis. Now he stood for the Nation, perhaps its only champion.

"Blasphemy! Oh, I know what has been said, 'It is not unlawful to claim to be a messiah.' That is correct. In the past, many have, some do now, and no doubt, many will in the future."

When Caiaphas realized he'd just echoed Gamaliel's words to him earlier, he'd almost tripped over the remainder of what he planned to say. Gamaliel would not approve of having his own argument used against him, although Caiaphas guessed he'd appreciate the irony.

"But this man is no ordinary prophet claiming to speak for the Lord. No, he claims to speak *as* the Lord. Understand, when he says he is His son, he does not mean, as we do, that we are all children of our Creator, he means His son, quite literally. In the Pagan world, he would be claiming status as a demigod. You can appreciate, then, the grave position he put us in. As more and more people are drawn into this spider's web, I fear swift and certain judgment will come down on us. Consider when in our past when we strayed from the path of righteousness. How did *Ha Shem* deal with us then? Dare we forget the Philistines, the Amelekites, or Babylon? Listen, it is the Passover. Shall we forget the captivity or wandering in the desert for four generations because our fathers worshipped a golden calf instead of *Ha Shem*? How, I ask you, how will He deal with us now?"

The silence in the room, he thought, spoke volumes. Let Gamaliel with his temporizing refute that.

"So, we are confronted with a dual threat, you see? The Nation at risk, either from the retribution dealt out by Rome or from judgment dealt by the Lord. The Lord's wrath or Rome's—which shall it be? Either would be terrible, but both? Both will spell an end to us forever." He'd spread his arms and gazed at the wall at the end of the room and boomed, "Is it not better, then, that this one man should die, than the whole Nation suffer?"

When Caiaphas said this, men leaned forward and, one by one, nodded. Only Josef shook his head, but with more "yes" than "no." Caiaphas had won the day. The room remained hushed.

One man sitting at the far end of the hall said, "But 'that this one man should die...' Even if we were to find him guilty of all the things he is charged with at a trial, we may not condemn him to death, High Priest." This comment set the room to murmuring. One or two of the Sanhedrin put their hands to their heads as if to ward off a certain strike by the Lord.

"Yes, yes, I know. But you agree, do you not, it would be appropriate, *if* we could?"

Most of them nodded and seemed relieved at the qualifier, the *if*. All, that is, except Josef who looked stricken.

"But a trial, Caiaphas," he said, "there must be a formal trial. The Rabban will tell us that we have our Law to maintain even if, as you say, we only employ it with the sufferance granted by Rome, still, we must keep to it."

Caiaphas had shrugged and turned away. "What must be—must be." And the deed was done.

Caiaphas strode across the Temple Mount. He felt exhilarated. The sun had just cleared the eastern walls; the fires were still banked at the Altar of Sacrifice. He'd had his day. More accurately, he had his day and night and now he was free to proceed. It had taken a great deal of effort and some calling in of favors, but he had managed to convene the Sanhedrin and hold his hearing on the rabbi at last. Equally, he had managed to avoid any meddling the Rabban might have provided. That had been a lucky stroke. Apparently Josef of Arimathea had spoken to the Rabban the previous morning, but Gamaliel had refused to attend. He said, as Josef told it, that he could not be impartial at a trial should there be one later, if he also attended the hearing.

Caiaphas knew enough about the intricacies of Law to understand that the case against Rabbi Yeshua would not stand up to close scrutiny during a prolonged trial. True, there had been the riot in the chambers of the money changers and that would count for something, but it would not create the sense of outrage and fear needed. So, there could be no trial. It was one thing for people with a grudge against rabbis in general and this Galilean one in particular, to testify free of constraint, but quite another if asked to repeat their testimony in circumstances which carried penalties for perjury. No, he required a different approach and after making his speech in the hearing the day before, he could now proceed without any interference from the Sanhedrin or the Rabban.

Caiaphas hurried on his way. He needed to secure his prisoner soon. If the Sanhedrin could not permanently end this Yeshua's nonsense, he knew that Pilate could. There was no love lost between Rome and Israel, but at the same time each understood the need for this forced symbiotic relationship. Pilate would solve his problem. He would make his case before the Prefect.

Chapter XXXV

Gamaliel also rose with the sun, but unlike like Caiaphas, the chill morning air held no appeal for him. He delayed leaving his house, preferring a leisurely breakfast and a quiet moment by his fountain. The Prefect could not be approached. Loukas said he would not be available either.

"I have, as you often fail to remember, a life outside yours, Rabban, and I have to take care of a few things before I have my Passover meal tonight. So, you will have to make do without me."

Gamaliel could think of no other reason to venture out. He'd been on the verge of inviting his friend to share the Passover with him and his sons that night, but let it slide. He lingered over his simple morning meal, consulted with Binyamin over what to serve that night, and dawdled over some scrolls. The Isaiah scroll tempted him but he rolled it tight and secured it with a cord. The leader of the Masad Hasidim would be traveling up from Qumran to pick it up sometime after Shabbat.

So, with no Loukas to discuss the hurdles they needed to vault in finishing the matter of the Prefect's difficulties, he decided it would be a better use of his time if applied to reflection and remembrance of other, deeper matters, rather than sorting through the sordid behavior of the Roman elite and their hangers-on. Still, the sudden change in the Prefect's status nagged at him. What had happened since they last met? Did the people who had traipsed after him and Loukas for most of the previous day have a connection with this abrupt change in the Prefect's status? And where had the missing boy disappeared to? Gamaliel did not believe for an instant he was what he pretended to be, but if not, then who was he? A slave in the Prefect's household, in the Fortress only, or something else. He did not sound like a slave, try as he might. Then again, what was a slave supposed to sound like? And the missing actors ought to be accounted for, if only to reduce a growing list of possible solutions for his puzzle. Gamaliel shook his head, too many unanswered questions and time was running out.

He needed an excuse to pay a visit to the Prefect, but it would have to be a legitimate one. He dared not risk confronting him straight on. No, he needed an excuse to call on the man but what, and how, and when? That had him stumped. What possible reason would he have for calling on Pilate today?

The answer came with an insistent knocking on his door.

Four Legionnaires, two on either side, escorted Gamaliel to the Antonia Fortress. At least he hoped escorted described it. When they'd arrived at his door the men refused to answer his questions as to the why and wherefore of their presence. They would only say that the Prefect required his attendance and then they marched him away.

With the orthodox Passover set to begin in seven or eight hours, the Temple Mount teemed with travelers rushing their sacrifices to the Temple and seeking supplies for the meal to be consumed at sundown. Unlike his previous trips to the Fortress accompanied by Roman soldiers, few of these people seemed to notice or care about its significance or Gamaliel's possible fate.

Pilate stood in the wide veranda where he heard the petitions and complaints from the people over whom he ruled. Rufus stood to the Prefect's right and to his left were two men whom Gamaliel assumed must be the mysterious visitors from Rome, the Tribune and Cassia, the accuser. A steep and broad flight of steps led up to the Prefect and his companions. Gamaliel paused before climbing them. His escort urged him on, not kindly.

Once at the top, Gamaliel paused to catch his breath. He

had no problem walking and did so every day, but climbing stairs, especially long flights, presented him with a challenge. The Prefect signaled him to approach and greeted him.

"*Ha Shem,* Prefect. Greetings. Excuse me while I gather myself together. Ah, there. You called for me. How can I help?"

Pilate rolled his eyes to his left and then made non-blinking eye contact. Gamaliel understood. Whatever matter they discussed, he should be careful.

"Rabban, your High Priest arrived here early this morning dragging a teacher of some sort with him. He wanted me to pass judgment on the poor man."

"Ah, Yeshua. Why bring this to you?"

"I suspect he has an agenda that only I can fulfill. He needs me to judge the man."

"And did you?"

"No, it seems the rabbi is from Galilee. Your King would have jurisdiction, not I. I sent him off to see Herod Antipas, but…"

"But?"

"If I know your King and your High Priest, the latter will be back with his rabbi before the sixth hour."

"Yes, that is very likely. I doubt the King has any interest in passing judgment on anyone since his disastrous mistake with the Baptizer. How does the High Priest's obsession with the rabbi concern me?"

"As he will return and as I will be asked again to pass judgment on the man, I called you here to guide me. I do not know your laws concerning the charges he alleges."

"I see." Since when did Pilate care a fig about Jewish Law and its application?

"You have been involved in an investigation of the man, I believe." Once again Pilate rolled his eyes left and then back to Gamaliel.

"Investigation…let me think…"

"There is an allegation of murder, I believe. This man was said to have been at the scene of a suspicious death. I believe you were looking into that."

Gamaliel rocked back on his heels. When Pilate wished to be clever, he did so very nicely. Unfortunately, his usual mode involved rudeness and bullying, not subtlety.

"I have been looking into that very issue. There are problems yet to be addressed."

"Indeed, what problems? Perhaps I can be of some assistance."

"Well, for one thing, a boy is missing and I believe he might shed some light on the…ah…the rabbi's situation."

"I see. When the…High Priest mentioned it I wondered about that too. You're asking about this missing boy, yes, and where he might be?"

"That and I also wondered if he were in the…um, rabbi's household, or in one of the rabbi's critics, or belonged to some other, independent group."

"Is it important?"

"I believe so. To whom did he answer, you see? Then there is the matter of who else knew where and when to witness the event, you could say."

"I believe the boy might have been of neither house, but local. You know how it is with your people. Here today and somewhere else tomorrow. So, not of the accused household, you see? I cannot respond to the second part of your question. Do you understand?"

"Perfectly. Another question, then, is it possible that the death of this person and the High Priest's push for judgment are not connected?"

"Pardon?"

Gamaliel realized that the Prefect had lost the thread. He tried again. "When the case was brought to my attention—"

"By the High Priest."

"Yes. As I was saying, when I first heard of the case, I assumed the killing and the need to judge the rabbi were linked. That is, that the people who witnessed it were involved in the broader charges, if you follow. It occurs to me now that that may not be the case. That the interest in the ah…rabbi's teaching and the murder might be separate and unrelated events. What would you say to that?"

Pilate frowned and appeared deep in thought. Then, his face brightened. "I see. That is very perceptive, Rabban. My friend, Rufus, has had a conversation with some people familiar with the event in question and tells me that there is every likelihood that you are correct."

So, the murder of Aurelius and the visitors' interest in Pilate were only coincidental. That meant that even if he could prove Pilate innocent, he still might be shipped off to Rome for some other offense. There could be more to celebrate on this Passover than anyone expected. Gamaliel did not know how much longer he could keep this up. Fortunately, at that moment, the two men standing to the Prefect's left drifted away, apparently bored with chatter about the fate of a rabbi. When they were out of earshot, Pilate waved Gamaliel into a corner.

"What Rufus discovered makes no sense except the Emperor makes no sense most of the time. I won't bore you with the details, but yes, they are two separate items."

"That is helpful. You cannot tell me what the Emperor is after?"

"Later, perhaps. You will not be pleased. I retract that. I believe you will be amused. Is there anything else? Be quick. Those two will not stay away for very long."

"Two questions. What do you know about drama?"

"Drama? Nothing. It is the preoccupation of the inherently idle and unemployed. It is a waste of time. Why do you ask?"

"There are elements of this mystery that smack of bad melodrama."

"If you say so. Your second question, and be quick."

"What was the man, Aurelius, doing in the corridor when he was killed?"

"Ah. I have no idea. Perhaps he was following me. As I told you—"

"I remember. Following you? Yes, that would fit."

"It would? Good. I have one question for you. Consider carefully before you answer."

Chapter XXXVI

The midday sun casts no shadows. Sarai paced the floor. No shadows outside, just those in her mind. Yakob. She worried about Yakob. He went out last night to one of his meetings and had returned very late. She knew it was not her place to question him. A wife must know her place and honor her husband. It was the Lord's wish. She muttered her way through Proverbs.

> *A foolish son is the calamity of his father: and the contentions of a wife are a continual dropping...A continual dropping in a very rainy day and a contentious woman are alike...House and riches are the inheritance of fathers: and a prudent wife is from the Lord...It is better to dwell in the wilderness than with a contentious and angry woman...It is better to dwell in the corner of the housetop, than with a brawling woman and in a wide house.*

She wanted to be a worthy wife. It was not her place to question what Yakob did at those meetings. Yet, she knew in her heart that nothing good could come from them. She feared he might even be taken from her. Then, what would she do? Perhaps she should consult the Rabban. But what could he say to her? "Be obedient and withdrawn, daughter. Know your place and rejoice that the Lord has blessed you with a noble husband."

What did an old Rabbi know about love, about surviving in the world? He lived in luxury, safe from want, from threats to his person. Had *Ha Shem* blessed her with a noble husband? Yes, he had and she did not want to lose him over the foolish idea that Rome was vulnerable to the plots and schemes of those rabble rousing former soldiers and outlaws who drew him away at night.

Yakob walked in and found her on her face praying.

"Get up, woman. What are you doing on the floor?"

"I am praying to *Ha Shem* that you will turn away from those people you conspire with when you leave here at night."

"Turn away? Don't be silly, woman. Those people are the only hope we have for freedom from these Roman terrors that daily bleed the poor and enrich themselves from the labor of a conquered Nation."

"What? That is not you speaking, husband. Those words come from some other place. We are safe here. We have shelter and wages and a decent master. Soon, we will have saved enough to have our own house and perhaps a business. I could bake loaves and sell them in the market. Everyone loves my—"

"Be still, I say. You are a woman. You cannot grasp the complexities of our situation. Bake your loaves if you want, but leave saving of the Nation to me, to us."

"But…"

"Enough of this, woman. I must be off. There is work to be done."

"What shall I tell the Physician when he returns? What if he has tasks for you?"

"I will be back in an hour or two."

"Where are you going? Please…"

"We are going to attempt to free Barabbas from prison."

"Free Barabbas? He is a brigand, an outlaw, and a murderer. He preys on his own people. Turning him loose would be like unleashing a wolf into the sheep fold. Would you invite this wolf into our house as well? Why would you do such a thing? It makes no sense."

"Why? Because when Barabbas is in the wilderness, it takes a full cohort of legionnaires to track him. He leads them around the hills, this way and that, and when they finally run out of water and realize they are lost…well, that's one less band of Romans for us to worry about."

"And if they do not become lost?"

"Then they are tied up out there and are not here to abuse us."

"And the innocent people who are destroyed by Barabbas and his band of cutthroats, what of them?"

"In a war, there are casualties. It cannot be helped. Now I must go."

Yakob slammed out the door. Was he truly off to free the brigand, Barabbas? How does one free a felon from the depths of the Antonia Fortress? He could lose his life in the attempt. Once a legionnaire…Why were men so stubborn? Sarai dropped to the floor and renewed her praying.

Gamaliel found Loukas loitering outside his door when he returned from his meeting with Pilate.

"Greetings in the Name, Loukas. Why are you standing on my doorsill? Is Binyamin not at home to let you in?"

"I didn't knock. I am in the open for a reason."

"Indeed? And what is that?"

"People pass by this house, many people. None stop unless they are calling on a householder nearby. Movement, you see. So, if someone lingers, someone like me, it is noticeable."

"Yes, that is so. Is someone 'noticeable' nearby?"

"That is the point. No one dare linger. They will be discovered at once, therefore, if anyone is curious about you or me and has the temerity to dog our heels, they will have to give it up here on this street or be discovered. Now, I will join you inside."

"Loukas, I congratulate you on your amazing plan to root out people who wish to keep us under scrutiny. A question, if they wished to keep an eye on us, they only have to drop out of sight around that corner and wait."

"You think? I believe by idling out here they would be equally fearful of discovery and confused by the behavior. 'What,' they will say to themselves, 'will someone think that man is doing loitering in the street?' They will vacate the area to ponder on the problem I have set for them."

"I see. Come in, I have things to report."

They settled in the great room. Binyamin brought them a cooling drink.

"Now," Gamaliel began, "I was summoned to the Prefect's presence this morning by four legionnaires. I must say that for a moment it seemed like old times."

Gamaliel recounted his odd visit with Pilate and the ruse of speaking about his case while seeming to address that of Yeshua.

"That was very clever of you, Rabban."

"Not I. Pilate initiated it. At the end, when his watchers grew bored and drifted away, we could speak openly. Our opportunities to do so in the future are severely limited, however."

"You learned some interesting facts?'

"Facts? I don't know about that, but I did find out that the missing boy was not from Caesarea. He may not have been from the Fortress staff either. Pilate was not sure. Also he confirmed that the interest his visitors have in him is not connected in any way to the murder."

"What then?"

"He said that Rufus, had overheard something or other, but he would not tell me what it was."

"Well, that's not helpful."

"Not exactly, but it raises possibilities for the future. In any event, there is nothing we can do about it. More interesting was a question he put to me as I left. He asked me to comment on a hypothetical situation concerning the relationship to gods in general and to *Ha Shem* in particular. I could not follow him at first."

"What was the question? We will parse it out and have it from him anyway."

"Possibly. He put this problem to me. If the gods were conspiring and if he were accused by one to favor the other but wished to assure it/he/she that he, Pilate, did not, in fact, favor him or her or it, how would he do that while maintaining his relationship with both?"

"I'm sorry. I have no clue as to what that means."

"Nor do I. I had him reframe it several times. His watchdogs seemed to be curious about our prolonged discourse and started to move toward us."

"What did you do?"

"I said, 'Are you asking me how one would assure one entity that your loyalty is to it and not to another when it believes it is not so? That you favor one of your gods over another?'"

"And?"

"He nodded. The two visitors had come too close by then for him to say anything more."

"And your answer was?"

"I said he should do something that made it imminently clear he had no interest in the second deity."

"Do something? What could you do to a god?"

"What indeed? I have no familiarity with their gods and their peculiarities. One does not question *Ha* Shem or try to deceive Him."

"You had no advice."

"Oh, I played his game. I suggested he could destroy something that god held dear, desecrate a Temple, release his enemy, or murder his offspring. Isn't that how they work things out in their dramas, their tragedies?"

"We are back to the theater."

"From the start of this enterprise, I'm afraid we may never have left it."

Chapter XXXVII

Pilate watched Gamaliel descend the steps to the Temple Mount, and then he pivoted and waved cheerily to the two men who had spent the morning watching him. He sought a quiet corner to think through what he'd been told. The Tribune and Cassia thought they had him, thought he'd been put in the arena with an assortment of lions and tigers licking their chops and eager for a meal. They were about to be proven wrong and the Rabban had handed him a way out. Gamaliel would have no idea that he'd done it, a fact he found very amusing. He'd managed to contain his glee until after the Rabban left and the Tribune and Cassia were out of earshot. The moment Gamaliel's response had left his lips he had the solution to the first of his problems. By that very evening, perhaps sooner if the High Priest didn't dawdle or Herod didn't stall, he'd clear the way to resume his position and perquisites. Pilate could hardly contain himself.

There was still the little matter of Aurelius' murder to be dealt with. He would have to rely on the Rabban for that. What really annoyed him was, if Aurelius Decimus had been a commoner instead of an equal, the murder would have been quickly dismissed. One tradesman or laborer more or less would not concern anyone, except the dead man's family. But as Aurelius held a moderately exalted position and purportedly the Emperor's favor, his death could not be easily swept away. He must first, however, take the necessary steps to disengage the primary mission pursued by Grex and Cassia Drusus. Once accomplished, he could turn his attention back to the murder. He made his way down to the prison cells.

"Who do we have in custody?" he asked the guard at the door.

"Two thieves and the son of a dog from the wilderness, Barabbas. The thieves have been condemned to be crucified."

"And Barabbas?"

"Also scheduled for a cross."

"What else can you tell me about the thieves?"

"They are local."

"Jews?"

"Yes, sir, I believe so."

"Anything else? Public enemies, murders? How about killers with multiple victims?"

"No, Excellency, just common thieves."

"Very well, prepare to bring Barabbas to me."

"Now?"

"Not now. I will send someone, but I want him produced the moment I do."

Pilate left and resumed his post on the broad plaza at the top of the stairs. A small crowd of supplicants still waited to plead their cases.

"Come back tomorrow," he snapped and waved them away. He was feeling good. He sat down and waited for the High Priest and his sad little teacher to arrive. If that rabbi's claims, outrageous as they seemed to Caiaphas, were believed by a sufficient number of those Hebrews, problem solved. It was an intriguing thought.

His wife's personal maid scurried over to him.

"You must come, Excellency."

"Must? Why must I come, Drucilla?"

"It is your good wife she..."

"She is in one of her states? How bad?"

"Very. She insists she will not rest until she tells you of this new vision."

Pilate glanced over the expanse of the Temple Mount below him. Caiaphas was nowhere in sight.

"For a moment only, then I must take up my position here. It is a matter of great importance."

Gamaliel broke a crust of bread and gouged out a wad of cheese from the large ball on the table. Loukas sipped at his wine. He'd made a point of adding a generous dollop of water. It was still early, and he said he did not want to have his faculties made fuzzy.

"Tell me your impression of the Prefect's question," Gamaliel said between mouthfuls.

"At this moment I cannot. What possible interest would he have in gods? As far as I know, he is not a serious believer in their pantheon or any other deity. Frankly, I don't think any of those people are. Why would they dispute over gods? If they need one, they just make one up. They have more gods than sand in Sinai. And why would he seek your opinion on the matter? He knows as well as anyone you have no interest, much less knowledge about their deities. Really, it beggars belief."

"It does, but even though he tried to hide it, he seemed delighted by my answer. If I didn't know better, I would swear he had found a way out of a tight spot. What's even worse, it appears that I may have given him the means."

"Did he tell you anything else that might suggest what that might be?"

"As I said, he agreed that the murder and the mission the visiting dignitaries had were not related. It had something to do with what Rufus, the eminently likeable but woefully inept official, overheard. He refused to elaborate."

"Or believed he couldn't. Is it possible that the news from Rufus and the relief he exhibited at your suggestions were related?"

"That is very good, Loukas. Congratulations, you have hit on it. Now, if we just knew what Rufus knew, we'd have our answer. Care to guess?"

Loukas helped himself to more bread and cheese. He popped a large portion of each into his mouth and chewed. Gamaliel was reminded of an ox with its cud.

"Sorry, I haven't a clue. This is excellent bread."

"Your Sarai made it. She sent some loaves with Yakob the night he walked me home. She could make a fair living selling them, I should think."

"Really?"

"I know little or nothing about being a baker or business, so I don't know whether she could or not. But they certainly are the best I have ever tasted."

Loukas shrugged and helped himself to another piece of cheese.

"To answer my own question, I believe Pilate's obvious delight in my answer and the news from Rufus is the only possible connection. That said, I have to wonder if, without realizing it, we had slipped back into the device of speaking about one thing in the guise of speaking about another. First we were discussing his problem while pretending to discuss Yeshua. When he asked me about the war between members of the pantheon. were we in fact discussing the dissonance between *Ha Shem* and their gods?"

"Sometimes, Gamaliel, you amaze me. At other times, you leap into the sea without checking for submerged rocks. How can you make such a jump?"

"In this case, it is the only solution that fits the time and place. Sometimes, if reason fails, one must rely on the unreasonable. He didn't want me to know what the two Romans were after, but somehow, he couldn't resist leaving a hint. I don't believe he was aware of that."

"But, if that is the case, then—"

Binyamin tapped on the door and slipped into the room.

"There is a woman here to see you," he said.

Gamaliel looked up. "A woman? To see me?"

"Sorry, no, sir. She wishes to speak to the honorable Physician. She says she knows he is busy with important matters, but she has news of some urgency to report. It is about her husband

and…she is a tiny bit hysterical, sir. She seems to think there is a plot afoot. She said something about releasing a wild animal. I asked her where this animal was caged and she only shook her head. She may not be all there, if you take my meaning."

Loukas rose and moved toward the door, happy for the water in the wine. "Did she give a name?"

"I believe she said her name was Sarai."

"Sarai? The Sarai who works for me?" Loukas stopped and glanced at Gamaliel.

"Show her in here, Binyamin," Gamaliel said.

Sarai required a cup of wine laced with one of Loukas' powders before she could manage anything coherent. Gamaliel could not be sure if it was her news or the company she found herself in that caused her hysterics. Finally she took a deep breath and blurted out her story.

"Yakob has gone to the Praetorium with some men intent on freeing Barabbas."

"But that is patently ridiculous," Loukas said. "How does he think he will manage that?"

"I do not know how. He did not confide in me, only he seemed certain it could be done."

"There is a more pressing question here," Gamaliel said. "Why would he want to do such a thing? Barabbas may be a nuisance to the Romans, but he is a terror to the rest of us. Releasing him does no one any good. Is your husband contemplating joining his band of cutthroats?"

Sarai blanched. "I do not know about that. He only said he thought that if Barabbas were back in the wilderness, it would force the Romans to chase after him, and that made them vulnerable."

"More misguided nonsense. If the Romans feel their ranks are too thin to handle the local population, they simply send in more troops, and there seems no end to them. Who are these men he has joined in this misadventure?"

"I am not sure, but I gather from what we've heard here and there that they are former legionnaires like him. Some of them have positions in the Fortress and others…well, I don't know."

"They have positions in the Antonia Fortress, you say?"

"Yes, I believe so, and in the city."

"Ah. How do they imagine they can free a dangerous man like Barabbas from the most secure prison in the country?" Gamaliel frowned and turned to Loukas. "On the other hand, suppose there was a commotion in the city or, better, on the Temple Mount, a commotion of sufficient size to require the local guards to leave their posts temporarily. Then these plotters with their intimate knowledge of the fort and its passages and access to the prison cells could simply whisk him away. Recall, Loukas, how we were brought in to see Pilate last week."

"But will there be a commotion? It is the Passover, Rabban. Who would dare start one?"

"Ah, yes, who?" Gamaliel frowned and stared unseeing at the remnants of his meal. His jaw dropped. "*Ha Shem*, forgive me, that's it. It must be. It is the High Priest who will create the confusion. Think about it for a moment. He will not mean to, but in his zeal to bring down the Galilean he will attract a crowd to the Mount. If Yeshua's supporters show up, there could be a small riot, a disturbance, at least enough to pull the troops from their stations. That would leave the cells poorly guarded long enough to whisk the man away."

"What shall we do?"

"We must stop it."

"How?"

Gamaliel shook his head. "For once, I do not know."

Chapter XXXVIII

Caiaphas needed a full cadre of Temple Guards to make his way from Herod's palace back to the Antonia Fortress. With Passover upon them, pilgrims clogged the streets to near impassability. Yeshua trailed serenely behind him, oblivious of the crowd and his shackles. As they neared the Temple Mount and the Praetorium, the crowd became closer and, if Caiaphas read their mood correctly, more surly. Someone must have spread the news of Yeshua's arrest among his followers.

"Make way for the High Priest," The guards shouted and manhandled those slow to respond.

"We should find a less crowded route," the captain of the guard shouted above the din.

"Press on, press on. We have nothing to hide or fear." Caiaphas stepped to the head of the column. "Make way…. Make way, now. I am the High Priest and I command you to step aside."

People grumbled. Most were not city residents and had only a vague idea who he was much less whom he escorted through the streets, but they resented the bullying by the guards and the High Priest's tone. He would make few new friends from this throng. The crowds did move back a bit, enough so that they could continue. A few, he supposed Galileans, began to raise a ruckus. He hurried on. Once he'd reached the Mount, he would be in safer company. He had given the remainder of the guard explicit instructions to prevent anyone who looked like they might be in Yeshua's party from approaching the Praetorium.

Josef of Arimathea pushed through the masses clogging their way.

"You cannot do this High Priest. It is contrary to—"

"I can and I will. You forget yourself, Josef. I am the High Priest. I am charged with maintaining the purity of our worship, our Temple, and our way."

"But the Law?"

"The Law is the purview of the Rabban. Talk to him."

"You are not above the Law, High Priest."

"Not above it, but in matters of faith, in matters that concern the way, the life and, in this case, the truth, I am the Law's final arbiter. Step aside. We dare not anger the Lord any longer."

He shoved the old man aside and motioned his guardsmen on.

Pilate found his wife huddled in a corner of their apartment. When she saw him she stood and pointed a wavering finger at him.

"Do not do it."

"Do not do what, wife?"

"Whatever it is you have planned for that rabbi. It came to me this morning after that ridiculous priest person left. He wishes to have the teacher from the north destroyed, and he would make you the instrument of his destruction. Nothing good can come from this. I saw the darkness. Wash your hands of it. I beg you leave that teacher alone."

"Calm yourself, wife. I know you set great store in your visions."

"You never listen to me."

"I do, but you know as well as I that not all come to pass. Remember last year when you believed the wine was poisoned? Was it? No, it wasn't. This matter holds little consequence for us. It has importance for me, but only incidentally." Procula began to whimper. Pilate put his hand on her shoulder. "There, calm yourself. You are not seeing this aright. I am doing nothing untoward beyond my sworn duty. These Hebrews have their own peculiar laws and customs. As Prefect I am obliged to support them in the pursuit of those laws and customs to the extent that I am able or required. Do you see? If the High Priest has a case which, under their law, requires a certain action, I have no choice but to carry it out. The High Priest and his fellow religionists will order the man's destruction, not I."

"It will destroy that man's future."

"Indeed? Which man's future will be destroyed and why should that worry us? Also, when is that likely happen?"

Procula's eyes rolled upward and disappeared. Pilate had seen it before. The eyes became all white, no iris, her teeth would start to chatter, she would moan, and then collapse. She would sleep for an hour or so and then, on awakening, would nag him about what she had seen for at least a week. He turned on his heel and left the room after giving a curt command to Hannah to tend to his wife.

"Woman, surely by now you know what to do next."

He managed to regain his seat on the plaza as the High Priest, his escort of Temple Guards, and his prisoner reached the far end of the broad platform that spread out before him to the south. They were bullying the crowds to move aside, but with little luck. Pilate relaxed. It could be awhile.

"Someone must warn the Fortress," Loukas shouted. "Sarai, did Yakob give you any names?"

"Names? I don't know. He told me some, but they are not real names." Gamaliel shot her a quizzical look. "They use made-up names in case one is taken prisoner and tortured. Whatever names the captured man gave out would be untraceable, you see?"

"Calm yourself, Loukas," Gamaliel said. He seemed serene in spite of the news they'd heard. "There is no way we can warn the fort. Even if we knew names and the plan in detail, and even if we did manage to reach them, who of that arrogant company would listen, much less believe us. In this circumstance, we would be considered the enemy or plotting something of our own. No, we must warn Caiaphas. He must delay his appointment with Pilate."

Loukas looked skeptical. "Do you really think you can dissuade him from pressing on with his plans by a disputation about the merits of his arguments or that his actions are unjust, unlawful?"

"That is not what I have in mind. We can discuss his case against the rabbi later. What he needs to know right now is that if he continues, he will be responsible for setting loose a worse scourge on the Nation than that posed by an insignificant, if radical, rabbi. Let's hope we are not too late."

Locals, residents of the city, and pilgrims from beyond its borders, Caiaphas discovered, occupied the Temple Mount. That came as a blessing. Whatever else may be said about Jerusalem, its citizens understood the importance of keeping strictly to the Law. The Temple was the Lord's dwelling place and the Temple dominated the skyline of Jerusalem. If the Temple were destroyed, the Nation would be destroyed. If Israel lost favor from the Lord, all would be lost. These people, with the exception of a few like the Rabban, would understand why Yeshua must be stopped before the wrath of an angry *Ha Shem* brought destruction to the Nation. It had happened before. This Temple constructed by the late King was technically the third of its kind and clearly the grandest, but Caiaphas knew that it could be swept away in an instant, should the Lord decide to punish his people for their faithlessness. It had been before. It could be again.

"Make way for the High Priest," his guards shouted. The people separated before them like the sea opening for Moses. A fitting simile, Caiaphas thought, given that the Passover would be observed that night.

The entourage had traversed halfway to the Praetorium when an obviously anxious Gamaliel stepped in its path.

"Stand aside, Rabban. This matter is no longer within your jurisdiction."

"That can be debated later and at leisure. I am not here to stop you. I wish only to delay this thing you plan to do."

"Delay? Never. It must be done. The Nation is threatened."

"You have so persuaded yourself, I know. I promise you I am not here to debate with you today. There is a much greater danger to us at the moment than this rabbi."

"Greater? What could be greater than the very destruction of the Nation?"

"If *Adonai* is angry with us over this man's teaching, He is not likely to strike during Passover, High Priest. There is no need to rush. But, please understand, your presence here will create a disturbance large enough to draw the legionnaires assigned to the Fortress' interior out onto the plaza. If that happens, we court disaster."

"Nonsense. What disaster?"

"There is a plot in place to free Barabbas. With a weakened cadre left to guard him, his friends plan to infiltrate the Fortress and free him. That poses an immediate and far greater threat than Yeshua. All I ask is that you delay a day or two."

"Free Barabbas from prison, from the Praetorium? Surely you are not serious. No one escapes the cells from that place. I don't care if all the guards are drunk or sleeping, no one can penetrate the depths of that sinister place for any reason other than that which the Romans allow. Pilate will leave Jerusalem soon and this matter cannot wait for his return. Step aside, Rabban."

Caiaphas signaled his guards to move on. Gamaliel was brushed aside and the party made its way to the steps leading up to the plaza where Pilate sat waiting.

Chapter XXXIX

Caiaphas, his prisoner and accompanying guards reached the platform and waited for Pilate to acknowledge them. Yeshua stood, hands still bound together and eyes focused in the distance. Pilate paced up and down, and came to a stop in front of the High Priest.

"I take it Herod was unsympathetic to your plan, Caiaphas? Fortune did not smile on you at Herod's palace?"

"The Tetrarch says he has doubts."

"Of course he does. Herod is not a complete fool. After his idiotic beheading of your prophet, the Baptizer, he has learned caution. I should think one martyr notched on his belt would be enough."

"I did as you required of me, Prefect. Now I am back with the request I made earlier."

"And that was? My memory is not what it used to be."

Caiaphas gritted his teeth. "This man mocks Caesar, threatens the Temple, disobeys your demand there be no disturbances during Passover. He is a known heretic and blasphemer. He must die that others will not be tempted to do the same."

"You wish me to crucify this man? Is that the essence of the thing? To do that is a very serious business. I believe I should examine this dangerous person before assigning him a cross."

Yeshua was pushed forward. Pilate stood close to him and glared. If it was an attempt to intimidate, it failed.

"*Iesus Nazarenus, Rex Iudaeorum.* Do you know what that means, King? No? In the civilized tongue of Rome, it means 'Yeshua of Nazareth, King of the Jews.' Your High Priest says you claim to be the King of the Jews."

Pilate pivoted around on his heel and faced the assembled Roman contingent.

"He says he is a King. He needs the proper costume. Bring him a robe and a crown."

Two Legionnaires disappeared and returned with a filthy purple robe and a crown which had long, sharp, protruding thorns. The robe was draped over Yeshua's shoulders and the crown pressed down on his head. Some of the thorns pierced his forehead, causing it to bleed.

"Now you look like a proper King. You are a King, then?" Pilate circled Yeshua, pulling at the wrinkles on the purple robe and giving the crown an extra downward push.

Yeshua stared at Pilate with black fathomless eyes and responded, "Is this nonsense your idea or are you just repeating someone else's?"

Pilate flinched, taken aback by Yeshua's insolence. His eyes flashed.

"The King is defiant. Tell me, King, why are you creating so much trouble? You understand, these men here want me to put you to death?"

"I came to testify to the truth."

"Oh? Tell me, what is truth? We'd all like to know that. So, perhaps you will tell us."

Pilate turned back to Caiaphas.

"High Priest, this man is annoying, but I find no crime here. Your Antipas doesn't either. He is impudent and clearly unrepentant for whatever you accuse him of, but I cannot crucify someone because you think he might get you in trouble with that ridiculous god of yours."

"Prefect, he must die," Caiaphas said softly.

"Must you say? You are mistaken. There is no must. Rome is known for its sense of justice."

"He mocks Caesar. He caused a riot in the Temple. You said that anyone who—"

"Well, yes, there is that to consider. I tell you what I can do... for the acts of disrespect and the riot in the Temple...a flogging. Guard, the scourge."

The guard retrieved the whip and twirled it around his head. It sounded like someone had knocked over a wasp nest.

Jesus was stripped of his purple cloak, his robe, and tunic. His hands, still bound, were fastened around a pillar.

"How many, sir?" the man with the whip asked.

"How many? Three should do it."

"Three lashes?"

"No, idiot, not three lashes,—three sets. Three sets of thirteen."

The man who wielded the whip did so with great expertise. He flicked his wrist at precisely the right moment. Instead of simply laying down a set of stripes, the stones fastened to the ends of the scourge's leather strips raked across Yeshua's flesh. Six lashes and his back was torn and bleeding. After a dozen, it was laid bare. At the twentieth stroke, he slumped against his ropes. The beating continued for the full thirty-nine. The scourge dripped blood, its wielder with sweat. A guard cut Jesus' bonds and he crumpled to the ground.

"Get him up," Pilate snapped. "Get the King on his feet and get him out of here."

A legionnaire brought a pail of water and poured it over him. Two others grabbed him by the arms and hauled him to his feet. The dirty purple robe was thrown over him. It darkened with blood.

"Stop. Prefect, this will not do. This man must be put to death."

"What is it with you people? A thorough flogging not enough?"

Caiaphas drew in a breath. Then, with all the dignity he could muster, he faced Pilate.

"You have your duty, Prefect, I have mine. This man threatens the whole of the Nation. I am fully aware of what you think of our worship and practices. But I say to you we have been faithful to the Lord since the beginning of memory. We have worshipped him in the high places when your ancestors were still turning over rocks looking for food. Whatever you may think of us, we are not a bloodthirsty people. The covenant calls us to obedience and we know if we stray from it, the Lord will punish us. This man presents himself as the son of the Lord, the one who may not be named. It is a blasphemy. It is dangerous and it will, if not put to an end by you, bring trouble to both our Nations"

"Ah, I see. He thinks he's a god. Tell me, High Priest, what King doesn't? Indeed, what god hasn't had offspring by some willing mortal?"

Rufus cleared his throat.

Pilate turned toward him and winked. "It will be fine, you will see, my friend."

Turning back to the High Priest, he added, "Very well, we will put the intricacies of gods who would be men and *vice-versa* to the side for now. Let us understand each other. I will crucify this man for you, but if I do this thing for you, you will be in my debt."

"Yes, Prefect."

"Deeply in my debt. I can expect you to guarantee certain things are done by your people on time and as requested?"

Caiaphas swallowed. "Yes, as you say."

Rufus stepped forward, took Pilate by the arm, and walked him to the back of the plaza

"This will get back to Rome. The letters, Pilate. A crucifixion on one of the people's holiest days, you dare not do it."

"But, don't you see? It will put an end to the Tribune's mission here. Besides, I am not going to pass judgment on this man—they are." He strode back toward Caiaphas.

"Guards, bring up Barabbas. Oh, and fix him up with a King's robe, as well. We don't want to be seen as playing favorites. Caiaphas, instruct your people to move closer."

Caiaphas spoke to his guards. People massed at the foot of the steps. Two guards dragged out a kicking and cursing Barabbas. The soldiers told him to be still or die. Another purple robe was produced and thrown over his shoulders.

"Bring him out here to join his countryman. Put one on my right and one on my left."

Yeshua and Barabbas were led to the front of the platform.

"Caiaphas, I am about to relieve you of any possible repercussions coming to you for what you have done to your rabbi."

Turning to the crowd, he raised his hands for silence. "People of Jerusalem, both of these men have been found guilty of crimes so serious, they require the death penalty." He paused for effect. "But it is your Passover and Rome would show mercy. We have a tradition on such important days, that one prisoner shall be set free, do we not?"

The crowd stirred. Caiaphas and the Temple officials frowned, the Tribune and Cassia with them. What tradition? No one had ever heard of such a tradition.

"However, it is difficult for me to choose between these two dangerous men, so I give the choice to you. Which would you have me free?"

He pointed to Barabbas. "Shall it be Yeshua Barabbas?" He slurred the 'bar' but said Yeshua loudly and clearly, Yeshua bar Abba...sss. As Pilate was not a Hebrew speaker, his pronunciation lacked definition. If you didn't listen carefully, it could have been heard as Yeshua, something.

"Or shall it be this man, *Iesus Nazarenus, Rex Iudaeorum?*"

Few, if any in the crowd spoke Latin and Pilate knew it. All they heard was something akin to "Yeshua, mumble-mumble" followed by a name that made no sense. The two men far above them on the platform were both bowed and beaten. Of the two, Barabbas appeared to be in better shape. After a pause, the followers of Barabbas, seeing their chance, shouted, "Yeshua Barabbas." Others, prompted by Caiaphas and his lieutenants followed suit. A few mistakenly believed they were calling for Rabbi Yeshua when they joined in.

"Yeshua Barabbas, Yeshua Barabbas!"

"You have chosen this man, Barabbas. So be it. Let him go."

Barabbas, stunned by the turn of events, watched in amazement, as his hands were untied and his dirty royal robe stripped from him. He raced down the steps into the arms of his supporters and disappeared into the crowd.

"What shall I do to the other?" Pilate looked at the High Priest and nodded.

Again he waited. Caiaphas, catching his drift, shouted, "Crucify him." His people repeated it and soon the crowd joined in, "Crucify him, crucify him."

Pilate looked for a long moment at the crowd in feigned amazement. "It is your decision then, not mine. My hands are clean in this."

He dipped his hands in a bowl of water and dried them with the towel.

"We are finished here," he said to Caiaphas. "Go away."

"The crucifixion?"

"Tomorrow."

"But I thought—"

"It is your Passover, High Priest. Go and celebrate your deliverance out of the hands of the enemies of your god. Go."

Chapter XL

Gamaliel and Loukas managed to intercept Caiaphas at the foot of the Praetorium steps. The High Priest swerved in an attempt to avoid them, but Gamaliel stepped in front of him and held up his hand.

"Stop, High Priest. Have you any idea what you have done? You would not listen, High Priest. Instead, against advice and common sense, you would plow ahead like an ox bothered by a wasp. Why must you be so stubborn?"

"I am the High Priest, Rabban. I know my duty even when others do not."

"Your duty is to attend to the Temple, its priests, and its worship. It has nothing to do with rooting out teachers with whom you do not agree. That is my job. Because you failed to grasp that concept, you have brought about the release of the most evil man in the Nation. Barabbas now has a license to prey on us again. I understand that a few people foolishly believe his release will thin the ranks of our oppressors, cause them to spend their resources in the wilderness, and therefore not be here to annoy us. They are wrong. Instead, it will only prompt the authorities to import even more troops. More soldiers mean more oppression, more taxes to pay for them, and all because you would destroy an insignificant rabbi whose great wrong lay in his power to attract followers where your chosen circle cannot."

"That is not the case. He is a blasphemer and a heretic. He

tempts the wrath of *Ha Shem*. And, just to be clear, it was not I, but Pilate who freed Barabbas."

"That is nonsense and you know it. I do not know what game the Prefect plays at. I suspect it has something to do with why those dignitaries are in the city. I will find out soon enough. Despite your disingenuous notion to convince the Nation that Yeshua poses a threat and Rome is to blame for his death, you and you alone staged this drama. You have unleashed a tragedy, Caiaphas, not unlike one of those epic Greek plays where an early act of hubris plays out in the lives of kings and princes over many years and inevitably ends in everyone's destruction."

"What are you nattering on about, Rabban? What drama? I merely asked for and received support from the Prefect in the matter concerning a rabbi who poses a threat to us and to him. Whether you will see it that way or not is immaterial. Drama? Of all the analogies to ever have proceeded from your mouth, that is the worst. Furthermore, just how can Pilate's freeing Barabbas pose a threat? Barabbas is no more than a brigand, a thief. It is only a matter of time before he will be recaptured and that will be the end of him."

"No, you are mistaken."

In the back of his mind Gamaliel's heard a familiar murmuring.

It will not collapse right away, Rabban, but the eagle that was once Rome is rapidly devolving into a guinea fowl. The majesty of your Moses has slipped into a quagmire of petty rules, and laws. Disputes between rival interpreters of it will slowly suck you down. Mark my words, Rabban...Gaze long and hard on your golden Temple for your generation will be the last to marvel at its glory.

The King's companion, Menahem, had said that to him. How long ago? Two, two and a half years? Is this what he meant?

"High Priest, this man, whom you dismiss as no more than a common brigand is very much more. The seeds of our destruction lay with him and what he represents, not with that rabbi you so despise."

"Don't be ridiculous. How can that be? He is nothing but a nuisance. You said so yourself."

"I have since learned that he attracts men to him, dangerous men. His following grows like that of Yeshua. The difference between them is that where the rabbi teaches peace, the thief teaches revolution and war."

"Revolution, you say? And is that such a terrible thing. Can we not hope for a release from these hateful people?"

"Do you remember our conversation last week about the Sicarii, the Dagger Men? His ranks are filling with them and with Zealots, and all sorts of foolish men who feel life has treated them badly and wish to lash out at someone. They believe that they can defeat Rome, that righteousness and fire in their bellies will overcome the reality of Rome and its legions. Many will die and then when the insurrection they have begun draws too many to its banner and becomes too intense, they will experience the might of Rome as never before. Legionnaires on the orders sent to their Centurions from Rome itself, will destroy us, the Temple, the Nation. Rome will, Caiaphas, not Yeshua and his band of fishermen. The end of the Nation as we know it may well be your legacy, High Priest."

Gamaliel turned and marched away before the dumbstruck Priest could respond.

"That sounded pretty strong, even coming from you," Loukas said as they forced their way through the crowd. "Very prophetic, if I may say so."

"I am no prophet. I do not pretend to be one, never have, but I know someone who is and he says, and now I agree, it will happen. It is just a matter of time."

"How much time? When will this cataclysm occur?"

"That I don't know. It is prophesy, after all—one month, two years, who knows, four generations? But it will come to pass. Enough of this. I must go home. I am tired and I have a Passover to prepare. We will talk some more tomorrow. I need to spend some time querying your servants, Sarai and Yakob. If they are forthcoming, and with any luck, we will be done with the Prefect after Shabbat. In the meantime, I will count my Passovers from now on. I fear that the ones I am to experience in David's city may be numbered."

"It is not like you to be a pessimist, Rabban."

"Perhaps some of the Prefect's 'pragmatism' has rubbed off on me."

Pilate stood at the top of the steps and watched as the High Priest descended to the Mount and struggled to compose himself. He had been hard on Caiaphas. It had been necessary and he had no regrets. When it came to abusing this people and their officials, he never had regrets. He ruled as a Roman governor, not some milksop. He did have some qualms when it came to the Rabban, however.

"Pilate," the Tribune called from within the Fortress, "in the light of the letters Rufus carries, would you care to enlighten us as to what you just did?"

"Gladly Honorable Tribune and Emissary of the Emperor. If I understand what I have been told about your mission here, I have made your day."

"How is that? I am unaware you have any knowledge of why Cassia, Aurelius, and I traveled to this forsaken outpost."

"Just so, but in this god forsaken outpost one is hard pressed to keep secrets. It is in the air. I believe you were sent to ascertain my loyalties to the gods of Rome and to make certain I have not converted to the inane religion of the Jews."

"Perhaps…"

"That being the case, please note, the man I will send to the cross tomorrow, condemned to it by his peers, by the way, and not I, claims to be the mortal offspring of their god. Many of the people here have come to accept the truth of that. I have seen to his destruction. I can hardly be believed to be one of them if I do that, now can I?"

"You will kill a demigod?"

"Many will think so."

"And the man set free?"

"Their worst nightmare. That man pillages, murders, and terrorizes his own people. To placate them, our legionnaires hunt him down. If we were to cease and desist even for a week, say...well you see how it might go for them."

"I see. You have a genius for survival, Pilate, but then we always knew that. I, for one, only wondered how you would do it. Now, I am interested in seeing how that same genius will extricate you from the charge of murdering your rival?"

"If you will make yourself available in the very near future, I will demonstrate it for you. Now, please excuse me. In all the excitement, I missed my midday meal. I must retire to my quarters and dine."

YOM SHISHI

Chapter XLI

The previous night, Gamaliel's sons, their wives, and children had spent the Passover with him. The evening had passed pleasantly enough, but Pilate's question nagged at him. His family departed, Gamaliel collapsed into his favorite couch. He loved this Holy Day and the story of the escape from Egypt and he loved his family, but this Passover lacked the bright optimism he usually experienced. He thought it might have had something to do with the outrage at the Praetorium.

After his morning ritual, he left to meet Loukas. His route usually took him across the Temple Mount and around the western wall of the Antonia Fortress. Occasionally, perhaps on High Holy days when pilgrims and worshipers filled the mount with their sacrifices, he would take a longer, but less busy route along the streets farther to the west and then work his way back to the Sheep Gate. Today he found he could do neither. Visitors packed the Temple area trying to have one last look at their Temple. Because the following day would be Shabbat, many of them would likely linger until the day after and the crowds would remain.

His alternate route seemed equally congested. He stopped a man dressed in a cloak which marked him as being from Cyrene.

"What is the hold up? Who are all these people and why are they clogging up the streets?"

"It is the execution, sir. They are bringing Rabbi Yeshua and two thieves to be crucified. The rabbi's followers and many others are here to witness."

"All these people are followers of Yeshua?"

"A few, but most are local—people who revel in the pain of others less fortunate than themselves. Crucifixions have become events like gladiatorial contests. People seem to enjoy bloodletting as long as it is not theirs. I'm sorry. Perhaps I spoke too strongly. It's just that I can't understand why watching a man suffocate and bleed to death while hanging on a cross is so attractive. Isn't there enough suffering every day? Why look for more and worse, how can one possibly enjoy it."

"It might have to do with their need to bolster themselves against their own misfortunes. You know what they say, 'That could be me.' It might also be argued they represent the inevitable end product of a brutal and bloody world. Human brutality has made too many of us insensate to the horror of death and dying, particularly if it is subsidized by the state. Children, who know nothing of the horrors of war, play at soldiering, dying a thousand deaths at the hands of other youths' wooden swords. I am afraid it has always been so. I pray it will not always be."

The three condemned men rounded the corner and staggered into view. Each reeled along the street to the jeers of the onlookers and was burdened with a rough wooden beam balanced across his shoulders. It would soon be joined to a tall vertical to complete his cross. Gamaliel started to back away. He had no desire to be a witness to Caiaphas' folly.

"Tell me, sir," the Cyrenian said, "isn't it unusual for a rabbi to be tried by a Roman official? Do you know what serious crime this rabbi committed that he should be on his way to that hill?"

"Alas, I cannot. Beyond offending a few people in high places and being a nuisance there was nothing I know of that warranted a trip to the Praetorium and Pilate. I do not understand why the Prefect even bothered to hear this case much less condemn the man to death. Say a prayer for him that he does not suffer."

"I will."

Gamaliel pushed through the crowd and headed back to the Temple Mount. It might be crowded but nothing like this street.

Loukas greeted him as usual, in his back court. "You are late, Rabban. That is not like you."

"I picked the wrong hour to travel. Yeshua and two criminals were being led to Golgotha. An enormous crowd lined the streets and the Romans escorting them were not interested in anyone's convenience. I had to double back."

"So Caiaphas' obsession ends today. You will no longer have to hear about the Galilean and his antics any more. I suppose that is a blessing in a way."

"You're right on one count. Yeshua will not fill my conversations with Caiaphas, but somehow, I doubt we have heard the last of the rabbi from Nazareth. So, are your servants ready for us?

"I will call them"

Yakob and his wife followed Loukas to the court. Sarai, nervous, Yakob surly.

"Yakob," Gamaliel said, "I assume you are delighted you did not have to risk life and limb in a futile attempt to free your hero, Barabbas."

"Sir?"

"Sarai did not tell you? She approached us yesterday to stop you from joining in the plot to free him. She feared for your life. She was right about that. But thanks to Pilate, Barabbas is free, and you are none the worse for it."

Yakob shot a dark look at his wife. He turned to Loukas. "With respect to you, Physician, what I do on my time is my business."

Loukas opened his mouth to respond, but Gamaliel signaled him to wait.

"Yes, that may be true, assuming your future wages hold no interest for you," he said. "However, I am curious why you and your comrades would contemplate such a rash idea."

"It was needed."

"I see. Not much of an answer. Still, you have your wish. Barabbas is free to harass and abuse the population once again.

How that can please you I do not know. Tell me something, Yakob, why do you suppose Pilate freed Barabbas?"

"He did not. The crowd shouted his name. The people wanted him free. They understand."

"The last part I seriously doubt. As to the business of the crowd making the decision, that is also nonsense."

"But they—"

"Pilate offered them two choices, Yeshua Barabbas and a name I cannot repeat because it was in Latin and my tongue does not have the skill necessary to reproduce it. No one had any idea what or who they voted for, if voting is what they did. Pilate rigged that choice for two reasons."

"Two?" Loukas said. "What possible reason would he have to do what he did?"

"Ah, that is his genius. I am not sure yet why he decided to honor Caiaphas' request to nail Yeshua to the Roman tree, but I am fairly certain it had something to do with why the Tribune and the other man are in residence. As for Barabbas, Yakob can tell us that. He can, if he thinks it through. Right at the moment he is confused. Tell me, Yakob, why would the Prefect want Barabbas on the loose?"

"I can't. We…I wanted him free to force the Romans to devote more of their forces to chasing him. Also there are other reasons…."

"Among those other reasons, he has attracted to him, dissidents and revolutionaries of all sorts and sizes. In time you believe their numbers will be sufficient for you and your comrades to overthrow the Empire."

Yakob shuffled his feet but remained silent.

"So, tell me, Yakob, speaking now as former legionnaire, tell us why that will not work?"

"It will."

"It won't and you know it. You hope it will. You dream it will, but it won't. Are you old enough to remember Sephoris? No? Well, not to dwell on it overmuch, but about three and a half decades ago an elderly man, Yehudah of the Galilee, decided, like you, that it was time to challenge Rome. He gathered a small band of like-minded rebels and attacked the armory in that town. They killed the Roman garrison. What do you suppose happened next?"

"I don't know."

"Come now, you can guess. You were a legionnaire. No? What always happens when Roman authority is challenged?" Yakob glowered at Gamaliel, but said nothing. "No answer? Loukas, would you care to guess?"

"I know the story."

"He knows, Yakob. What do you say?"

"They sent troops."

"Exactly. Within a week, a substantial cohort of soldiers arrived in Sephoris. They defeated the rebels and his men, sacked the town then burned it to the ground. They raped and murdered the women, killed the children, and crucified all the men. They say the crosses stretched all the way to Nazareth. Knowing that story, what do you suppose will be the fate of Jerusalem if or when you and your Zealots try to follow in the footsteps of Yehudah of the Galilee?"

Yakob rolled his eyes heavenward, but said nothing.

"You see how it is. Pilate has everything to gain and nothing to lose. If Barabbas returns to terrorizing us, he will be a necessary presence because his soldiers are the only protection we will have. Your colleagues will not attempt to take him. He is your creation. So, Rome becomes our savior. Is that what you wanted? I don't think so. Instead, we are placed in Pilate's debt. If Barabbas and those like him are too successful, Rome will simply dispatch more troops. If it gets too bad, well..."

Yakob lowered his eyes. "You do not believe in freeing the Nation?"

"Oh, I do. I do not believe it will come by the use of violence. At this moment in history, there is no force on earth strong enough to defeat Rome. So, we must wait. In the Lord's time, we will be free. It is not our place nor is it wise to anticipate *Ha Shem*. In the meantime, bands of outlaws and those who would be our saviors— the Zealots, the Sicarii—can only make things worse. Magi would tell us that the stars are set in their courses. Pilate has set in motion events that will ultimately destroy us. The worst part of that is he has no idea what he's done. I tell you, unless we find a way to alter those courses and right now, we are doomed."

"Do you believe that, Gamaliel?" Loukas asked.

"I don't know. Dare we take a chance? Yakob, look to your wife. She cares for you as you clearly do not care for her."

"I do care for Sarai"

"Do you? Then stop risking your life and quite possibly hers, and enjoy life together while you still can."

Chapter XLII

Morning broke cold and clear. The fire pit held only a few coals and ashes. Pilate blew on them and added a handful of straw and then some sticks and branches. The room filled briefly with smoke and then the draft caught and the smoke drifted to the ceiling and out the smoke hole. He groaned. He'd celebrated his success the previous night with a fine dinner in his apartment and, after several hours of too much wine and many murderous looks from his wife, he went to his private study and slept. Now, he had to cope with a fierce headache and fuzziness of thought. It was not a new experience for him, but he thought that as he grew older the after effects of such indulgence weighed more heavily on him. Soon they would out-strip the pleasure that prompted them, and he would officially become an old man. He held his hands to the fire and attempted to force his mind into a full state of consciousness. It took him a moment to remember exactly what he had done and another to remember what he had yet to do. Passover was ended. Tomorrow Shabbat would begin. That meant Gamaliel would not be available until the following day. He needed to speak to the Rabban before then—today. His time as a free man would not last much longer. The murder of Aurelius hung over his head like that mythical sword, the name of which he could never remember. The Tribune might allow him to find a reasonable surrogate murderer if the victim were a native of no consequence, but Aurelius came from an important family and had the ear of the Emperor. Pilate dressed and called for his steward.

The steward bustled into the room bearing a tray which held a cup filled with a liquid Pilate knew would taste terrible, but which would repair the damage he'd done to his body the night before. He needed to clear his head.

"Dagon, I need the Rabban delivered to me immediately. Send legionnaires to his house and have him brought here at once."

"Yes. Excellency."

"And find that boy."

"What boy would that be?"

"You know, the one assigned to me when we arrived, the slave from…I forget where…that boy."

"I assigned you a boy?"

"You did. You must remember…tallish boy, dark hair, his was name Marius."

"I do not know of any boy assigned to you that fits that description or who has that name."

"You don't know…? What are you up to, Dagon? When my wife and I came down from Caesarea you provided servants, women for her, some servants, cup bearers, dressers, and so on for me, and the boy."

"I am sorry…It must have slipped my mind. I will make inquiries."

"You do that, Dagon, and don't come back until you can deliver him. Now, get me the Rabban."

◇◇◇

Loukas dismissed Yakob and Sarai. Gamaliel followed them into the house and stopped Yakob at the door sill. He spoke softly. Yakob stepped back and his eyes flashed. Gamaliel shrugged and pointed to his wife. Yakob frowned and nodded. Loukas raised his eyebrows. It was not like Gamaliel not to share. The conversation ended and Gamaliel returned to Loukas' side.

"Is there anything I need to know?"

"Need to know? You mean about my little chat just now with Yakob? An errand I asked him to do. Do you think your man learned anything this morning? Shall we see him settle into quiet domesticity?"

"Making the transition from a lifetime serving in wars and conflict, from killing and pillaging to…what did you call it… 'quiet domesticity'…cannot be easy. Roman legionnaires are many things and serve many purposes, but in the end they are killing machines. Who they kill is never their choice, only how efficiently and how often they do it. So, to answer your question, I hope so. Only the Lord knows."

"Can you imagine a society where the majority of men were first soldiers before they were householders?"

"No."

"No, nor can I. It is not a pretty thought. Well, we need to be off. We still have work to do. We have not found the means to exonerate the Prefect yet."

"Will we?"

"As it is with the possible pacification of Yakob, only *Ha Shem* knows. There is a piece we are missing and need to locate before it is too late."

"A piece? What would that be? Not another trip to the hippodrome?"

"No more horses and it is not a what, but a who. We must find Marius, the boy. I am certain that he is the key to this mystery and I have serious doubts he even knows it."

"Marius? What possible information could he have?"

"A great deal. Now, before Pilate's agents find us and haul us off to the Praetorium, let us be off and searching. Another trip to the Souk will be a good start."

"You do not wish to speak to the Prefect now?

"Not now, no. He told me all I needed to know yesterday. To spend time now would be to waste it. We must get back into the streets."

"And will we be shadowed again?"

"Probably not, at least not by those clever men and their place-changing maneuver. I hope, by another, but we will see. Come along, we need the boy."

"How do we go about finding him?"

"We will look for him in a few likely places. He is not a seer or a scholar by any means but when he discovers that Barabbas is on the loose and Pilate restored and then turns those facts over in his mind, I believe he will find us."

"A few likely places?"

"Two. No, make that three. Come along, Loukas, I have an uncomfortable feeling that Pilate's minyans are approaching. We do not wish to be found."

Marius did not, in fact, qualify as any of those things Gamaliel suggested. The others in his troop called him Ox. Not because he was as strong as one nor as big, but because they believed him to be that slow. He had adopted that role as a means of self preservation. If people thought you stupid, they were less cautious around you. They would let slip bits of information they believed you could not understand. Marius used that to his advantage on more than one occasion. All of which explained why he had been targeted by the men when they'd arrived in Jerusalem. Any of the company could have played the role, but his apparent ingenuousness had sealed it. On his second day in the city, he'd been whisked away and locked up. The room had either been carved out of a hillside or lay near water. The floor stayed wet the whole time he was in it. The walls sweated and the green slime which covered them added the only color he could make out in the dim light that filtered over and under the ill fitted door that separated him from the sun and freedom

He did not know how long he had been there when three men had entered the room and had put the proposition to him. They had an assortment of arms strapped to their bodies and all of them looked dangerous. Marius did not know much about soldiering, but he had traveled enough to recognize that these men had an assortment of blades that evidenced they had some close familiarity with both Rome and its enemies. The three had stared at him without saying a word for what he believed must have been several hours. In truth it was more like a hundred heartbeats.

"You are a patriot, boy?" the tall one, who seemed to be their leader, had asked.

"Sir?"

Marius had no idea where this conversation would lead, but the weaponry led him to believe that a wrong answer could mean a quick and painful death.

"You wish to see the Empire destroyed and the Romans sent back to their river home?"

"Yes, I do." That had been the easy question. Everyone wished for that, didn't they?

"You can be a part of that," the tall one then said, the man he later discovered they called the General. The General then told him how. Not him alone, naturally, but as part of a team. They had a plan, only they called it a campaign like soldiers would. Marius decided that's what they were, or what they had been at one time or another, perhaps not all of them, but some—the leaders.

He'd studied the men in the room. Marius had survived growing up in the streets of the Empire largely by his wits. He was alive because he had learned to play the fool when necessary. This had become one of those times. He'd listened to the General explain the role he expected Marius to play in the campaign and how important it was. He thought about how to answer no would affect his life expectancy and, since the only other choice he had was to die on the end of one of those numerous blades—they'd never let him go after revealing their intent—he'd agreed.

Marius had never been cast in such a heroic role. In spite of his misgivings, he admitted to being a little flattered. His part, while complex and requiring at least one switch in personalities, he'd been able to master in a day's time.

When the Prefect's party had arrived at the Practorium the following week, it had been an easy task for him to blend in with the other servants and slaves assigned to the Prefect and his wife. No one questioned him. After all, what kind of blockhead would pretend to be a slave?

Chapter XLIII

The crowd which had gathered to witness the men being led off to be crucified had largely dispersed by the time Gamaliel and Loukas regained the city streets. A few stragglers still hurried to the Gannath Gate which led out of the city and to the place which someone with a vivid imagination had named Golgotha or Skull Hill. Even though Loukas and Gamaliel were still inside the city walls, they could hear jeering and shouting by the more raucous witnesses in the crowd gathered outside on the hill.

"What is it about State sanctioned death that so fascinates people, Rabban? Death, anyone's death, cannot be pleasant to witness."

"Public executions, gladiatorial shows in the circus, an obsession with conflict…? I was asked that earlier today and I have no answer beyond the suggestion it reflects the times we live in. Our history, Loukas, is hardly one of peaceful or negotiated settlements with our neighbors. We conquer, we are conquered. 'Saul had his hundreds, David had his thousands' the Book tells us if you remember. And you know the reference is not to sheep, but to the Philistines each is credited with dispatching. National heroes are almost universally warriors. Emperors and Kings rise to power on the cold, dead bodies they have laid at their feet."

"That is a very dark view of the world."

"I wish it were not so, but to date, can you think of an exception?"

"I wish I could. Will there ever be an end to it?"

"I think it unlikely. Not in my lifetime anyway. Changing the subject, have you noticed anyone in the street demonstrating an inordinate interest in us?"

"We are at this again?" Loukas paused and, as unobtrusively as he could, glanced both ways. "I cannot tell. There are many people, and some are looking at us. I doubt any of them would be after us."

"No, if they were, the last thing they'd do is make eye contact. Did you happen to see a tallish woman?"

"Did I see…? I may have. Shall I look again?"

"No, no, keep walking. We will make our way to the amphitheater now."

"The amphitheater? We are going to that cesspit because…?"

"Because, as unlikely as it may seem to be, I believe Aurelius' murder began in that place weeks ago."

"At the theater? Weeks? How on earth could that be? Aurelius and the other two did not arrive but a little over a week. They were not expected. How does one plot a murder if you do not know if your victim is going to be where you may get to him?"

"An excellent question, and one I shall answer when two things happen."

"Two? Only two or two that may lead to many more?"

"The former, although I cannot say anything for certain just now."

"Care to share the two?"

"Ah, we have arrived. When you visited this place before what didn't you see?"

"Pardon me, what did I *not* see?"

"Exactly."

"You jest. Very well, I did not see any evidence of hippopotami, eagles, respectable citizens, fruit trees—"

"I do not jest, and you are wasting precious time. I mean, what was missing in that theater that you would have a reasonable expectation of seeing."

"Not hippopotami, then. Let me think…what did I not see… what was missing, you meant. I don't know."

"What about actors?"

◇◇◇

The boy had, in fact discovered how the release of Barabbas would affect his future. Thus, he was in the streets this morning making himself as inconspicuous as possible while keeping close tabs on Gamaliel and Loukas. They might be, he thought, his only hope of staying alive. But could he trust them to keep him safe or would they turn him over to the authorities? He dared not return to the Praetorium under any circumstances.

Besides allowing himself to be drawn into the net of these dangerous men, his problems really began when he discovered that his usefulness to the General had come to an end. He'd returned to the hut outside the Sheep Gate as he'd been told. By chance or luck, before he pushed through the curtain that served as a door, he'd hesitated. The voices within brought him up short.

"He has to go," one of them had said. He couldn't be sure which. The only voice he really knew was the General.

"He is just a boy. What harm can he do?"

"He can tell Pilate's people where to find us."

"Pilate will be gone in three days. Then it will make no difference. It will be months before we have a new Prefect and by then…" the voice trailed off.

"We cannot risk it. What if Pilate escapes the charges? What if it turns out they don't care if he killed one of his own? What if the Rabban succeeds in clearing him?"

"What are the chances of that?"

"If he finds the boy, very good."

"Oh. I see. Do you think he will?"

"The Rabban is not a stupid man like our High Priest. If he has enough time, he will sort this out."

"If only the assassination had worked as we drew it up."

"Or if only you'd sent someone competent to do the job or at least had a little more patience, we might not be sitting here worrying about this."

"Too late for that now. We press on. Very well, kill the boy."

When he overheard the men's talk, he knew that unless he fled immediately, he would not see another day. The Dagger Men would soon be on his trail. Shabbat was not a special day for him, but even so, he'd like to see it and live beyond as well.

Marius sped away into the city as fast as his legs would take him. He needed to hide, to flee. He changed his attire and took to the streets in search of a way to save his skin. The obvious next step would be to leave the city immediately, to attach himself to one of the hundreds of pilgrims packing and pouring through the city gates and roads on their way to the sea or northward to the roads that would take them east and west to their homes. He would have done so, but couldn't. He had no money. He might have been welcome to join any of the departing families, but he could hardly expect them to feed him. His life before and then since becoming a slave in the service of these people meant he had no means to acquire coins. He could try to cut a few purses, he supposed. It wouldn't be the first time, but he hesitated. To be caught in that would also end in his death. Returning to Pilate was out of the question. First, he would be trading what little freedom he currently enjoyed for safety in a life of slavery. Even that didn't sway his decision not to go to Pilate. After all, there was a certain security in slavery. That is if you could pick the right master. But since the people who intended to see him dead also had free access to the Fortress, he knew he wouldn't last a fortnight no matter in whose household he served.

That left continuing to live by his wits in the streets in the hope his pursuers would not find him and eventually give up trying or trusting someone like the Rabban or his friend the Physician to help him. But could he? More importantly, would they? The Rabban worked for Pilate and was trying to find out who killed that other Roman. How likely would they overlook his involvement? Wouldn't it be simpler for them to turn him over to the Prefect? Their task would be completed. Marius had a difficult decision to make, and he didn't have much time to make it. Which way to turn? If he had money he could leave this wretched city forever and his problems would be solved.

His world pivoted on that *if.* Thieving was an occupation he never really developed, though he had tried on occasion, and he had few marketable skills otherwise. If he just had something to sell…who would buy it?

When he turned a corner he spotted the Rabban and the Physician. He stayed close to the storefronts and stalls keeping the Rabban and the Physician in sight while simultaneously scanning the street for men carrying daggers. He needed time to decide whether running into the two men constituted good or bad luck.

Chapter XLIV

By most cities' standards the amphitheater in Jerusalem would be deemed a disappointment both architecturally and artistically. It lacked size and style. Furthermore, classical drama whether comedy or tragedy, Greek or Roman, did not play well to the sober tastes of the city's religious population and there were barely enough gentiles and Hellenized Jews to keep it open year-round. Because of that and its general lack of panache, it could not generate an audience base sufficient to sustain anything more than traveling troupes of actors performing the classics and other entertainment of dubious merit. In the past, one or two attempts had been made to stage *Exagoge*, the play depicting Moses' freeing the Jews from Egypt. It had met with little success. It would have been appropriate for the time and would be mounted in the laxer spirituality of Alexandria and Damascus to great acclaim, but not here. Not in the city of David. Not in the very shadow of the Lord's dwelling place.

Gamaliel paused before the entrance and studied its façade. A slight wind stirred the dust on the street and the faded banners strung across the theater entrance. The sunlight, which had nearly blinded him a moment earlier, began to fade. The streets and building before him were plunged into darkness.

"Loukas, what is happening?" Gamaliel feared nothing of men, but an act of *Ha Shem* was another matter.

"Rabban, it is a phenomenon of the stars. An itinerant astrologer told me about it. Somehow the moon crosses the sun and momentarily blots it out."

"You're sure about that?"

"What else could it be?"

"I am considering the possibility that the High Priest was right? That Yeshua has angered the Lord."

"Really, Rabban, is that the Lord you fall before, one who punishes his creation because it occasionally strays?"

"In a word, yes."

"I see. Well, fear not, the light will return any moment now… There you see, it is finished. The Lord has not moved against us yet."

"Nevertheless, it is very disconcerting. The moon blots out the sun, you say. I imagine the pagans are having a field day with that one. Apollo's chariot collides with Selene's. A catastrophe. Listen to the wailing and moaning."

"I would have wagered any amount that you, of all people, would have no idea who those deities were."

"And you would have lost a great many denari. It is my duty to know these things if I am to refute them."

"Yes. Well, tomorrow is Shabbat, Rabban. After that astral display, I expect many of the lapsed will return to the faith, at least for a while."

"Possibly. All we need now is an earthquake and 'for a while' could become for a lifetime."

"You have more confidence in conversion from fear than I do. Now, before you ask again, Rabban, the Master of the plays, manager, or whatever he is called, is named Mordekay. I have no idea where he comes from originally. His accent could be Greek or slightly farther east and his name is obviously an invention he believes will ingratiate him to the citizenry. He will not tell you the truth even if there is no reason to lie. That should tell you the sort of person you hope to pry information from."

"I wasn't going to ask, but thank you for all that anyway. When you questioned him before, he did say there was no troupe currently in residence?"

"Not exactly. I asked him if any were missing. I assumed a troupe did, in fact, exist. He said no one had gone missing which confirmed my assumption. If no one had gone missing, naturally there had to be something not to be missing from."

"I see, very clever. Did you ask when the players arrived?"

"I saw no reason to. Should I have?"

"At the time, I didn't think so, but now, yes it might be an important piece of information. One more question, when you interviewed him, did you actually see anyone else?"

"Now that you mention it, no I did not. That is strange, isn't it?"

"Probably not as much as you might think. Remember, Loukas, that if the actors are not acting, if there is no audience to pay admission, they wouldn't get paid. No pay, no eat. If the troupe arrived and then, because of the Holy Day or an official edict of some sort, they were denied work, they would have to spread out through the city and look for work, money, something, until they were called to perform or found the wherewithal to move on."

"That is not much of a life."

"No, it is not. Now let's ask this Mordekay person when this troupe arrived in Jerusalem."

"And that will tell us what, exactly?"

"When the plot that ended in the murder of Aurelius was first hatched."

"I know you think Aurelius' murder was premeditated because of the dagger. What has a troupe of players to do with it?"

"Think a moment. Pilate's dagger is stolen. Only half the torches in the hallway were lit. The Centurion denies any involvement in sending a message. Later men, including your servant Yakob, hatch a plot to free Barabbas. It is all of a piece, Loukas."

"Barabbas? Really, Gamaliel, that can't be true. How can Barabbas be connected to the death of the noble Roman?"

"That, my friend, is what we must discover. But I assure you that both Aurelius' death and this amphitheater are smaller segments of a much larger picture."

"And the link that connects them is Mordekay?"

"Mordekay? Certainly not. He is as ignorant as a stump. Mordekay will provide a date and some meetings with the actors that will link us to the boy. The boy is the connection to the murder."

"Marius?"

"The same. Now, we go in."

Eyes were watching him, following his every move, burning a hole in his back. They had found him. That must be it. Marius spun around searching for the watcher, the threat. He couldn't pick out anyone in the crowd. Of course he couldn't. Those people were trained to blend in, weren't they? Assassins had to or they'd never succeed at what they did. No one walked the streets with a placard declaring them to be a murderer, did they? The boy panicked and started to run. He no longer cared what happened to the Rabban and his friend. He needed to find a place to hide and think. His headlong dash brought him to a narrow but relatively tall building. He pushed through a half open door and slammed it shut. After the bright sun he found himself in near pitch black darkness. He tried to slow his breathing while his eyes adjusted to absolute dark. Not even a sliver of light shone through the crack between the door and the sill. Marius was too frightened to notice.

After a moment his panic subsided and his vision improved. He could make out the shapes around him. He realized he had barged into the *scaena* at the amphitheater. He recognized the musty smells of dusty fabric, paint, and bygone actors. The door, which he'd just closed, creaked open. His panic returned. He glanced wildly around looking for a hiding place. He knew he had almost no time to become invisible before this new person's eyesight would adapt to the dark and he could be seen. He scurried as quietly as he could to a corner, crouched down, and drew what he thought must be the flap of a tent over his head.

He could hear voices outside on the stage or in the orchestra. He strained his ears first to listen for someone moving about in the dark and secondly to the conversation outside.

"So, Master Mordekay," Gamaliel said, "This troupe which you do not remember being here, can you tell me when it would have arrived in the city, if there had been one?"

The manager frowned and shook his head. "Sir?"

"If you insist there is no troupe of players in the city, so be it. I need to know when this nonexistent troupe arrived. You will save me a great deal of time and yourself a great deal of inconvenience and pain if you answer my question. When—two weeks, three?"

"Three."

"Good, now we understand each other. Please describe the members of this troupe that is not here."

"The players only or including the people who came with them?"

"The players first. If I need the others, I will tell you."

"Well, the usual. Five men, three boys, all players. They had with them three dressers who also formed part of the chorus and six others who were part of the chorus and occasional players when the drama called for crowds."

"Tell me about the boys."

"What's to tell? They were boys. You know, they had parts if called on. Otherwise they worked the masks."

"Can you describe them in any detail?"

"I'm sorry, but they were not here long enough to even form an impression. When they heard that any play making they would do would have to wait until after Passover and the Shabbat following that, they disappeared into the city."

"While they lingered, did you notice anyone else showing any interest in them—soldiers perhaps, or people from the Praetorium, Pilate's servants, perhaps."

Mordekay shuffled his feet and kept his eyes fixed on the floor. "No, no one."

"Thank you Mordekay. You are a very bad liar, but in spite of your attempts not to seem so, you are a veritable fountain of information. Come along Loukas, it's time to repair to my house. I am expecting the boy any moment."

"The boy? You expect the boy to present himself at your House?"

"In a manner of speaking, yes. We must be on our way."

Marius thought he recognized the voices. It must be the Rabban. He didn't hear the Physician speak so the other voice must be the man in charge of the theater. Why had they come here? What had they discovered? He was doomed. Either those men who'd forced him into that terrible business and who now wished him dead would find him, or the Rabban would and turn him over to Pilate. Whichever came to pass, he was a dead man. He made himself as small as possible. His covering smelled like its last user had been a camel. He lifted the edge of his shelter to access some fresher air. He thought he heard footsteps. There was enough grit on the floor to signal the movements of anyone not treading very carefully. There it was again. A scrape, a thump followed by a muttered curse. Whoever was out there must have barked his shin on a crate.

Marius held his breath for as long as he could. He exhaled. His shelter flap fluttered. Another step, close by, almost on him. He froze.

A hand clamped down on his shoulder. The pain caused him to cry out. Another caught up the fabric across his chest and hauled him to his feet.

"You need to come with me," a hoarse voice on the other side of his camel blanket said.

Marius fainted.

Chapter XLV

"I know I will sound the fool, but what makes you think Marius will magically appear on your doorstep? We have had no contact with him for a week or more. He is Pilate's slave and yet even the Prefect does not know where he is. What did the Master of the Plays say to you that led you to believe the boy would suddenly surface? I heard every word that passed between you and I recall nothing about the boy"

"No? I asked about boys, if you stop and think about it. All troupes of players include a few boys among their number if they can."

"Yes, I remember. You think Marius was an actor at one time?"

"Not at one time, Loukas. Marius is an actor even as we speak."

"But, he is Pilate's slave."

"So he says."

"So Pilate agrees. What are you imagining?"

"First, to be clear, Mordekay told me only what I expected to hear. Second, he told me in the amphitheater. Never underestimate your location when you ask a question that might produce the answer that solves your puzzle. Third, we were there in order to draw the boy to us and, just as importantly, in the one place where he imagined he'd be safe. Finally, earlier I also had words with your Yakob, if you remember."

"You castigated him for being involved with the Zealots."

"Among other things, yes. I also spoke to him afterwards, if you recall. I said I would tell you about that conversation later."

"And you will tell me now?"

"Yes, well, I described our Marius to him, or a variation of him and—"

"A variation? Pardon, but what does that mean?"

"Patience, my friend. You will see. So, shortly after we left he set out on our trail. I assumed the boy lurked somewhere nearby. In fact, I believe he has been doing so for days—with an occasional absence to report to one or more of his masters. I also assumed that sooner or later the possibility he would be threatened or worse by his recent acquaintances would cause him to panic and run. If I guessed correctly, Yakob will deliver Marius to us within the hour. I hope so because Shabbat will soon be upon us, and I will be helpless to do anything about him or our task for a whole day."

"You astound me, Rabban. How can you possible know all this?"

"Tut, it is not difficult if you refuse to be led by the nose. Think for a moment. If Pilate is a murderer, fine, it all fits, not well but adequately. Or, if the murder was committed by someone else to discredit him, also fine. But if either of these two possibilities are not the case and he is not responsible for Aurelius' murder, nothing of what we have been thinking then makes any sense."

"He is caught red handed and…oh, I see, if he isn't. We assume that. Very well, if he is not then…then what? I am lost."

"We have been looking at this backwards, Loukas."

"Sorry, backwards?"

"Backwards, yes. Now, it is nearly the ninth hour and we have not had our midday meal. I am famished. If we hurry along, I can have Binyamin fix us something to eat while we wait for Yakob and the boy to arrive."

"And you are sure they will?"

"I am hopeful, yes…what?"

As Gamaliel spoke the earth shook under his feet. Loukas grabbed at a wall to steady himself. Three roof tiles dislodged from their moorings and shattered at their feet. A fourth followed and grazed Gamaliel's shoulder. The masonry under Loukas' hand cracked and then buckled. He jerked back in time to avoid a shower of rubble from the disintegrating wall. People screamed and looked this way and that for safety. In an earthquake, there are no safe places. Some ran only to stumble and fall. Finally the shaking stopped. Gamaliel rubbed his shoulder.

"Are you alright, Rabban?"

"Bruised I suspect, but still in one piece."

"Well, you did mention an earthquake as a recruitment device to increase the faithful. Shall we expect a hoard of new converts?"

"Possibly. I wonder how the High Priest is reacting to all this."

Whether it had been the last or the first of many, the slap to his face brought Marius to his senses. When he saw the man who'd delivered it crouching over him, he nearly fainted again.

"Please don't kill me," he squeaked. "I promise I will never tell anyone what I know. No, I mean, if I did know anything, which I don't, I wouldn't ever tell anyone. Please, I don't know anything. I just did what you asked. I don't even know your names—"

"You've said a good deal already, boy. You would be wise to close your mouth and keep it that way until we get you to the Rabban of the Sanhedrin."

"Who? No, I mean I know him but…why am I being taken to him?"

The earth trembled. Boxes and crates tumbled from shelves. Heavy stands and candelabra crashed to the floor. A long pole that held a curtain against one wall snapped in half and the curtain ripped in two, top to bottom. Masks careened across the floor and ended in an untidy pile against the opposite wall.

"We have to get out of here," Marius yelped, but he didn't move. Fear locked him in place.

The strange man increased his grip on the boy. "Sit still, boy. Listen to me. If you believe in a god or *the* God, pray to him or her. Pray that the roof on this cattle shed doesn't collapse."

"It isn't a cattle shed, it's—"

"I know what it is, imbecile. I also know what it smells like."

The earthquake subsided. The man stood and hauled Marius to his feet.

"Are you going to walk with me quietly, or will I need to knock you senseless again, and haul you to the Rabban's house like a sack of grain?"

"I can walk." Marius decided if he was to be killed, he would face it with honor. Until that moment, he would stretch out the time to his demise for as long as possible.

◇◇◇

Loukas put his cup down on the table and sighed. For a moment the food, the wine, and the comfort of Gamaliel's dining area had let him forget the earthquake and his chronic confusion about what his friend was up to.

"You said I was looking at the situation backwards. What did you mean?"

"Not you, we, and not we were, we are. We are looking at it that way, you, me, and Pilate. After dismissing Pilate as a murderer, we have assumed that Aurelius was murdered by someone else and Pilate set up to take the blame. We further assumed that the motivation had to do with that same someone's desire to unseat him and take over his Prefecture."

"We did. But you're saying that is not the case? If not, what then? We have nothing."

"Actually, we have more if we do. Listen, if we stay with the backwards theory, then instead of assuming all our witnesses were lying, we assume they were all telling the truth. Priscus the Centurion says he sent no message to Pilate. If he is telling the truth, who did? What if Aurelius was not the intended victim? Then who was? If the murder was not an impulsive act but a premeditated one, what do we conclude? And one last thing, who knew that the official party from Rome was on the way? Pilate says he didn't, so who? Did anyone? Perhaps that is the reason why Aurelius is dead."

"That is too much. I have to think each of your 'what ifs' separately. So, you're saying backwards leads us forward."

"It is a paradox, but yes. Start over with the same set of facts, and you will see where and how this must have happened."

Loukas did not seem convinced.

"Ah, someone at the door. Binyamin, the door. Show our visitors in here. Now you will see, Loukas."

"I will see what? You are going to unravel this problem and win the favor of the Prefect and the enmity of your countrymen?

"The first I hope, the second, I expect not. All will be revealed. And here is Yakob and our Marius, or should I call you Maria today?"

SHABBAT

Chapter XLVI

For most of Gamaliel's life, Shabbat had been spent in prayer, reciting the psalms, or quiet contemplation of scripture, with family and, lately, alone. But from the moment the third star had blinked into view the previous evening it had been one interruption after another. Keeping Shabbat with the boy in residence turned out to be nearly impossible. First, Binyamin complained at having to prepare extra food at the last minute. Then, Loukas refused to stay and divert the boy so that it fell to Gamaliel to instruct his guest in the rigors of Shabbat. In that respect, the boy did not appear to be a willing student. As the day dragged on Gamaliel had to fend off the boy's questions and complaints. Only the fear of what might be waiting outside kept him from bolting out the door.

He had questioned Marius at length the previous evening, right up to the time the shofars sounded from the pinnacle and he had to stop. Loukas lingered and tried to explain to Marius why the Rabban could not violate Shabbat by continuing his questioning. It was a form of work, he'd said and prohibited by the Law. The boy frowned and asked a dozen more questions. Finally, Loukas had to excuse himself and leave. The boy attempted to question Gamaliel repeatedly and finally dropped off to sleep. He was at it again the first thing in the morning.

In desperation, Gamaliel instructed Binyamin to keep an eye on the boy, and he left his house. Peace, if there was to be any, would be found at the Temple. It had become a frequent retreat from the complexities of life for him, and if ever there was a time to seek peace, it was this moment. He had not gone more than a hundred paces from his door when any thoughts of a quiet afternoon were blown away by a gale named Rufus, Pilate's friend and, today, his messenger boy.

"Rabban Gamaliel," Rufus began. Neither the title nor the name came easily to him, and he cleared his throat as if he'd just expelled something unpleasant from somewhere deep within.

"Honored sir," Gamaliel said and nodded.

"You are to come with me."

"I am afraid that is quite impossible."

"This request comes from the Prefect himself."

"Even so…"

"You fail to understand me."

"Oh, I know what you are asking. It is just that I am unable to comply with Pilate's request, as you describe it."

"Then understand this. It is not a request or a wish. He orders your presence at once."

During the exchange, Gamaliel had managed to gain the Temple Mount. His path led directly to the Temple. The crowds were thinner than the week before. Pilgrims had either started on their way home or remained in their camps and tents.

"Oh, I know what your Master wants. I offer my regrets at not being in a position to give him it, but it is Shabbat and I cannot. Tell him that. He will not be happy, but he will understand. I suspect he knows it already."

Gamaliel turned on his heel and stepped into the Temple courts. Once in the Court of the Israelites, Rufus could not follow him—not without consequences, at least. Rufus was left to fume in the Court of the Gentiles. Gamaliel did not turn to catch his reaction. He might need Rufus the next day when he finally did confront the Prefect.

"You cannot deny him, Rabban," Rufus shouted. "In two days, he is to be taken to Rome. He will be ruined. He might be assassinated."

Gamaliel wheeled around and raised his right hand. "He will not be going anywhere, Rufus. Tell him that. Tell him I will call on him tomorrow and I will require the presence of his guests as well."

He turned and disappeared into the Temple.

Loukas had been Hellenized in his youth and had never really embraced the strict observance practices of his neighbors. Jerusalem differed from the rest of the country in that. The Temple served as the city's focus and primary business, as it were. Orthodoxy characterized its inhabitants. Elsewhere, for example in the Galilee, observance of the Law was more relaxed. So, he did not keep a strict Shabbat. And that explained why he'd left Gamaliel with the boy. He'd spent one Shabbat with the Rabban and vowed he never would again. For Loukas, Shabbat meant a relief from work, not a prohibition of it. It meant no patients to visit unless they represented an emergency. He would spend his day catching up. His bag needed replenishment, bandages, potions, powders, and balms. He also needed to sit down with Yakob and have a serious talk about Zealots and Sicarii. It would not be a pleasant conversation. Given his servant's volcanic temper, it might even be dangerous. Either he would end up with a faithful servant and ally or with no servants at all. He had no prescription in his bag to relieve his dislike of confrontation, no powder or pastille to ease its execution. Gamaliel, he knew, would throw himself into any verbal conflict. In fact, he would frequently invite it. It is what rabbis did in each other's company. The art of disputation fueled their lives as wine did that of a drunkard, but Loukas had a more conciliatory nature and heated argument did not sit well with him.

"You wanted a word, sir?" Yakob stood before him in as near a posture of servility as his pride would allow, which wasn't much.

"Yes, I do. Sit."

Yakob seemed taken aback. Servants rarely were allowed to sit with their masters. But then, this Greek Jew didn't fit anyone's mold. He sat.

"You may find this difficult, Yakob, but bear with me. You served the Empire for many years, not because you wished to, but because you were forced to. I understand that. As a Physician, I know how painful old wounds can be and how long some take to heal, if they ever do."

"Yes, sir?"

"Yes, well it is like this. I need a servant whose loyalty is to me first and foremost. Such a servant sees my enemies as his, my friends as his. I must depend on him for support and even defense should that ever be necessary. Do you understand?"

"I was a legionnaire, as you noted, for many years. What you just said is what we were taught. We were to serve Rome. Rome was the master, but the lesson was the same."

"Good, then we understand each other. If, back when you marched against Rome's enemies, you were to have divided your loyalties, perhaps offered succor to your enemy or aid to another army, what was the likely outcome if you were to have been discovered?"

"I would not see the next sunrise."

"Exactly. Yakob, I expect no less than the same loyalty from you albeit, if I do not receive it, your life will not be in danger, only your livelihood. As you know, the Rabban and I are working to salvage the Prefect's life. That cannot sit well with you. I also know you are in contact with certain radical elements in the community. As my servant, whom I hope will be with me for a long time, I cannot have a divided loyalty. Irrespective of your feelings about the Prefect and your sympathy for the ideas of these Zealots, I must ask you to set them aside and be of service to me and the Rabban. Can you do that?"

Yakob's scowl would have done an angry Zeus proud. Loukas could almost hear the thoughts knocking against one another in his servant's mind. At last, his expression softened.

"I did as the Rabban asked yesterday. I will again. To tell you the truth, sir, I am weary of fighting, weary of carrying this hate around. If you will always be honest with me, I will serve you as you ask. Also, Sarai has had these same words with me. I do not wish to lose her."

"Thank you. That could not have been easy for you to say. Now, go and enjoy a quiet Shabbat. Tomorrow, I fear, might be trying for you. We go to rescue the Prefect. As much as I am sure you will dislike doing it, you might be called on to help us in that undertaking."

"Yes, I will, but I would ask one question? Why did your Rabban want me to scare that woman half to death and then drag her to his house?"

"The woman is not a woman at all. He is a boy named Marius and he is an actor. He dressed as a woman for several reasons, but when you found him, it was to hide—to hide in plain sight. Why he did will be made clear tomorrow, I hope."

YOM RISHON

Chapter XLVII

They made a strange procession. For the occasion, the Rabban wore his robes of office, Loukas a toga of homespun, and definitely not Israelite. Yakob wore the plain tunic one associated with an off duty legionnaire, and his somewhat worse for wear broadsword sheathed at his side. The three were flanked by a quartet of legionnaires, preceded by Rufus, and trailed by a crowd of noisy Israelites. The presence of the soldiers inspired Yakob to march a little straighter, a little taller, shoulders back, eyes forward. Marius had been left behind. He would be called to testify, but only if and when the Rabban had extracted a promise from the Prefect that he would be granted immunity from prosecution if he did so. Gamaliel did not tell him that Pilate's promises were as substantial as smoke. He hoped to keep Marius out of the equation altogether, but he could not predict the behavior of the other Roman officials.

They paused at the foot of the steps that led to the platform where only two and a half days earlier Barabbas and the Galilean rabbi had met their respective fates, Barabbas freedom, Yeshua death. As they ascended, they heard and then saw a commotion of some sort had erupted at the top. Gamaliel recognized Caiaphas in an animated conversation with Pilate. Pilate's face had turned bright red, a shade Gamaliel knew from experience could well have a tragic end for the source of his anger. Caiaphas flapped his arms and stamped about in a mad choreography unaware that he danced on the rim of a volcano.

"It was your guards," Caiaphas screamed.

"You think my guards care a fig about your rabbi. Your people must have slipped them a bribe. Then they stole the body away. My guards are gone—in the wind, High Priest, but if I find them, it will go hard on them."

"What is the problem, Prefect, High Priest?"

"Yeshua."

"The High Priest's rabbi."

They answered together and then glared, first at each other and then at Gamaliel.

Gamaliel raised both hands as if to ward off an impending deluge of words. "The rabbi is dead. Surely he can bother you no more, High Priest."

"The tomb that Josef provided was empty this morning. Now his followers claim he rolled the stone back and is alive. Some hysterical woman or women are rushing around claiming they saw him and he is alive, that he did not die."

Yakob cut in. "With respect, your Excellencies, they do not claim he did not die. They claim he did die but then rose from the dead."

"Really? And you know this how?"

"My wife, Excellency." Yakob caught Gamaliel's eye and shrugged. "She is close to some of Yeshua's people."

"I see." Pilate said. He seemed oddly delighted at the news. "Well then, perhaps what they said about him was true after all. He was a demigod. Demigods sometimes do that you know, return from Pluto's realm. There is Osiris and Orpheus and—"

Caiaphas seemed on the verge of apoplexy. "Yeshua is not one of your ridiculous pagan deities. He claimed to be the son of the Lord," he yelled.

"Yes, well, your Lord, my Jupiter, his Zeus, Hades, Pluto, what is the difference, and more to the point, who cares? Rabban, calm this man down before he explodes."

"High Priest, I am sure there is a rational explanation for all of this. In any case you will not have it resolved here by abusing the Prefect, or until after we have a chance to interview some witnesses. It is not all that unusual, you know. There are instances in the Book and the culture of this sort of thing happening. Loukas, here, as you know, is a Physician. He can give you many examples of this phenomenon."

"Actually, Rabban, I cannot. But, as the Prefect has noted, I have heard of this sort of thing in other religious disciplines."

"There, you see, Caiaphas. Now you should retire to the Temple and see to the backlog of sacrifices the Passover has engendered."

Caiaphas' jowls shook in frustration. Then, the color drained from his face as the realization dawned that he might have overstepped and he should probably quit the Prefect's presence before he uttered one word too many. He stormed down the steps and across the mount to the Temple.

"So, Rabban, you are here at last. Rufus has informed you of my imminent departure unless you can answer some questions on my behalf?" He turned and stared at Yakob. "And who is this man who presumes to address the Prefect about the status of a dead rabbi without being asked?"

"This is Yakob, formerly in the service of the Empire and ah, um…Loukas' bodyguard."

"The Physician needs a bodyguard?"

"These are trying times, Excellency, and to answer your question about Rufus, he has so informed me and I can."

"Good. I will send for the Tribune and Cassia and an amanuensis. I want this proceeding in writing."

"Was the rabbi really not in his tomb this morning?"

"That is the report."

"Interesting. It seems we have not heard the last of him after all."

Pilate ushered them into a room set to one side of the public platform and signaled to Rufus to fetch Tribune Grex and Cassia Drusus. Pilate had anticipated the meeting. Whether he had that much confidence in Gamaliel, or a backup plan should the Rabban fail, may never be known. At any rate, the room had had its furniture arranged in the fashion of a court. Two heavy chairs had been pulled up behind a table. Here the two dignitaries were seated. Opposite them Pilate had placed a third chair in which he was now seated. Gamaliel and the other two men were left to stand to one side.

"You may proceed, Rabban," Pilate said.

"One moment." Cassia stared at Pilate. "Are we to understand that you have trusted your case to this Jew?"

"Yes."

"I see. And you, what is your name, Jew?"

"I am Gamaliel, son of Simeon, grandson of Hillel the Elder, and Rabban of the Sanhedrin. With me is Loukas the Physician, and his manservant Yakob ben Nathaniel, formerly a legionnaire who loyally served the Empire for two decades. I have been given the unenviable task of establishing the innocence or guilt of your Prefect." Pilate nearly catapulted out of his chair when Gamaliel mentioned guilt. "After many days of arduous investigation, I have finally unraveled the tangled threads that led to the murder of Aurelius Decimus."

"And why, Rabban Gamaliel, son of Simeon ben Hillel, should we believe anything you say to us? You have no standing. You are not a citizen of the Empire and therefore cannot plead anyone's case."

"Yet, you will hear me out for two very important reasons."

"And they are?"

"Citizen or not, I am the chief officer of the Law in this land. I adjudicate its interpretation every day. It is our Law, to be sure, but in this land it is *the* Law. Your Emperor has so decreed, and so it must be."

"I must think about that. And the second reason?"

"You will know I speak the truth because I have absolutely nothing whatsoever to gain from an exercise which may exonerate the Prefect. In fact, I may lose my position and reputation if I do so. You must understand, then, that I have more to gain by finding Pontius Pilate guilty than innocent."

Pilate squirmed in his chair and shot Gamaliel an injured look.

"Very well, Rabban. We will accept your credentials for the moment. You may proceed. You do understand we require that you follow the rules of our trial system?"

"I would if I could, your Excellencies, but as I have only a glancing acquaintance with them, I cannot promise to do as you wish. I will proceed with as much order as this tangled case allows. Perhaps I should summarize and then go into specifics."

"Please do and quickly."

"Very briefly, then, I will show that the plan to commit the murder originated here in this city at least two and more likely three weeks ago. In any event, well before the Prefect left Caesarea Maritima. It directly involved three men and a boy. The men were intimately involved with inner workings of the Fortress. Due to Aurelius' overarching ambition, he found himself in the wrong place at the wrong time and became an incidental victim of a more ambitious plot."

"What do you mean, 'incidental' victim?"

"Aurelius Decimus was not the intended target".

"What? You are not making any sense Rabban. He had a dagger stuck in his ribs. Pilate's dagger to be precise. How can you say he wasn't—"

"The Prefect's dagger is the most interesting piece to this puzzle. When we met on the first day and I heard that it was his dagger that had been used to murder Aurelius, I felt certain of your Prefect's innocence."

Chapter XLVIII

Gamaliel suppressed a smile as his words registered on the Roman's faces. In his mind, precious little difference existed between disputing a man's innocence or guilt and disputing the interpretation of an obscure Talmudic passage. He took a breath and stepped into the center of the room to address the two Romans. The difference in their status and his, the threat they posed to him personally if he offended or failed, mattered little to him now. He was in his element.

Cassia scowled. "How can the fact that Aurelius Decimus met his end with the Prefect's knife possibly indicate Pilate's innocence? I would think the reverse would be the case."

"I had a long conversation with an erstwhile assassin and also an armorer. They both assured me that if they wished to dispatch your friend the last weapon they would select would be a dress dagger, the Prefect's or any other. Those daggers have, as a rule, no edge and dullish tips. At the very least, using one would make murder difficult. All my experiences with the accused have convinced me that whatever else may be said of him, he is not stupid. If he wished to kill his rival, he would have used a more efficient blade. More importantly, what sort of fool uses his own dagger to kill a rival? Would either of you? No, if you had murder in your heart and had thought about it, you would use an anonymous dagger, one that could not be traced back to you. Aurelius had the Prefect's blade stuck in his ribs, *ergo* someone else killed him in what may be thought a pathetic attempt to implicate your Prefect."

The Tribune snorted. "That is your entire case? Pilate you have not done yourself any favors calling on this man to be your advocate."

"Excuse me, Tribune," Gamaliel said, "but that is not the case. That is the presumption I needed to make before I took the case. If I had believed at any time that Pilate was guilty of the crime, I would not be standing here. I do not consider myself a stupid man either, and as I said, defending the man most hated by the residents of Jerusalem benefits me not at all. If he were guilty I would have said so at the outset. Now may I continue?"

The Tribune shrugged but the smirk that had signaled his doubts about Gamaliel lingered.

"This murder was planned weeks ago and begins with the Sicarii. You are familiar with those men, I believe."

"Fleas to be squashed."

"Possibly, but more importantly for Rome and us, they are a common enemy. They, like the bandit released several days ago, prey on both camps equally. The Sicarii believe that terrorizing the population by killing the people they label as collaborators, will make your rule more difficult and perhaps even provoke a rebellion."

"That is nonsense."

"Of course it is. No one but a fool would attempt to stand against Rome. Not, at least, without a substantial army at its back. It will never happen here. We may be unhappy with your rule, but we are not foolish. We will wait. Zealots, on the other hand, whether in Britannia, Germania, Gaul, or Israel are not so rational. For them, passion displaces common sense. So, moving on, a small group of these men, situated in this very Fortress, hatched a plan to assassinate a certain Roman official. To do it and also to make a statement about their brilliance, the decision was made to use the Prefect's dagger as the lethal weapon, fully aware that it could make the task more difficult."

"Ridiculous."

"Perhaps, but hear me out. How would they get their hands on such a closely guarded item?" Gamaliel paused and stared at Pilate for a moment. "Your Prefect knows how they did it but has yet to complete the thought. Prefect?"

Pilate drummed his fingers on the chair arm. His scowl, which had creased his forehead since the subject of the dagger came up, became darker. Then, it disappeared.

"The woman," he said to the two officials at the table. "Procula, my good wife reported a strange woman in our company. That woman has never been seen again. She must have taken it."

"You want us to believe a strange woman slips into your company and you do not notice?"

"And never seen again, but familiar somehow, wouldn't you say, Prefect?" Gamaliel said. "Bear with me for a little longer, your Excellencies. When Pontius Pilate comes to Jerusalem he brings with him a few of his household from Caesarea. Once here they are joined by the servant staff in residence and supplemented with temporary employees taken on for the occasion. It would be easy to insert a stranger into the mix. All you would need is a willing supervisor. Remember, I said at the beginning that the planners were located in the Fortress."

"Very well. What next? The woman steals the dagger. What has any of this to do with premeditation? All of it could have been worked out in an hour and done specifically to throw suspicion off Pilate. You said yourself he was not stupid."

"But now you concede that there can be some doubt about his involvement?"

"Not enough to release him."

"No? Then we continue. I have, in my custody, the person responsible for lifting the knife. If necessary, he will testify to that."

"He? You said woman took the knife."

"Yes, I did. May I have something to drink? Talking makes me parched."

Gamaliel was brought a drink. He sipped. The officials hearing Pilate's case stirred in their chairs. When he had stretched the time out as much as he dared, he placed the cup on the table and continued.

"I did say he, I did say a woman, and I did imply premeditated. Some weeks ago an iterant troupe of actors, the *dramatis personae,* you would say, arrived in Jerusalem hoping to offer plays at our amphitheater. They were rebuffed. Their number included several men and three boys. If you are familiar with the theater, you know that the boys wear the colors of youths and because their voices have not yet changed, often assume the roles of women. One of these boys, Marius, the tallest, was coerced to pose as a woman, steal the dagger, and then stay on playing the role of a slave assigned to the Prefect."

Pilate stood. "What are you saying? That boy was not a part of my household?"

"You recall, Prefect, that your wife reported a strange woman and then on second thought decided that the face was a familiar one after all. Familiar because she ran across the boy almost daily in your company."

"You have the boy?" the Tribune asked.

"He is in my custody, yes."

"He must be brought to us. If he is party to murder, he must be punished."

"Yes, I supposed you would say that. However, there is a jurisdictional problem here. He is also guilty of a serious transgression of one of our Laws. First, he must be tried in our court, you see? I doubt there will be time to turn him over to you before your departure. I will offer him to the Prefect later."

"Rabban, we do not need all these tiresome details. Just tell us who murdered Aurelius if not Pilate."

"Very well, the sequence of events is as follows, the boy is suborned and steals the dagger. It is passed to an assassin, one of the Sicarii, I believe, who lies in wait in the darkened hallway. Another of their number, this time posing as a legionnaire, delivers a message, purportedly from Priscus the Centurion to Pilate requesting they meet. The Prefect, suspecting nothing amiss, goes, but he is late. When he arrives he finds Aurelius dead and you arrive shortly thereafter. I must ask Cassia Drusus a question at this point. What prompted you to go to that corridor when you did?"

"Me? I received a message from the Tribune that I should."

"I sent you no message."

"It was delivered by a legionnaire from the local barracks, was it not?"

"Yes, as a matter of fact it was."

"That is the final piece. The legionnaire who delivered both messages might have been a legionnaire at one time. I am told that a few Jewish legionnaires come here after fulfilling their service time or have defected. I am also told that some of them are less than happy with their former masters and are easily recruited to the Zealots and Sicarii. At any rate, Priscus denies he ever sent a message, and it is now evident he told the truth."

"But Aurelius, what possible reason had they to murder him?"

"Well, he was a highly placed Roman. Ordinarily that would be reason enough, but as I indicated, he wasn't the intended victim."

"Wasn't? Who then?"

"Pilate was the target. The Sicarii have been, until recently, considered no more than an annoyance. Their activities have been directed to low level and easily approached targets, but to murder the Prefect? Well, that would change everything, you see?"

"We will have to take your word for that. Go on."

"They send one of their own, disguised as a legionnaire. They know he will not be discovered because it is common knowledge that the Prefect cannot tell one legionnaire from another. Pilate receives the message. And later you receive a similar message. You were supposed to discover Pilate's body lying on the floor with his dagger in his heart, a touch of intended irony. But Pilate is late and doesn't get his own dagger stuck in his ribs, Aurelius does."

"But what was Aurelius doing there?"

"Ah! Before he was the assassin's victim, Aurelius was the victim of unbridled ambition. I am sure he overheard the message given to Pilate by the false legionnaire. The meeting had been labeled important and he thought he might hear something which could improve his chances to supplant the Prefect. Thus, he goes to the corridor and into the shadows to eavesdrop on the Centurion and Pilate. Our murderer lurks, in the same shadows waiting for the Prefect. But instead, Aurelius arrives first and slips into the dark to spy on his rival. The murderer sees only a Roman of obvious stature with his back to him. Who else could it be but the Prefect? He stabs him and leaves, his mission accomplished. Imagine the plotters' annoyance when they discover that they have killed the wrong man. Then, they are rewarded when it appears you have decided to arrest Pilate. He may not be dead, but disgraced and gone will do."

"That is an amazing story. You can verify the details?"

"All of them."

"The role this supposed bodyguard you brought with you is…?"

"He will indicate which of the names written on this wax tablet you will want to question."

"Wax tablet with names. How did you come by…never mind, I have heard enough. Pontius Pilate, you will want to resume your duties and bring these people to account. I expect you will find a few more candidates for your Skull Hill. We are done here."

Chapter XLIX

Loukas reclined on a leather-covered couch he had come to view as his own. Binyamin had prepared their midday meal and now, sated, they relaxed with a plate of early fruit.

"What just happened?"

"We extracted the Prefect from the quicksand he was cast into."

"That's it?"

"The plays you pretend to abhor, but about which you seem to know a great deal, the one about Clytemnestra is part of a trilogy and is not the third about justice? In *Eumenides* isn't there a trial and justice is meted out to Orestes for the murder of his parents or something?"

"Yes, so?"

"Like the goddess Athena, we found justice among the Romans in spite of the Fates that is all."

"I'm impressed. I had no idea you patronized the theater."

"I don't, but I read."

"I see. By the way, you were very convincing this morning, Rabban. You even sold that story to me. Pilate should be pleased."

"What Pilate thinks or does not think is of little interest to me."

"You aren't serious."

"No, I am not, but it wasn't a story. Everything I said was true. I did omit a few pieces, I admit, but they were not needed to free the Prefect."

"I see. Only a few pieces? Very well, one or two those pieces

I would like explained. You said the boy is under arrest for a crime. What crime would that be?"

"Loukas, I could not turn him over to those men. He is a boy, not a criminal. He doesn't deserve to die. I decided to keep him out of their clutches if I could. So, I made that up. It's not entirely a lie. There must be a stricture against assuming the persona of a woman somewhere in Leviticus. That would be the crime. If that is insufficient, I will find something."

"I see, and you think you will get away with that?"

"It worked."

"But what if Pilate sends for him?"

"He will not. He will be on his way to Caesarea Maritima and away from those two hunting dogs the Emperor set on him as soon as he possibly can. Besides, the boy may be about to change his name and disappear. Tell me, Loukas, now that I have tamed your servant, Yakob, how does the idea of acquiring an apprentice strike you? Marius is bright and eager. He has no future in the theater and he knows that."

"Me? Take on the boy as an apprentice?"

"You could raise him up as your old master raised you. It would be like giving back."

"An apprentice? You are sure he can do the work."

"I am only sure he will try."

"Very well, I will think about it. Tell me something else. You claimed that the fact that Pilate's dagger was used to murder Aurelius was the moment you knew he was innocent. That is not what you said to me at the time."

"No, it was the second or third thing and it only occurred to me. No, the first thing that made me to doubt his guilt was Procula's vision."

"The Prefect's wife. She is mad. What in her vision made you think him innocent?"

"I would like to say the content, but that is not so, although it did turn out to be prophetic. No, the fact that she intervened in the first place. She may be mad, but she is not a fool. If her husband had been guilty, she never would have accosted me in the hallway with such a cracked idea."

"Still, it's pretty thin. How prophetic?'

"She said that she saw the murder, that a Tribune was responsible. That part was right. Not a Roman Tribune, she said, but another. The Sicarii are organized like the army. One of their more important leaders is referred to as the General, which would translate to Tribune. The boy told me."

"Oh."

Loukas stood and made to leave but paused. "What was the business about Yeshua all about? Why did Pilate accede to Caiaphas' insistence that the rabbi be crucified? It isn't the sort of issue he normally considers. It concerns the Sanhedrin, not Rome and Galilee, not Judea."

"Ah, that is the interesting part. You might ask why those three visitors from Rome were here in the first place. You know the Emperor is said to be on the verge of insanity. He has secluded himself on some island and governs from there. The stories about his behavior are scandalous. Do you remember the merchant's nonsensical story Agon told us, about the Emperor fearing the power of *Elohim*? With most stories that become wilder with the retelling, there is always a kernel of truth in them. According to Rufus, Tiberius took it in his head that our Prefect had become enamored with 'the god of the Israelites.' He thought that because of our reputation for defiance and our well known lack of cooperation with their rule, not to mention how the Lord challenges his own notion of divinity, he would order those three to come and investigate. Aurelius was more than happy to join them. In fact, it might be that it was he who put the ridiculous notion in the Emperor's head in the first place. There is a certain irony in that, if true. Everyone knew he lusted after Pilate's position. The other two did so because they feared what an annoyed Tiberius would do to them if they didn't."

"Surely not, and what has that to do with Yeshua?"

"Yeshua made claims about his relationship to *Ha Shem*. To a pagan, to Pilate, and to the remaining two officials—*Ha Shem,* forgive me—those claims sounded god-like. Pilate reasoned that if he killed one of the Hebrew's demigods, which was his idea of what Yeshua represented, he could convince them that he was not in league with the Lord. So, he made up that story about a tradition of freeing one prisoner on Passover, and then gave the vote to condemn to the assembled crowd. Then by misdirection, he had the result he wanted but with no cause to blame him for the result."

"It's nonsense."

"Yes, but it worked."

"And Barabbas goes free. Tell me, why on earth did he choose him? Wouldn't it have been more prudent to offer one of the others due to be crucified? There were the two thieves. Releasing Barabbas can't be good."

"Even that. Remember, Barabbas is a common enemy, theirs and ours and, once again, we made the choice to free him, not Pilate. A common thief poses no real threat to the people. But to turn loose the terror known to all? Now we must rely on our overlords to recapture the bandit. Pilate becomes our benefactor in the process. For me, it is a blessing."

"A blessing? Sorry, how so?"

"The difficulty I faced in this whole idiotic matter had to do with how the Nation would judge me if I successfully defended the one man they all wish dead or departed. The only way I could come out of this in one piece would be to find a perpetrator who was more feared than the Prefect. At this moment in time, it is the Sicarii. Barabbas' freedom falls on his head and on the High Priest. I, on the other hand, attempted to prevent both of these abominations from happening."

"You say you had to come up with…the Sicarii really did plot to assassinate the Pilate? You didn't make that up just to…?"

"The Prefect said I was *iustus*. Would a just man fabricate something as devious as all that?"

"No, a just man would not. More appropriately put, would the Rabban of the Sanhedrin? I must go. I will think about the boy, and if I can find room for him in my life, I will send Sarai or Yakob to fetch him."

◇◇◇

As he expected, Caiaphas appeared at his door before sundown. Gamaliel greeted him and offered refreshment.

"I came to thank you, Rabban. My temper nearly cost me my position as High Priest, maybe my life."

"Pilate's face had achieved the shade of crimson that normally would have had you confined in the Antonia Fortress dungeon. It was fortunate you left when you did."

"I suppose so. So, now what do I do with this nonsense about the man failing to die?"

"Yeshua? At the risk of sounding like I am saying, 'I told you so,' what else did you expect? Your obsession with that man has turned him from being an effective, if mildly heretical rabbi, into a martyr. There is nothing you can do now but wait it out."

"But they say he has been seen in the streets, that his disciples gather and meet with him."

"They would wouldn't they. Two possibilities present themselves. First, his disciples somehow stole the body and are making all this up to keep alive the ministry he established. You know the appeal it has particularly to the underclass. Why don't you ask the disciple who turned him over to you what really happened?"

"He has disappeared. What is the second?"

"Yeshua, they say, had a disciple who looked a lot like him. Tomas. I was told they called him the twin. It is possible that these sightings are simply Tomas and not a risen Yeshua?"

"Possibly, but I doubt such a theory will hold up very long, especially when another hysterical woman claims to have seen them together. No, I will go with your first suggestion. I will insist that guards were bribed and the body was stolen and buried somewhere in the wilderness, perhaps with the connivance of Barabbas."

"I would leave that last part out. Barabbas as an ally would certainly sully his name, but at the same time remind the people that you were responsible for his release. That, in turn, will prompt more questions than you have answers."

"I suppose you are right. Let's see if we can convince the people to blame Pilate for that."

"Caiaphas, you get in trouble when you attempt cleverness. Let it go. In the meantime, it appears you will have to deal with Yeshua for a while longer."

"You think it will pass in time?"

"I believe it unlikely. In any case, that is up to *Ha Shem,* High Priest, not you, not I, and not even the Emperor himself. Now, I must prepare this Isaiah scroll for our friends in Qumran."

"They are not our friends."

"Perhaps not, but I doubt the Romans would make that distinction. Anyway it is really wonderful workmanship. If they take care of it, it should last for thousands of years."

Appendix

Jesus' Trial—The Timing

Masad Hasidim or the community at Qumran, that of the Dead Sea Scrolls, was a group of dissident Jews—a denomination not unlike the Pharisees. Commonly identified as the Essenes, they were believed to use an older calendar to calculate Holy Days and Feasts. It is generally believed that they would have celebrated Passover on Tuesday rather than Thursday of the week now referred to as Holy Week or Passover. That would explain the textual differences between John's Gospel and the three Synoptic Gospels. This narrative assumes Jesus celebrated the Last Supper with them and would have had Passover later in the week. (Tradition places the Upper Room in the Essene Quarter). This assumption allows ample time for the events described in the Passion Narratives to take place. One major difficulty with those narratives lies on the time available and the process guaranteed Jews accused of serious crimes, as Jesus was. It is highly unlikely that his trial and condemnation could have happened between late Thursday night and Friday noon, but if it began Tuesday and carried through to Friday, it would work.

The timetable used in this narrative is as follows:

Passover Week

> Yom Rishon (Sunday), Jesus enters the city riding an ass to the cheers of the people.

Yom Sheni (Monday), Jesus teaches in the Temple.

Yom Shlishi (Tuesday), Jesus cleanses the Temple and celebrates the Essene Passover.

Yom Revi'i (Wednesday), Jesus is brought before the Sanhedrin.

Yom Chamishi (Thursday), Jesus is brought to Pilate and Antipas (Orthodox Passover).

Yom Shishi (Friday), Jesus is crucified. (Mark writes at the ninth hour.)

Yom Shabbat (Saturday)

Yom Rishon (Sunday), the Resurrection.

Speaking the Name

Orthodox Jewish custom prevents a person from saying the name of God. The pronunciation of the Hebrew, הוהי (the tetragrammaton, YHWH) which designates the Almighty is sometimes pronounced Yaweh (I Am), Jehovah, or some other circumlocution. Even today, orthodox Jewish literature and web sites will print God only as G*d. Because our protagonist, Gamaliel, would have been at least as orthodox as modern day practice, the term Lord, or the Lord, *Adonai,* or *Elohim,* is used instead of God in order to make this distinction. Sometimes a greeting would be even more circumspect and the person initiating it would merely say "Greetings in the Name, or just "The Name" (*Ha Shem*).

Hours of the Day

A day was divided into twenty four hours—twelve for daylight, twelve for night. Day began at sunup and ended at sunset thus making a full twenty-four hour cycle. The hours were of indefinite lengths depending on the season, shortest in the winter, longer in the summer, but noon, when the sun stood at its zenith, was designated the sixth hour.

The Antonia Fortress

Traditionally, the Fortress named by Herod the Great for his onetime ally and friend, Mark Antony, is thought to have been located at the northern edge of the Temple Mount. It served as the headquarters (Praetorium) for the legionnaires permanently assigned to the city and the Prefect, Pontius Pilate, when he traveled down from Caesarea Maritima.

The Dome of the Rock is assumed to be sited on the location of Herod's Temple and as such it is a major sticking point for many orthodox Jews and Christians who feel that the site should revert to the Israelis and be made available should a new Temple be built. Whether such a project would or even will be cannot be discussed here beyond noting that the location is hotly contested and relates to the claims each side makes as to where the Temple stood and then which building would take precedence, should it be decided that both shared the same location.

Josephus, the Jewish historian writing in the first century, describes the Fortress as being located in the current position now occupied by the Dome of the Rock. Josephus, (Jewish Wars 5.238-247) describes the Fortress' location as being on the highest point on the hill. Islamists refer to that place as Mount Mariah, the point from which Mohammad was lifted up to heaven. It is there the Dome of the Rock is located, built in the seventh century.

If, as Josephus claims, that the Antonia Fortress was built on a rock 25 meters above the Temple Mount floor platform, the Antonia Fortress must have been located where the Dome of the Rock is sited and the Temple must have been located further south, possibly where the El-Kas fountain is (was). The rock formation on which the Dome of the Rock rests harmonizes exactly with Josephus' description, being about 25 meters high, the measurement he avers the Fort of Antonia was built on and that means the current floor of the Dome of the Rock is 23 meters above the Temple floor in Jesus' day.

Further tradition holds that the Western Wall (the Wailing Wall) lies opposite the location of the Temple. An aerial view of the wall and the current Temple Mount places it well south of the Dome of the Rock.

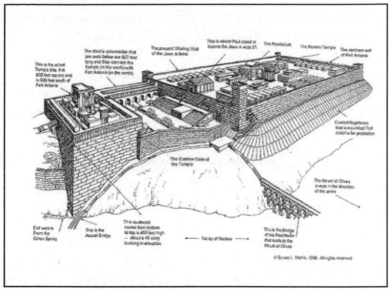

A prospect of the Temple and Antonia Fortress as viewed from the Mount of Olives as described by Josephus

If one reads the eyewitness accounts of Josephus, the Temple and Fortress would appear as illustrated. (Illustration used with permission).

Keeping Time

We do not know with any certainty when the rabbi from Nazareth, Jesus, was born. We have fairly substantial evidence that Herod the Great died in 4 BCE. If it was he who ordered the slaughter of the innocents (Matthew 2:16), then Jesus had to have been born sometime before that. The story is set in the year 30 CE on the assumption that the earlier date is correct and Jesus was in his mid-thirties when his ministry was in full flower. But the date is admittedly arbitrary. It should be noted here that there are scholars who place Jesus' birth as late as 6 CE and cite Luke's reference to Quirinius as governor of Syria, an office he held around 6-9 CE. But Quirinius is believed to have served in some official capacity in Syria twice: 6-4 BCE and then again in 6-9 CE so the earlier birth date can stand. The identifiers CE (Current Era) and BCE (Before Current Era) are now used in lieu of BC and AD because of this.

Scripture

Unless otherwise indicated, Bible verses are from the King James version but occasionally altered either for clarity or for textual reasons.

Historical Characters

Barabbas

One of the more ironic coincidences in the Gospel narrative involves the person of Barabbas. It was the name of a bandit, a robber, and possibly one of the forerunners of the *Siccori* or assassins. The gospel tells us his full name was Yeshua Barabbas, that is, Jesus Barabbas. In Hebrew the word *bar or ben* means son of, and *abba* means father. Therefore, Yeshua Barabbas could easily be translated, or heard as, Yeshua (Jesus), son of (the) Father, particularly if enunciated by a non-Hebrew speaker.

Caiaphas

Yosef bar Kayafa: High Priest of the Temple 18 CE to 36 CE. Although removed from office by Caligula, he saw his sons succeed him in the office later.

Gamaliel

Gamaliel the Elder, Gamaliel I: Served as the Rabban (chief rabbi) of the Sanhedrin, the ruling body of Israel. While believing the Law of Moses to be wholly inspired, he is reported to have taken a broad-minded and compassionate stance in its interpretation. Gamaliel held that the Sabbath Laws should be understood in a realistic rather than rigorous fashion. He also maintained, in distinction to his contemporaries, that the Law should protect women during divorce and urged openness toward Gentiles. Acts 5:38-39 relates that he intervened on behalf of Saint Peter and other Jewish followers of Jesus. He died twenty years before the destruction of the Temple in 70 CE.

Josef of Arimathea

A member of the Sanhedrin, supporter of Jesus, and in whose tomb Jesus was placed after his crucifixion. There are many suppositions about his relationship to Jesus. One source asserts he was uncle to Mary, the mother of Jesus. Legend has it he took the chalice used at the last supper to Glastonbury England. He is said to have stuck his walking stick into the ground where it rooted and became the Glastonbury thorn which blooms every year at Christmastide.

Loukas

A fictional character based loosely on the Third Evangelist and… who knows?

Pontius Pilate

Prefect (Governor) of Judea appointed by Tiberius and recalled in 36 CE by the Emperor Caligula.

Procula

Procula is just one of the names traditionally given for Pilate's wife. The others are Claudia and occasionally Claudia Procles or Claudia Procula. She appears briefly in Matthew's Gospel as having had a dream/premonition warning Pilate not to persecute Jesus.

Tiberius

Roman Emperor from 14 AD to 37 AD. He moved his headquarters from Rome to *Vila Jovis* on the Isle of Capri. Tradition has it that he was paranoid (at least) and had his enemies thrown to their death from its parapets to the rocks below. Lacivious and wanton living have been ascribed to him as well.

Yehudah

Judas Iscariot. Yehudah, like Jesus (Yeshua) was a common name in the first century Israel/Judea. The traditional treatment assumed Judas was from a village named Kerioth, presumed to be in the southern part of Judea. No satisfactory location for the town has ever been established. Some scholars take Iscariot to be an adulteration of *Siccori*.

This author assumes Iscariot is a variant on the Aramaic word *skyr*, which is roughly translated as red or ruddy. An admixture of the Aramaic and the Greek suffix –ote (like, -ish) would yield: h skiriote, pronounced as eh-skiri-ote, Iscariot, Judas the Red [ish]. Thus, Judas the Red, as in, Erik the Red. Early Byzantine icons commonly depict Judas with red hair.

Yehudah of the Galilee
Little is known about Yehudah (Judas) of the Galilee except he is mentioned in Josephus with regard to the raid on the armory in Sepphoris. This insurrection resulted in the crucifixion of many men and the town itself being razed. There is an additional reference in the New Testament (Acts 5:36 ff.) where Gamaliel describes him as a false messiah. His uprising in 6 C.E. is thought by some scholars to be the opening battle that would culminate in the Jewish Wars in 66-67 C.E. and the destruction of the Temple and the leveling of Jerusalem in 70 C.E. Sometimes referred to as, Yehudah of Gamala

Yeshua ben Josef
Jesus of Nazareth.

Sicarii

The Sicarii, (Hebrew סיקירקיס) the Dagger Men, were a group of Zealots which operated during the Roman occupation of Palestine (Israel today). They were terrorists, nationalists, and feared equally by the Romans and the Israelis. The Sicarii are mentioned by Josephus in his *Jewish Antiquities*: "When Albinus reached the city of Jerusalem, he bent every effort and made every provision to ensure peace in the land by exterminating most of the Sicarii (xx.208).

Hippodrome

The name hippodrome (Latin = Circus) is derived from the Greek words "hippos (ἵππος; "horse") and "dromos" (δρόμος; "course"). Originally a Greek stadium built for horse and chariot racing, the Greek hippodrome was usually set out on the slope of a hill, and the ground taken from one side served to form the embankment on the other side. One end of the hippodrome was semicircular, and the other end square with an extensive portico in front of which, at a lower level, were the stalls for the horses and chariots. At both ends of the hippodrome there were posts (*termai*) or pylons around which the chariots turned.

Miscellany

Gehinnom

Garbage, trash, offal, and waste were dumped in this valley outside Jerusalem. When the rains came much of it would be washed eastward toward and finally into the Dead Sea.

Garum

A pungent paste made by crushing the roe and liver of fish and then and fermenting them in brine and used to flavor other dishes. Garum was popular in the Roman world.

Mikvah *(pl. mikva'ote)*

Orthodox Jews cleanse themselves periodically by immersion in this ritual bath. Some ascribe this practice as the forerunner of the baptismal practice instituted by John the Baptizer.

Neqqudot

To recycle papyrus, a sheet would be sanded and re-polished. If the task were not done carefully, a bit of ink might be overlooked (a *neqqudot*) and when a new word was written, that mark might be introduced which could easily change the meaning of the word or the entire sentence.

Perjury

Under Jewish law at that time, bearing false witness was a serious offense. If a witness were caught lying to a court, he would receive the punishment the accused would have received if convicted.

Earthquakes

Since it sits on the old African Rift, Israel has had its share of earthquakes over the centuries. One major earthquake in Jerusalem has been dated to 32CE and because the gospel narratives cite an earthquake on the day Jesus was crucified, the crucifixion is sometimes arbitrarily fixed to that year. It is more difficult to find a coincident eclipse of the sun.